DIRTY
gentleman

from the author of *The Harbour Series*

CHRISTY PASTORE

Publication Date: April 22, 2022
Dirty Gentleman
Copyright © 2022 Christy Pastore

Book formatting provided by Stacey Blake of Champagne Book Design
champagnebookdesign.com
Cover designed by Letitia Hasser r.b.a. Designs
rbadesigns.com
Editing provided by Missy Borucki

This is a work of fiction. Names, characters, places, brands, media, and incidents are either a product of the author's imagination or are used fictitiously. The author acknowledges the trademarked status and trademark owners of various products referenced in this work of fiction. Any trademarks, service marks, product names or named features are assumed to be the property of their respective owners and are used only for reference. There is no implied endorsement.

Warning:
This book is intended for mature audiences.

Author's Note

According to the Human Trafficking Institute an estimated 24.9 million people are victims of sex and labor trafficking.

To report a trafficking case in the U.S. and U.S. Territories call the National Human Trafficking Hotline: 1-888-373-7888. The hotline is available 24/7 to take confidential and anonymous reports. Interpreters are available. Text: "BeFree" 233733.

More resources:

THORN—A nonprofit organization founded by Ashton Kutcher and Demi Moore. THORN builds technology to defend children from sexual abuse.

NCMEC—All information regarding child sexual exploitation should be reported to the National Center for Missing and Exploited Children. 1-800-THE-LOST (843-5678).

European Commission National Hotlines—Numbers for countries including Estonia, France, Greece, Italy, Latvia, Poland, Spain, United Kingdom, and more.

Hope For Justice—Hope For Justice runs anti-trafficking projects all over the world, working directly with victims and survivors.

Polaris Project—A nonprofit organization founded in 2002 leading a social justice movement to end human trafficking.

DIRTY (adj.):
Unethical or corrupt; sordid: *dirty politics.*
Lewd or lecherous: *a dirty mind.*
Acquired by illicit or improper means: *dirty money.*

GENTLEMAN (n.):
A man of refinement.

DIRTY
gentleman

CHAPTER
one

Lauren

T HE WORLD IS BRUTAL, BUT IT'S HARD TO SEE THAT FROM WHERE I'm standing.

Paradise.

I feel so free. This is me living my best life.

"Hurry, hurry," my friend Cynthia calls out as we grab our spicy mango margaritas from the bar.

Nerves of excitement flutter in my stomach as we cross the dance floor. My sister Katrina is missing out. The two of us were supposed to come to Isla Mujeres for the music festival, but she had a work thing that she couldn't reschedule.

I'm glad that my work is super flexible. Of course, it doesn't hurt that I've racked up a ton of PTO.

I wanted fun and sun and the chance to meet a sexy guy who loves country music, tequila cocktails, and chips and salsa as much as I do.

Cynthia moved into my building late last summer. We met at the pool. I'd been babysitting my nieces, who, for the record, are holy fucking terrors. They wouldn't listen to me to save my life. Kat had to fly to Dallas that afternoon for a conference. Unbeknownst to me, they turned into little monsters since the last time I'd seen them.

Just as I was about to lose my shit, Cynthia appeared with squirt guns and vodka popsicles. The water guns were for Cora and Thea. The booze was for the two of us.

She handed me a watermelon flavored popsicle and said, *"If this doesn't work, I'll help you drown the little beasts and make it look like an accident."*

We became fast friends. A shared love of iced coffee lemonade (yes, that's a thing), cinnamon doughnuts, and *The Crown*.

This vacation has been unforgettable. I'm just sad that tomorrow is our last day on the island.

Loud beats of music pump through the speakers. Clapping and cheers erupt through the crowd as Them Vibes take the stage. Cynthia bops her head and shakes her ass. I jump up and down when they start play the opening notes to the song, "Electric Fever."

"This is my favorite song," I yell to Cynthia.

"I know it's your jam." She tosses her head back in a laugh and raises her drink into the air. "Whoop!"

"I'm so glad we're here together."

Cynthia smiles. "Me too."

My eyes scan the crowd and I spot a tall guy with dark hair staring right at me. At least I think he's looking at me. I take another drink and let the alcohol do its job.

When I look back in his direction, he's gone. *Oh well.*

Guess I'll be going home with my virginity firmly intact. I shouldn't be upset, but at twenty-four it's beginning to feel like a burden. I look over at Cynthia, who's having the time of her life. I should be more like her. She's not lost her V-card yet, either. But as a proper southern lady from Alabama, she's waiting for marriage.

In my twenties and a virgin. Some might think I'm pathetic.

Laughable, right? In high school, boys didn't ask me out. My guess is that they'd heard about my curfew being nine p.m. and how strict my father had been, so why bother?

Back then, I can't say I blamed the boys. Everything would have been a hassle from a logistical standpoint. What teenage boy wants to think about having a dinner date with a girl at five p.m. then maybe make it to the movies at seven o'clock? If it were a two-hour movie, we'd need to leave early.

A sharp pain hits my arm, sending my drink splashing onto the sand.

"Oh hey, sorry," a cheery voice drawls out. I look up to see a burly guy wearing a Brooks and Dunn T-shirt smiling at me.

"That's okay." I investigate my cup. "Some of the drink survived."

He laughs and pulls down the brim of his black hat. "Lemme make it up to you and buy you another drink."

"Oh, you really don't need to."

He steps closer and smiles. "It's the least I can do. And just so you know, I'm not one of those guys tryin' to pick you up with a cheesy line."

"You can try a cheesy line on me. I don't mind." I laugh, and Cynthia grabs my arm and pulls me toward the stage. "Ouch," I squeal. "You're pinching my skin."

She lets go of my arm and I rub the spot. "Sorry, but you need to be careful. That guy looks like a predator."

I shake my head and roll my eyes. "I dunno, he looks harmless to me."

The band finishes their set and I down my drink. A rush of heat climbs up my spine and settles in my neck. The warm sunshine feels good on my skin. I'm not looking forward to going back to the chilly winter in Chicago.

Sweat pours down my back and my bikini top sticks

uncomfortably to my skin. Okay, so maybe the wintry weather won't be so horrible.

"I need another drink." Cynthia leans in and checks my cup. "Looks like you do too."

"Well, I was going to get one from that guy—"

Cynthia holds up her hand. "Stop it."

Aside from my sister Katrina, Cynthia is my closest friend. I'm kind of a loner. I'd blame my job, but I love working from home. I'm a virtual concierge, so I never have to go into the office.

We weave through the crowd, and my arms feel heavy. I let out a long yawn, making my eyes water.

Too much sun? I've only had three drinks. I don't even feel buzzed. Not to mention, I spent all morning hydrating. I made sure that we stocked up on plenty of water. Thank goodness the hotel's sundries store had glass bottles of Perrier.

Sweat grows wet on my skin, then cools. When we get to the bar, I tap Cynthia's shoulder. "I think I need a bottle of water." The last word comes out through a yawn. I grab a napkin from the dispenser and wipe my forehead and back of my neck.

She eyes me up and down. "That's a good idea. We should get out of the sun for a while. Let's go up to our room and cool off."

We reach the elevator. My legs feel like weights are attached, holding me heavy footed with each step. Blood rushes in my ears and dizziness hits me in a wave. My hand grabs the rail and I shake the haziness from my head.

"Hey, you okay?" Cynthia looks at me with a smile.

Colors dance in my eyes with streaks of white and sickness hits my stomach. I nod at my friend and find my footing.

"Oh, you poor girl," she whispers.

When we reach our floor, Cynthia grabs my arm.

"Is she okay?"

"Just a bit too much sun and drinks."

Fuzziness coats my brain. Cynthia says something, but I can't quite make out the words.

I hear my own voice. It's above a whisper and scratchy. My chin hits her shoulder, and my teeth clamp together. Suddenly I feel as if I'm falling. Strong, rough hands grab at my skin.

Swallowing, I try to open my eyes, but everything seems heavy. Voices carry around the room. At least I think I'm in a room. My fingers touch soft leather, and I realize I'm back in our hotel suite.

I think.

I'm so tired. The voices fade into murmurs, and I sink deeper into the couch.

I blink my eyes open, and darkness surrounds me. In a foggy haze, I turn my head and find myself sitting in a room. The lights from the table lamps paint neon blue streaks across the wall.

Stale dampness washes over me, and I wonder if the smell is me.

There's a bed in front of me, covered in a dusty pink bedspread. The thread makes a diamond-shaped pattern across the fabric.

Moving slowly, I peel my sweat-soaked thighs from the slippery faux leather seat. Fuzz coats my tongue. My head throbs with a dull ache.

Distress pumps into my veins when I see my arms strapped down with duct tape. I try to wiggle free, but the tape digs in deeper, pulling at the hair on my arms.

What the fuck?

Where am I?

Unable to shake the dread, my head swivels around the room.

A soft glowing light pours from behind me. Twisting my head to the left, I see a shower and vanity area.

My stomach rumbles, and I wonder how long I've been here. Wherever *here* is.

I hear footsteps outside the door before it flings open, casting a dull yellow light across the faded green carpet. It gives me a minute to better study my surroundings. It looks like a motel that hasn't had a makeover since the eighties. Wood paneling lines three of the four walls. An air conditioning unit sits below the oversized leaf patterned curtains.

A scream rips through the air and I jerk—the wail is undoubtedly female. An angry voice grinds out words I don't understand. Cries and choked sobs follow.

Fear crawls all over my skin like icy spiders.

"No, please, I want to go home!" The words from the unknown female voice hang in the air.

Oh god, I've been drugged and taken . . . kidnapped.

I've seen the movies. I've watched the news reports. I know how this will end.

A man in a red button-down shirt appears in the doorway. He takes a puff of his cigarette and then blows the smoke into the air. Inky black hair hangs down to his shoulders. His dark eyes cut to mine as he motions and speaks a foreign language I do not understand.

What ungodly things will they do to me? Beat me? Break me?

Bile rises in my throat and my eyes snap shut. Horrors of my childhood come zipping back. My father loved beating the hell out of me and my sister. He did not need alcohol. His ugly, black heart and vile disposition were all he needed. And our mother's unwillingness to defy him.

It is possible our mother was uglier than our father. People would stop us almost everywhere we went and tell her what beautiful daughters she had.

One day, a woman in the grocery store told my mother that I had the prettiest long hair she'd ever seen. After thanking the stranger for her compliment, my mother hauled me out of the store and down the street to the local beauty salon. She told the hairstylist that I never brush my hair and all I do is cry when she'd brush it out.

All lies. I cried once when she had pulled so hard on my scalp, and I asked her to stop. She didn't like that, so she cracked me over the head with the brush. That's why I cried.

"Cut it off. Make it short."

"No, Mommy, please, no. I don't want to cut my hair off!"

I stood red-faced and screaming in the middle of the salon. She threatened that when we got home, not only would I get the belt from our father, I'd also have to wash my mouth out with soap.

A woman in a blue cotton dress brushes past the man. She's carrying a garbage bag, and she drops it onto the bed. The woman doesn't look at me. And she's in and out so quickly that I barely get a look at her features.

Red Shirt leans against the doorframe and puffs on the cigarette, then tosses it onto the cement floor. Smoke billows up from the glowing embers. His boot lifts and then the smolder disappears under the weight of his sole.

Probably a symbolic gesture. A warning that they can snuff my life out at any time. That *he* can crush me.

Red Shirt prowls into the room. Panic coils through my blood. I blink and bite back the bile rising once more. He looms over me, his teeth stained brown. Reaching behind him, he reveals a sharp blade. Flinching, I rear back and almost topple over in the chair.

Blades cut things.

Carve skin.

Mutilate.

He leans down. The smell of cigarettes and tequila are heavy on his breath. Red Shirt grunts and grabs my chin. I twist away.

"You're a pretty thing." He sniffs my skin. "You smell like coconut and sweat." The words roll off his tongue in a thick accent. My eyes dart to his neck tattoo: *The devil doesn't sleep.*

The knife presses against my skin and he begins to cut the duct tape. My eyes squeeze shut and sickness rolls in my stomach. It takes no time for the tape to lift from the wooden armrests.

"You. Shower." He grabs me by my elbow and drags me to my feet. His free hand dumps the bag onto the bed. Shampoo, a comb, soap, and an oversized white T-shirt inside.

"Then we bring food."

My eyes swing to the shower. The cracked green tiles and glass doors stare back at me, and I wonder how many other women have showered here.

He stalks out of the room and the heavy door shuts and locks behind him.

A shiver passes over me. Slowly I rub at my wrists and carefully tear off the tape. It burns as I peel back each tiny section.

The last piece comes off my skin and I look for a trash can in the bathroom.

Taking a deep breath, my eyes drift to the switch on the wall. I flip the switch, blinking through the brightness. The buzzing sound is loud out first and then settles into a low hum. My fingers rub at chipped flecks of paint on the wall.

I glare at my reflection. "What happened?"

I remember dancing and standing at the bar with Cynthia. *Cynthia! Do they have her too?*

Fear clutches my heart, but I shove it down as I scramble around the room, looking for a clue as to where I might be. In a rush, I pull open the drawers from the nightstand, which are all empty.

Two paintings hang slightly askew on the wall. One is a

parrot, and the other is of a hut on an island with women carrying baskets on their heads. My hands grip the frame and position it upright.

Taking a step backward, the back of my knee hits the mattress. I'm afraid to look under the bed.

There's another light switch by the door. I flip it on and light scatters across the room. I crouch down and lift the bedspread. Nothing, not even a bug.

My eyes dart to the curtains. *Of course!* I can study the landscape. It'll be helpful for the police when I give my statement.

A heavy breath leaves my lips. "If I get out."

Feeling defeated, I walk toward the curtains. I yank back the fabric only to reveal a brick wall.

I'm trapped.

The reality hits me like a tidal wave.

CHAPTER
Two

Lauren

AFTER MY SHOWER, I DRY OFF WITH THE DULL, RATTY TOWEL. I stand at the vanity combing out my long blond hair. My thoughts float to Cynthia. My friend. Is she in this hell too? Or, god forbid, *dead*. When I think about it, tears threaten to spill down my cheeks.

No. I won't give them my tears. I haven't yet, and I won't. Despite this bleak and terror-filled situation, I force down the tears.

There's a knock at the door and the heavy metal clacks. Tension ripples around the room as a woman steps inside.

"Food. Eat. You have fifteen minutes before we take the dirty dishes." She places the tray on the desk and then leaves.

My stomach rumbles at the smell of the vegetables and meat. There's a stir-fry dish, warm bread, and water to wash it down.

I inhale my food. Not caring about how it's prepared. I could be eating rat for all I know. Swallowing hard, I force out the nasty thoughts.

Taking a mouthful of food, I steel myself. I think about

something more useful, surviving if I can, before being sold to the highest bidder.

Amid all the uncertainty, it's the one thing I know will happen.

If I had never appreciated my freedom before, I do now.

In all the years of my life, if I did not appreciate the sunshine, fresh water, and clean sheets—I do now.

Time had become both my enemy and my friend.

When dinner fails to come tonight, I feel my fate has been decided. Someone has purchased me. The question is who?

A sex-trafficking ring in the Philippines.

A Taliban leader who keeps his bed warm with virgins. Until they're not.

Or a ruthless Chinese billionaire who loves to practice throwing knives at my head.

Sinister chuckles echo outside my door. That's when the loud banging begins and screeching of heavy metal music thumps.

I heave myself onto the bed and crush the pillow over my head and I scream. The tears fall from my eyes and my heart jackhammers in my chest.

CHAPTER
Three

Lauren

ALL THE SCARE TACTICS AND EMOTIONAL TORTURE BLEED together.

When Red Shirt raises his hand threatening to slap me or calls me a whore, it doesn't matter. He calls all of us whores. In the grand scheme of things, his words are meaningless.

I don't believe him.

When my father struck me at eight years old and told me that he hated me, I believed him.

That hurt.

A knock at the door pulls me from my thoughts.

"Food. Eat." Is all she says and then leaves the room.

This will be my tenth meal since my arrival. It smells good. Warm bread and a vegetable soup.

Despite how the food warms my body, ice continues to flood my veins. I need the ice to protect me. But it won't. It didn't when I was a kid. Why would it protect me now?

Red Shirt busts into my room along with two other men. Before I can scream or protest, they bind my wrists.

One of the men takes a strand of my hair and sniffs it, just like Red Shirt did before. "Fuck, you smell good, whore." His other hand paws at my shoulder.

The man I don't recognize chuckles darkly. His tequila-laced breath passes over my face, and I cough. He smooths his palms down his blue shirt and licks his lips. Waves of sickness creep up from my gut, and my legs shake beneath me.

Crossing his arms, Red Shirt leans against the door frame, amused at the scene in front of him.

"Come on, boss," the one holding my hair says. "Close the door and let me have a taste of her sweet cunt."

They mutter something in their native tongue and laugh. Fisting my hair tight, he pulls me against him and his hard cock grinds against my ass. My stomach clenches in disgust.

The man releases his hold on me, and I fall forward. I stumble and Blue Shirt catches me. His hands slide up my ribcage to my breasts, where he squeezes.

Red Shirt stalks toward me. "Move, bitch."

Why I feel the need to dig my feet into the carpet in protest is a mystery to me.

He leans forward and lowers his face to mine. I stare into his black eyes. I see nothing. Vacant and cold. Soulless. Devoid of any emotion.

"You want to play that way?" he asks.

"Move, obey your master." Blue Shirt pushes at my back.

Red Shirt tugs me into the hallway and shoves me against the wall. My head hits the brick and I wince in pain.

"Where are you taking me?"

"None of your business," he snarls. "Move now, whore."

Mustering all the courage I can, I remember that these people are criminals.

Simple thinkers.

Money. Crime. Eat. Sleep. Fuck. Kill.

My pulse thuds with every step as Red Shirt drags me down the narrow corridor. The familiar confines of the room I'd been in grow farther and farther away. We pass a large room with dirty mattresses and chairs. It must have been a lounge at one point.

He shoves me forward into the barely lit entryway past the elevators. Chairs litter the space along with garbage. A blue and yellow flyer sticks out: *Visit Belize.*

Belize! Are we in Belize? Somewhere close?

When we reach the stairs, he readjusts his hold on me. "Walk." He leans in close, smelling of fried food and tequila.

I can barely see the wooden stairs, but I know they're unstable. They creak with each step I take. Ripped sheets of wallpaper decorate the stairwell and when I turn toward the next flight, half the railing is missing.

"Stay close to the wall. Can't have you falling to your death."

That might be the best thing for me at this point.

Red Shirt drags me across a mezzanine level. This is the nicest part of the building. I'm stunned at how clean and unscathed by time this area is.

He heaves me across the open room. The red and gold carpet feels good against my feet. The leather couches and chairs look so cozy. And there's a fully stocked bar with flat-screen televisions. A man in a white dress shirt is standing behind the bar cleaning wine glasses.

Footsteps and cries echo down the staircase. More women arrive. Horror paints their faces at the sight of the chains. I look around for Cynthia. A lot of women and girls have their heads down. Curtains of blond, red, and brown shield their faces.

Some of them can't be more than sixteen years old.

Teenagers. Were they stolen from hotel rooms while their parents were out drinking and dancing? Were they abducted in plain sight from cafés while the locals watched? Were any of them at the festival like me?

A woman with dark raven hair and olive skin beside me kicks at the man who has a hold of her. An angry growl rips from his throat as he ties her arms behind her back.

"Ti ucciderò," she screams.

The man laughs. "Whore."

Her accent is thick as she repeats the words again. Grinding my teeth, my mind races and I stare at her. Hoping she looks at me. Hoping she understands the silent message I'm conveying.

Fighting back won't do any good.

Rough fingers touch the top of my head. Massaging my scalp with tenderness.

Words on repeat drift over the shell of my ear.

Laughs filter in the space. Clammy hands jerk at my chin and then I feel something soft brush against my cheek.

Something wet trails across my lips. Salt and musk meld together in my nose.

The smell makes me want to gag.

"Enough!" a deep, gritty voice calls out.

There's a scuffle and metal bangs against metal.

"Sick fucking bastards," a sweet voice mumbles.

Cynthia?

I feel something scratchy drift over my lips and cheek. My eyelids pop open and I stare into the blackness. The bulb from the lamp in the corner flashes.

The mattress dips and I burst upright. My hands fly out from my body, ready to strike.

"Hey, *hey*. It's okay."

My eyes blink through the fuzzy light to see a woman with green eyes and dark, stringy hair. She smiles and I relax.

A slow breath leaves my lungs as I twist off the bed. "This isn't my room." Throbs of pain beat behind my eyes.

"No." She stands and wipes her hands on the towel she's holding. "Welcome to my humble abode. I'm Bianca."

"Lauren." I rise to my feet and stretch my arms over my head. "Do I even want to know what they were doing to me?" A cold chill climbs up my legs.

"Probably not, but you should know. One guy, I call him Ingo. He made me watch while he jerked off in my shower. Then painted your lips with his semen."

My stomach lurches in disgust. I run toward the bathroom sink and flip on the water. Scooping the water into my hands, I splash my face and mouth.

"Feel better?" she asks, handing me a towel.

"Not really." I dry off my face and try desperately not to throw up.

Her room is bigger than mine. Two beds with brilliant green bedspreads fill the space, and a flat-screen television hangs on the wall. There's even a bar area with a sink. This must have been a suite.

I slump onto the bed and fight back the tears. "The last thing I remember is being on the Mezzanine level. Were you there too?"

"Yeah. Do you remember eating or drinking anything?"

My eyes squeeze shut, and I try to remember what happened. "Not really."

"It was some kind of fruit drink. I'm sure it was laced with something." She hands me a plastic bottle. "Here's some water and a piece of bread. It's the best I can do."

"Thanks." I study her. Trying to remember if I'd seen her before. "How'd you get this stuff?"

Bianca huffs a laugh. "I bribed the guy who delivers my food. His name is Carlos."

"What did he want in return?" I shudder, thinking the worst.

A smirk turns up her pink lips. "I flashed him my tits. I know, I know—classy. But after my first night, I realized I needed to do something to get information. Carlos brought me an extra bread roll the next day. So, I figured I could use it to my advantage."

Bianca's mood is cheerful. What could make her keep a sun-shiny attitude in this hellhole? Hope?

As I take a few sips, a million questions flicker in my head.

"Where'd they take you from?" I pass the bottle back to her and she takes a long drink.

"Grabbed me while I was at a club with my friend, Janie. Next thing I know, I'm here." Her hand gestures around the space. "I'm pretty sure someone roofied my drink. Bits and pieces are fuzzy. But I was definitely dancing and taking shots."

My eyes squeeze tight at the memory of my own kidnapping.

"What about you?"

"I was at the Island Time Music Festival in Isla Mujeres with my friend Cynthia. Have you met anyone by that name? Blond hair, brown eyes, petite build."

"No. You're the first person I've talked to since I've been here. Aside from Carlos."

My fingers pick at the smooth corner of the bedspread. "Do you know where we are? I saw a travel flyer for Belize in one of the rooms."

Bianca moves behind the bar and waves an orange in the air. "Yeah, we're in Belize. Thanks to my Spanish skills, I've picked up on some of the conversations, but it's not much. Some overlords speak a dialect of Creole. It's gotta be local, like slang."

I nod. "What *do* you know?"

She peels back the layer of orange, and the citrus scent makes my mouth water. "There's going to be an online auction. It's complete with our pictures and stats. From what Carlos tells me, virgins are the ones that get super high bids. There's apparently a guy who owns an island in the Caribbean bidding. A regular. He's got a place that they refer to as fantasy island. Super rich. Super handsome. I guess he's looking for his next wife."

"How do they know if we're virgins?"

"I'm assuming they'll have someone examine us."

Flinching at the thought of some stranger, one of these men prodding around my lady parts makes me want to throw up. I take the orange slice she hands me. "Thanks. When is the auction?"

"I heard in a few days, but who knows." Bianca pops an orange slice into her mouth. She hums a song that I don't recognize. Leaning forward, she hands me a few more orange slices.

"I wonder why they took me from my room and brought me here?"

She props her long tan legs up onto the bed I'm sitting on. "Probably to make room for new hostages. I'm sure they're out kidnapping unsuspecting women right now."

My eyes close and I finish the remaining orange slices. "Can I ask you a question?"

She nods and swallows. "Isn't that what you've been doing?"

"You don't seem scared."

She arches a single dark brow and finishes peeling the orange, setting aside the remaining pieces. "Is that your question?"

I swallow and stifle a laugh. "Are you scared?"

Bianca drops her feet to the carpet and tosses the orange peels into a brown bag. "Yes, but nothing they, or whoever buys me, do to me can be any worse than my previous life."

Previous life. She's already accepted her fate.

She walks toward the bathroom, climbing on top of the toilet seat. With a swift tug, the vent lifts, and she shoves the bag inside. "My mom's now third husband, Ken, in addition to cheating on her, has driven her to spend her days drunk and stoned. She barely knows I'm alive. The son of a bitch had me fired from her company, and then he cornered me in my office and tried to force himself on me. Step-daddy's robbing her blind and she's too stupid to kick the piece of slime to the curb. And the cherry on top, I'm the spoiled bitch who lies. So, fuck them both."

Surely, Bianca can't think that the life of a sex slave would be any better. At least if she's rescued, she'd have her freedom.

"What about you?"

My brows scrunch together. "What about me?"

"Are you scared?"

"Totally."

She pops another slice into her mouth and chews slowly as she stares at me. When she swallows, I mimic the same action.

"Get rid of your fear, Lauren. It won't do you any good."

CHAPTER
four

Lauren

AFTER OUR THIRD EVENING MEAL TOGETHER, THE DOOR OPENS and a man wearing a black shirt and faded denim walks inside. Relief passes over Bianca's face, and she hops up from her seat.

"They're on a smoke break. Quick, give me your garbage," he whispers.

Bianca sprints into the bathroom and removes the brown bag from the hole. The bag has peels from at least six oranges that I counted. She quickly replaces the grate and then jumps back into the room. "Thanks, Carlos. Any new information?"

He looks over his shoulders and then steps further inside. "It's happening tonight."

Panic swirls inside my chest. "What? What's happening?" The words rush from my mouth.

Carlos takes a step back. The yellow glow from the hallway light passes over his face. He's young, maybe twenty-five. "The auction. But first, the physical exams—for your health report."

My head drops back, and I stare at the stained ceiling tiles.

If he's this nice to Bianca, why doesn't he go to the police and set us free? He knows this is fucked up.

"The doctor won't hurt you and she's female. Try not to panic," he whispers. "Gotta go."

The metal door shuts and locks. He's gone and my head spins with anxiety.

"Why doesn't Carlos just let us out of here?" I stomp my foot against the floor.

"Because they'll kill him." Bianca's eyes meet mine. "It's either us or him, and he's just trying to survive a life that he was born into and probably doesn't want."

"You think that I'm going to feel sorry for him? These people that are about to stick us with needles and check our hymens? It's so fucking archaic."

"I just hope they don't put tracking devices in us. I watched a documentary once about these slaves in Europe. It was horrible."

Stop talking. I want to shout at her. But this is her way of dealing with what's going to happen.

She blows out a puff of air. "Guess my value will decrease when they find out I'm not a virgin."

After they take our dinner trays away, we sit in mostly silence. I stare up at the television, thinking about what I'd be doing right now if I were at home. My mind swirls with thoughts of ordering a cheese pizza and watching *The Crown* with Cynthia.

Cynthia.

"Do you think your friend Janie is looking for you?"

"Nah, she's probably at home in her bed sleeping, not giving me a thought."

"Were you the two of you good friends?"

"I met her about five months ago. She was hired by my mom's company in the marketing department. She rescued me from an embarrassing 'coffee meets important files on the break room floor' disaster."

Kind of how Cynthia rescued me from my pool-terrorizing nieces. I'd give anything to be at home with Katrina and the girls right now. I wouldn't even care if they were acting like little hellions.

All my memories halt when the heavy door flies open, and Red Shirt grabs my arm, pulling me from the room.

"What the—" I clamp my mouth shut when my eyes meet Red Shirt's dark ones.

"Time to go, bitch." He shoves me forward into the hallway. I blink back at the light that my eyes have yet to adjust to.

"Where are you taking her?" Bianca demands.

A man with greasy blond hair and a barbed wire neck tattoo grips Bianca by the arm and hauls her out of the room.

Screams, cries, sobs, and wails filter down the long corridor.

My heart aches for each of them. It's a waste of feelings though. Most of them will be dead soon.

We take the same path we've taken the other two times. Carlos said exams were tonight. If the auction is soon, I can't imagine that we're about to have another round of whippings. Yet here we are.

Looking around the room at the women, the hope of seeing Cynthia fades. I'm sure she's dead or sold to another group of traffickers. I've seen enough news and documentaries to know that the window of saving a life is short. And it's been at least three weeks now.

The group is small. I count twelve bodies, including myself and Bianca. She stands tall and steels her spine.

"Quiet, whores," a voice shouts.

"First, you will shower. Then the doctor will examine you," Red Shirt instructs. "This will all be over, and soon, you will be with your new masters."

Flight and fight both coil in my gut.

Red Shirt pulls me forward and grips my bicep. "Time to get the stink off you."

I don't really understand what's meant by that comment. We've been allowed to shower every day in our rooms. We shuffle down the dark hallway. Silent sobs and cries fill the space, and I want to scream at them to save their tears.

Red Shirt smirks as he opens the door. Horror strikes me when I see the pool area covered in dirt and overgrown plants. Lounge chairs and tables float in the mucky waters of the deep end. We trek along the deck, and I worry they're going to shove us into the pool and turn the hose on us.

When I tear my eyes from the pool, I see a sign for the locker rooms. Relief washes over me. But it's quickly replaced with apprehension.

All the shower doors have been removed.

"Strip," he commands.

My knees lock in place and I'm rooted to my spot.

Shake the fear, Lauren.

My eyes search for Bianca. She's already naked.

Of course she is.

"Obey me, whore. Unless you need some new bruises." He clicks his tongue and licks his lips. My skin crawls and that's all I need to move. Who cares if he sees me naked?

He won't touch me.

"—*virgins get super high bids.*"

For once I embrace my virginity. Gathering strength and courage, I drag the sweaty tank top up over my head.

Fuck you. Fuck you all to hell.

"Good girl, you'll fetch a decent price," he sneers and grabs me by the shoulders. He drags his gaze up and down my body. "You've got nice tits. I hope you're not lying about this cunt of yours. I could use some *virgin* money."

Ignoring his grotesque comment, I walk forward. He slaps my ass when I step into the shower stall.

I jerk at the contact, but I don't stumble. The warm water curls around me, and I try to forget what's happening for a little while anyway. I find the bar of soap and lather my skin.

After rinsing the shampoo from my hair, I turn off the spray.

Red Shirt grunts and hands me a towel. "I've decided that you're worth at least two million dollars."

Two million, huh? If he wants it that badly, he will not hit me.

Naked and unashamed, I stand in front of my trafficker and smile. "You'll burn in hell one day for all that you're doing. I only wish it could be me that jabs a dagger into your throat and sends you there."

A sadistic smile paints his face. "Hell. I've been there ten times over."

"What's your name?"

He eyes me with a pointed stare. "You think I'm dumb enough to give you my name?"

Yes. I think you're dumb. One day, you will get caught.

"No, I don't think that you're dumb," I lie, and it tastes so damn bitter on my tongue. "I'm asking because I want to remember it when I'm with my new owner. When I look at myself every day in the mirror, I want to be able to chant your name over and over. And one day, when I barely recognize myself anymore, and all I'm left with is the image of you staring back at me, I want to be able to say, fuck *you*, to your evil living existence."

"Lots of people call me Catch." He reaches up and pinches my nipple with his thumb and forefinger. "I'd rather have you scream out my name over and over while I pound that virgin pussy." His rough hand palms my breast. "But then again, Catch don't fuck what he releases."

"I. Hate. You." I wrap the threadbare towel around my body and squeeze the water from my hair at his feet.

"You've got fight in you. I like that. Your master will too." Catch grabs his cock and bares his tobacco-stained teeth. "Now, move."

He pushes me down the locker room toward a set of double doors. The hallway is well lit and there's a sign on the wall that reads *Salon and Spa*.

Cries float down the hallway and I try to ignore the frantic shouts for help. One woman pushes her handler against the wall, but he scoops her up and tosses her over his shoulder like a feed sack.

Fighting isn't going to do any good. An avalanche of sorrow hits me hard. This is really happening. I'm going to be branded like livestock. My captors will punch my data into a computer, and then I'll be sold.

One by one, the women disappear into the room and never come out. Their handlers walk off and never look back.

Catch yanks my arm and propels me into the room. A woman with dark hair that hangs below her chin wearing a surgical mask stands at an examination table. She snaps on a fresh pair of rubber gloves and eyes me. When Catch heaves me into a chair, I toss him a scowl.

"Leave us," the woman orders.

Oh my god—she's American. What the actual fuck?

Catch stalks out and closes the door.

"Okay, let's get your height and weight. Please stand on the scale."

Her accent is decidedly *northern*. It reminds me of Minnesota. I step up onto the scale and take a deep breath as she fiddles with the apparatus.

"Good. Now, sit here." She pats the exam table, which is just a massage table.

Her brown eyes bore into mine as she examines every inch of my skin. "Open your mouth and stick out your tongue."

I do as I'm told. Who is this woman? Why would she help these men?

One reason—money.

The doctor takes my blood pressure and listens to my breathing, making notes as she goes along. It's the standard annual checkup process.

"Okay, now this is the uncomfortable part," she says, and points to the stirrups.

My lips bite back the scoff that threatens to burst from my mouth.

"Lie back. This shouldn't take but a few moments."

I swallow and turn my face up at the ceiling. Fuck. I hate this. *Fuck you all. Fuck you all.*

Doctor Lady performs the normal procedure, and thankfully, it did not hurt too much.

"Did you stick me with a tracking device?"

"No. All done. You can step down."

"Great," I mumble, pulling my towel tighter around my body. My heart pings when I see the picture of me and Cynthia in my folder.

"Hey, have you seen this woman?"

A scowl paints her face as she glances at the picture. When she flips the picture over, her eyes widen.

"What? What is it? Is it bad?"

"No, I've not seen her." Doctor Lady takes off her gloves and then scratches notes into my file folder. "Now, you're going to be fitted for your dress."

My brows scrunch. "My dress?"

Ignoring my question, she fumbles with my file and then taps the door behind her. A woman in a black pant suit and black sunglasses opens the door and Doctor Lady hands her my file.

"Come with me," Pant Suit Lady orders in a heavy German accent.

I follow her down the corridor. The smell of lavender infuses the air and soft music plays from the speakers in the ceiling. This part of the building is so clean. It's like I'm in another place altogether.

We step into the salon, and I almost can't believe my eyes. A team of people dressed in black is fluttering about applying makeup and styling hair. The stylists wear big, rimmed glasses just like the woman who brought me here.

"Faster," she says with a snap of her fingers. "This way."

Out of sheer curiosity, I fall in step a few paces behind her. We arrive in a huge room packed wall to wall with racks of black-and-white dresses.

"Blond hair, blue eyes." She clicks her tongue and walks toward a rack. "Come here, young lady."

I gulp and slink toward where she stands.

She plucks a black dress and shoves it into my hands. "This is your size. Put it on in there."

My gaze pings to the dressing room and back to my dress. It's beautiful. A black velvet halter with an open back. I've never worn something so gorgeous.

"*Now,* we don't have all night."

My bare feet slide over the carpet, and I hurry inside the room. Slipping off my towel, I step into the dress and pull it up over my hips. My fingers shake as I zip up the side.

This is it. Steps closer to my new life. My hands smooth over my face and tears threaten, desperate to shed. I fight to keep my eyes dry.

"Does the dress fit?"

I toss back the curtain and step out. "Yes, ma'am."

Yes, ma'am? Geesh.

I can feel her eyes moving up and down my body as she inspects me. Her hands pull and tug the fabric around my shoulders and waist.

"Beautiful, you should get a decent price—a *high* price."

That anger returns, flaming my cheeks. I sniff and stand taller. "I'm not a damn piece of cattle headed to market."

Yes, you are.

Her lip curls up and she grasps my arms, turning me to face the door. She shoves at my back and then grabs my wrist hauling me down the corridor and into a room. A lady in all white stands by a massage table.

"Wax her legs and clean up her pussy," Pant Suit Lady barks out. "And fix those eyebrows."

Two men lurk from the shadows and pin me onto the table. Instinct has me fighting back, but soon they lock my wrists down.

They don't care. *She* doesn't care.

After the torture of plucking and waxing, Pant Suit Lady takes me to the salon.

"Time for your hair and makeup."

Her words are delivered exceptionally casual, like this is a goddamn society event. Like a wedding. My heart clenches behind the cage of ribs its prisoner to. And I think of a wedding that I'll never have. A moment that's being removed from my life.

Two men stand at the salon entrance with dark sunglasses and guns strapped to their chests. When we enter the salon, no one pays me any attention. Pant Suit Lady shows me to a chair and when I sit, I spot Bianca in the corner. A woman curls the ends of her dark hair, while another paints her lips pink.

She's gorgeous.

No! This is not a good thing.

I hate them. I hate this. I hate everything.

Do something then.

What?

I have this conversation with myself for about five minutes. I think about stripping the curling wand from one of these bitches and burning the fuck out of someone.

"Hola." A woman approaches and weaves her fingers into my hair. "You have beautiful hair."

"Thank you," I mumble.

Thank you?

Really, Lauren? Where's the hate you just had?

"I think I will curl your hair back here and here." She sweeps long strands of hair away from my forehead. "This way, we can show off your eyes."

What the ever-loving fuck?

Why are these women so fucking *nice*? Are they nice? I feel like I'm going insane.

I smile at Bianca, and she smiles right back.

Finally, after an hour of primping and styling, I'm *ready*.

Ready for my looming death sentence. Because, let's be honest, that's where this is going. We're trafficked human beings. Sex slaves. And all this is just smoke and mirrors. There's nothing glamorous about what will happen to the twelve of us.

Pant Suit Lady claps her hands together. "Ladies, I need you to form a single file line at the door."

Ladies? A single line?

Jesus.

Bianca is the first in line. She's either crazy or badass.

For whatever reason, my feet don't want to move. The women line up one by one in silence. There are no cries or pleas for help.

Someone whizzes past us in a flurry. When my eyes focus, I see a woman with a lint brush. She's working frantically on our dresses. Two more women with lint brushes appear. They split the line.

I sigh when the brush hits my stomach.

Damn it.

My heels clip over the tile as we're led to wherever we're going. It's an online auction, I remind myself.

The velvet fabric whooshes over my skin with every step I take, making everything inside me stir with agitation. We arrive at two black lacquered doors.

We step inside, and I note that this was probably a ballroom once.

Drifting on a log of hope, I think about the happy occasions that happened inside these walls.

Parties. Weddings. Retirement celebrations. Are those memories living in here like ghosts?

Dear Ghosts, if you're listening, my name is Lauren Sanders. I'm sure you've seen terrible things in this room, but if you can just give me a little bit of hope, I'd really appreciate it.

When a woman pins a ribbon with the number eight on my hip, reality hits me—I'm going to be sold.

Maybe the buyer will at least be someone kind.

Or maybe he'll be someone who doesn't understand what buying another human really means.

Maybe a lonely prince who needs someone to share his life with.

Grow up, Lauren. This isn't a happily ever after situation.

Like lambs to the slaughter, we're paraded up the stairs and onto a stage. A spotlight moves under twinkling lights. There are two giant cameras in the space. Industrial, the kind you see in the news stations.

A man with a perfectly pressed suit appears in front of a microphone stand.

"Six, five, four, three—" comes from an anonymous voice.

My knees shake and threaten to buckle beneath me. Sweat forms at the back of my neck, and my heart beats a furious rhythm in my chest.

"Distinguished viewers, welcome to the auction." He sweeps his hand toward us. "You have the files at your fingertips. We'll start with—*item* number one. The bidding starts at three-hundred thousand."

My hands ball into fists. Item?

Item!!

Her name is Bianca.

I hope all of you burn in hell.

CHAPTER
five

Lauren

SOLD.
    Sold.
    Sold.
My life is no longer my own.
$3.2 million.
That's the value my life is worth. What would my parents think of that?

Ha!

Knowing they could have sold me for such an enormous amount would certainly piss them off. Guess I have worth after all.

After the cameras are turned off and the lights come up, we're shuffled into a small room. Navy blue carpet with patterns of gold leaves span the space. There's no furniture.

Some of the women are talking. Others sob quietly. Barely breathing, I still myself in a corner.

Minutes bleed into more minutes.

Tick. Tick. Tock. Tock.

After what feels like an hour, the door opens, and Pant Suit lady appears. Men in black suits enter and stand behind her.

"Ladies, we have completed your contracts."

You mean our sale transactions—you fucking bitch.

I bet she's behind this whole goddamn twisted illegal operation. A woman selling other women. I mean, this is just the icing on the cake for women on women crime.

More men in black suits enter the suite, and one by one, they haul women out with their wrists bound and blindfolds over their eyes.

Screams of panic rip through the air.

A man approaches me and nods when he's given a silk mask.

Before I'm blindfolded, I see Bianca one last time. She does nothing as they bind her wrists and place a silver mask over her eyes. Nine hundred thousand dollars, that's Bianca's worth.

My heart splits into fragments. I hope she survives her master.

The man places the mask over my eyes and leads me to wherever we're going. Outside? Another room? I have no idea.

The salty breeze whips across my face, and then a chill weaves up my spine. Soft voices exchange information as I'm shoved into the back of a vehicle. I have no idea where I'm going.

Yes, you do, your new life. Who the hell spends $3.2 million on another human being?

I squirm against the slippery fabric. My binds and blindfold are removed, and I'm face to face with a man in a . . . yep, black suit and sunglasses. He handcuffs one of my wrists to a handle affixed to the center console.

"Good evening. Are you comfortable?" His elegant accent licks over my brain. I can't quite make out the dialect.

Stunned at his politeness, I nod.

"Would you care for some Champagne, madam?"

Madam? Is he serious?

"Who are you? Did *you* buy me?"

He chuckles. "No, I don't have that kind of money. Between you and me, I find this whole thing revolting."

"Yet here you are, a willing participant."

His long fingers wrap around a Champagne bottle, and he pours a drink.

"I insist," he says, handing me the flute.

I scoff and take the glass from his hand. *Fuck it.*

"Cheers," I tell him and raise the glass to my lips.

We glide through the streets of whatever city in Belize we're in with ease. I swallow down the rest of my drink. It's sweet and the bubbles tickle my throat.

A sigh leaves my lungs as I stare into the black of night. Beams of light reflect off the earth and bounce into the limo.

Suit guy takes the glass from my hand and pours me another drink. Not caring, I swallow down the second glass.

We arrive at an airplane hangar where a private jet awaits. A giant "K" decorates the tail. We exit the limo, and my limbs begin to feel heavy. Just as they did before I was taken.

Damn it.

"Did you put something . . . *zomethang* . . . *my* drink?" I lick my lips and swallow. All my words come out in a slur.

I'm floating up, up, up.

A fog descends and my eyes grow tired. The roar of an engine shakes beneath my ass as I try to fight the pull of sleep.

CHAPTER

six

Lauren

OVERWHELMING PANIC HITS ME AND MY BODY JOLTS UP. There's a dull ache in my head and my neck. Shaking out the cobwebs, I sit upright with my palms at my side, looking around my new space. The surroundings are bigger than the previous prison I'd been held hostage.

The room is a palette of white and gray, except for two of the four walls are covered with floor-to-ceiling blackout shades. Soft lights from the ceiling illuminate two other walls, which are a natural stone. A black fireplace spans one wall, and a flat-screen television is anchored above it.

Clean.

Modern.

The bed I'm sitting on has a black metal frame and the white sheets feel good against my skin. A touch of sandalwood and sweet citrus rush over me when I slide my palms over the fabric.

Looking down, I'm still in the black dress. My legs wobble as I set my feet on the white rug beside the bed.

My eyes fall to the nightstand. There's a bottle of Acqua

Panna water and two pills. Beside it lays a note that says: *Take these for your headache.*

I pick up the bottle and the cap clicks as I twist it from the metal ring. A sigh of relief rushes over me as I wash the pills down with half the bottle. Walking around the room, I relax as much as possible.

What is this place? Is it my destination? Or just another pit stop on the road to my new life? Or is simply a mirage for Hell on Earth.

The sound of heels clipping over hardwood has me clutching the bottle to my chest. Uncertainty coils around every part of me.

A woman with blond hair and blue eyes appears from around the corner. "Hello. Nice to see that you're up," she says in a heavily accented voice.

Polish maybe. There's a large Polish community in Chicago. The way she pronounces her vowels makes me think Polish.

She moves to the desk and picks up a remote device. The blackout shades begin to lift.

"Um, hi." Trepidation drips from my voice as I watch the blinds rise.

"I'm Anja." She straightens her posture and picks a piece of lint from the sleeve of her navy jacket. In a slim fit pant suit with a cream blouse and her hair tied in a low bun, her appearance reminds me of Pant Suit lady.

Shivers race over my skin.

"I'm the head of staff here at the manor." She clicks a button on the wall.

The manor? How grandiose.

Light gushes into the space and spreads across the room. The shades reveal two giant floor-to-ceiling windows. Snow falls like powdered sugar over cake, coating the land. Trees and not much else are spread out before me. Endless white with splashes of green.

"Where am I?"

"Europe."

Duh. But where exactly?

She smiles and sits the remote back onto the desktop. "I know what you're thinking, but no, I will not tell you the exact location. Master Kallas won't permit it."

Master Kallas. My master.

"How long have I been here?"

"About ten hours," Anja tells me, matter of fact.

What the hell happened? I remember the limo. The Champagne. The smell of salty air and the roar of engines.

An ache gnaws at my stomach.

She levels me with a pointed stare. "How are you feeling? I'm sure that you're starving."

Okay, seriously, can she read my mind? I am hungry though.

"I could eat. That would be nice."

Anja smiles. "Very well. The shower is through these doors, and you'll find the closet is full of clothes in your size. If you need anything, don't hesitate to ask."

I'm in a glass box. Is this torture? Allowing me to see the world spin and change without me in it?

"Um, will I be locked in this room?"

Anja cocks a brow. "No, you're free to come and go as you please in this house."

In this house.

"What about outside the house?"

Anja pins me with a soft smile. "If you want to go outside, arrangements will need to be made."

I puff out a breath. "Right, because I'm a prisoner here."

"Prisons have bars. You have windows."

"Why am I here?" I blurt, hating the sarcasm that licks over her voice.

"You should ask Master Kallas when he returns."

Returns? The man who bought me isn't even here. My hands ball into fists, and the tips of my nails puncture the skin.

"Now, how about some food? Do you have any dietary restrictions? Allergies?"

"None that I know of."

"Very well. How does tomato soup with baked bread sound?"

The food throws me off. It doesn't give any clue as to where this place is. But it does sound delicious, and I'm starving. One of my favorite meals is tomato soup and grilled cheese.

"That sounds good." My shoulders relax a little.

"You'll like it here, I promise."

Hmm. Sure I will. Stockholm, here I come.

I slip off my black dress and read the laundry instructions on the tag.

I fling open the doors to the closet. White and more white, but nonetheless, this space is gorgeous.

Two giant crystal chandeliers hang from the tray ceiling. Two large leather ottomans sit directly underneath the chandeliers.

It's bigger than my apartment in Chicago. I would much rather be in my one-bedroom apartment than in this ice castle, even if it is gorgeous.

Rows of denim, blouses, pants, and dresses all hang on wooden hangers. The back wall is filled with shoes. My hands pluck a brown boot from the shelf. Size EU 39 . . . US 8.5. My size. My *exact* size.

I pull open a drawer to find cotton underwear and socks. Next drawer more intimates. Lace and padded bras and matching silk and delicate panties.

My heart jerks in my chest and panic assaults my brain.

Sex. This man . . . *master* will expect it from me.

Oh god.

I don't want this.

I think about ripping everything from the hangers and tearing the clothes into tiny fragments of fabric.

Then, you'll have a big mess and nothing to wear.

Pick your battles, Lauren.

I don't even know what this Master Kallas wants from me.

Sex, dummy. He's going to fuck you and beat you.

Destroy.

Rape.

Torture your mind, body, and soul until you are a ghost of the woman you are.

My hands shake as I hang my dress on a hanger. I'll look for the laundry basket later. Tears cloud my vision and I choke on the air around me.

I need to calm down.

It's the fear of the unknown. You have no answers to make you feel *safe?*

Safe.

My legs shake and my knees give out from beneath me. A sputter of laughter bubbles and clogs my mouth.

I slap my palms on the carpet and gather my thoughts.

Forget everything except for getting answers. Information is the most valuable commodity.

As I step inside the amazing bathroom, I take a long look at myself in the mirror. Could this man who bought me have done so to save my life? Maybe there's a chance he rescues people. A good humanitarian.

Excitement flutters in my stomach, sending butterflies zipping through my lungs. Anja was nice and so was the man who brought me here.

You mean the guy who drugged you?

Aside from that part, he *had* been nice.

Think of the ballroom ghosts. I try grasping onto hope, but it flickers and vanishes. Pain grips my heart as I struggle to breathe.

My legs shake and wobble across the tile of the bathroom. The floor beneath me rolls like a wave, and I stumble over the rug, crashing into the vanity.

Breathe.

All you can do is forget the past. Focus on the present.

Live. You need to find a way to exist here.

CHAPTER
seven

Lauren

ANJA CALLS ME FOR LUNCH, AND I WALK DOWN THE STAIRCASE when icy needles prick up my spine. It's as if all the warmth in the room suddenly disappeared.

"Ah, Lauren. Welcome. Come sit with me." The man stands and gestures for me to sit in the chair beside him.

Tall and domineering in the large space, it almost has me squirming in fear of his presence.

"You are more beautiful in person. Just a stunning creature."

"Who are you?" I demand, knowing more than likely the answer.

He's not ugly. He's older than I expected. Strands of silver pepper through his dark hair. His suit is black and screams power and money. Obviously from the looks of this place, he has a lot.

Anja brings me a bowl and places the warm bread in front of me. I take a seat and his dark eyes bore into mine—soulless.

"I'm Valter Kallas."

"Okay, Mr. Kallas. Where am I exactly? And please don't say Europe. I've figured that much out."

"You're in Stuvica, Vutreila."

I'm in the Baltics.

Starving, I take a few bites of the bread and when Valter pushes his bowl back, I ladle some onto my spoon. It's delicious.

Anja comes back into the room and the two of them exchange a few words as she takes his bowl and places it in the sink.

"This is one of my many homes. I hope you find these accommodations satisfactory."

Satisfactory is an understatement.

"Yes. Your home is beautiful."

His finger slithers down my arm. I flinch at the contact.

"Don't worry, Lauren. I don't plan to fuck you, unless that's something you want. All you have to do is ask." He raises a dark brow. "And you'll address me as Master Kallas when we're alone."

The soup and bread in my stomach roil.

"No, Master Kallas, that's not something I want from you."

"Very well. Perhaps one of my sons would be better suited to take your virginity."

"I would rather you kill me than be subjected to rape."

His icy stare slides over me. "You've got a little bit of fight in you. Maybe I should keep you for myself."

Oh god, please, no. I don't want to lose my virginity to this man who probably fucks everything that moves.

"I'm sure your wife wouldn't like that very much."

He snickers. "My wife is no longer with us." He moves to stand in front of one of the glass windows.

This place is surrounded by glass. His ice castle.

"I have a lover, so I suppose I don't need your body for pleasure. But if you change your mind, all you have to do is ask," he says over his shoulder.

No longer able to eat, I shove my bowl toward the middle of the table.

"Master Kallas, *why* am I here?"

"I believe that I do owe you an explanation." The muscle in his jaw ticks. "Let's take this into the other room." He gestures toward the seating area behind us.

Pressure builds in my chest and my hands start to tremble. I don't want to be afraid, but how can I not be?

Pull yourself together.

He said he's not going to rape you. He won't touch you.

Famous last words.

"This past summer, your sister Katrina and her husband Gregory came to Vutreila on vacation."

He knows Kat and Greg? I didn't know the two of them came here on vacation. Summer? I remember Kat said Greg had a conference in June and that she was going with him, but that was in Berlin. She never mentioned Vutreila.

Anja walks into the room and sets a mug in front of Master Kallas.

She looks at me. "Would you care for tea or coffee, Lauren?"

"No, thank you."

She exits the room and Master Kallas raises the mug to his mouth, blowing the steam away. "Gregory was reckless while he spent time in our casino. He got involved in a high-stakes poker game. Millions of dollars in the pot. I floated him a loan."

Silence falls over the room.

I'm afraid of the answer. Even more afraid that I already know the answer, but I ask anyway. "Did Gregory lose?"

A ghost of a smile plays on his lips before taking a drink. "Yes. I gave him forty-eight hours to repay the loan. Incredibly generous of me. Don't you think?"

"I don't understand what his loss has to do with me?"

"Gregory and Katrina couldn't pay back the loan, which is exactly why you're here."

My eyes pop wide and sickness swirls inside me. "Are you

telling me that my sister's husband sold me to you over a gambling debt?"

My family? My own *family*.

"No, not Gregory. Your sister Katrina."

The words slam into me with the force of a tidal wave. My head spins and spins.

No. He's lying. Katrina would never do this to me.

"You're lying." I hear the shakiness in my voice. The muscles in my stomach clench and my palms mist with sweat.

"I'm not lying." He sets the cup on the coaster. "Your sister told me that you're a highly intelligent young woman. But what makes you most valuable is that you have a photographic memory."

Knots of anger bubble inside me.

"Katrina convinced me you could be extremely useful to me."

This is fucking nuts.

"Master Kallas, what *exactly* are you asking of me?"

"I have grand plans for you, Lauren. You're going to be my most valuable asset. That photographic memory of yours is going to help me get my hands on everything I want."

My hands wring together, and my heart clogs in my throat. "For how long? How long will you keep me?"

"Until I decide."

"Will I ever get my freedom back?"

"You're free here."

"I mean, can I leave here and go home?" The desperation in my voice makes me hate myself.

The imposing man leans forward, resting his weight on this on his forearms. "Why would you want to go back to a family who sold you?"

He asks a good fucking question. And points out the painful truth. *Alleged truth.*

"Okay, so let's say that I help you get what you want—at that point, will the debt be paid?"

"Yes."

"Then, if the debt is paid, can I choose to leave?"

"I don't think you'll want to leave. If you leave, you'll go back to a world without my security and comforts. I believe you'll stay."

Swallowing thickly, I choose my next words carefully. "Here's the part I don't get. If my family owes you money, why go through the hassle of abducting me in Mexico? Why buy me?"

"Who do you think runs the trafficking ring? Whose bank do you think all that money pipes into?"

At the realization, my heart smashes into the pit of my stomach. So he buys me with his own dirty money and funnels it back into his own system. Wash. Rinse. Repeat. It makes perfect sense. He's a genius. An *evil* genius.

"It was you or sweet Thea and Cora. Your sister couldn't bear the thought of your nieces becoming sex workers."

Oh my god. This man smuggles children, and he has no shame in the skin trade.

"Cora and Thea? You would have taken my nieces and made them sex slaves? They're only children!"

I expect him to answer the question, but he doesn't. He doesn't have to. He's a criminal and apparently a mad man.

"Give me what I want, Lauren, and you'll have an incredible life here."

I feel the color drain from my face. "Do you plan to make me a sex worker?"

"No."

"What happens if I don't help you?"

"I will bend you until you break." He stands and straightens his French cuffs. "Take a look around. It's the beginning of winter here. Temperatures will continue to drop. I can take away the heat at first. Next will be the blankets and firewood. Followed by hot water. And eventually your clothes."

My eyes bulge from their sockets.

"You'll last maybe two weeks at best, and that's if I remember to have Anja bring you food and water."

My eyes sweep to the window. It's snowing, and from what I know about this part of the world, with the wind gusts and the sea, it makes for a miserable winter. I swallow hard. As much as I want to protest and fight, this is not the hill I want to die on.

Literally.

"Do we understand one another?"

I shake off the shiver that runs down my spine. "Yes, Master Kallas. We understand each other."

I understand that you're a coldhearted bastard.

"Good. Tonight we dine at le Rideau Bordeaux. It's a member's only club that my son Wystan owns. You'll meet him and my eldest son, Damen, at dinner. Now to everyone else, you're Lauren Bainbridge—a college student taking a gap year. You're here as my guest. Is that understood?"

No, it is not understood. I fight the urge to scream at him. Instead, I simply nod.

"You'll need to wear a gown, of course. First impressions are everything. Anja will help you with anything you need. My driver will arrive at six-thirty to collect you."

His *sons* are probably just as evil and vile as he is.

My teeth grind and I feel like the floor will cave beneath me. I don't want to be agreeable, but it's better for me to agree than fight back—for now.

"Thank you. I look forward to a lovely evening."

He turns on his heel and walks away.

My eyelids sink closed, and I swallow the wave of rising bile. What will he make me do?

CHAPTER
eight

Damen

I STAND IN FRONT OF THE WINDOWS OF MY OFFICE, LIFELESS LIKE A robotic shadow. The sun dips below the mountains, snuffing out the glint of snow caps.

Our city is beautiful at this time of day.

Sipping a glass of Stoli Elit, I wait as the darkness of night takes over the city. Snow floats down, blanketing the land. The streetlamps glimmer, casting shadows of light illuminating a pathway for the people to make it home safely. My eyes flick to the scene below. People scurry over cobblestones, likely headed toward their destination for special dinners with friends and family.

Family.

Weeks ago, my father struck the deal of the century. A broad market sell-off. Now Vutreila owns the largest bank in Eastern Europe. More money for us. More money for our businesses.

And the Kallas family business is crime. My father is the head of the Kallas crime family and while my brother, Wystan, and I have our separate businesses from the "family" business, we're still called upon for certain appearances.

My speaker phone buzzes. "Mr. Kallas, line two is for you."

"Thank you." I walk toward my desk and hit the blinking button. "What's going on?"

"The mayor just called. He's booked a room for tomorrow afternoon."

"Okay. Give him anything he wants. Just be sure to escort him and his guest through the kitchen."

"Very good, sir."

The old Swiss clock on the wall strikes half-past six.

"Sir, is there anything else you need?" My assistant Ingrid stands just to the right of the roaring fireplace. Shadowy flames from the fireplace lick up her long legs.

"No, thank you, Ingrid. Enjoy your weekend."

Ingrid gives me a brief smile and bows her head. A curtain of blond shields her dark eyes.

"You do the same, sir."

Offering a curt nod, my attention turns back to the window, and I finish the rest of my drink.

I drop into my desk chair and shove the glass aside. My phone hums a familiar tune and the vibrations force my eyes to the screen. It's my younger brother Wystan.

We have dinner with Father at the club in an hour. Don't forget.

How can I forget? It's one of the Kallas family traditions.

As I enter le Rideau Bordeaux, I notice the usual crowd.

The *family* is here.

My uncle Lorence, my father's right-hand man, and his mistress Sana sip cocktails in the dining room among the wholesome mix of elite members of society and not so reputable business owners.

Talking shop and talking shit. Striking deals and making plans.

Each of these lowlifes is essential to my own business. I'll happily take their money. All their money.

Despite the harsh winters and the less than tropical summers, Vutreila has transformed into a playground for the rich and powerful. People from all over the world come to taste the forbidden and get drunk on it.

Lorence throws lavish parties for his friends, takes their money, and they all still come back for more.

What will happen when the parties end?

Even with his numerous errors, Lorence remains untouchable in the family. While I don't want to inherit the tarnished dynasty, it may be unavoidable. Lorence has always been my father's favorite brother, and even with his reputation, he still retains the full confidence of the patriarch.

Although if I were to become the *king*, my first order of business would be to read Lorence the riot act, then strip him of his power and put Wystan in his place.

Slipping through the crowd of patrons, I nod to Lorence as I make my way toward the private dining room.

When I enter the room, my eyes land on the most beautiful woman I've seen in my entire life.

She's young. A blond beauty with dazzling blue eyes. She looks like a Grecian goddess wearing a glittering silver gown. The neckline plunges and the silk fabric clings to her breasts.

She's sitting beside my father, but that doesn't stop my lingering stare.

So, he's got a new plaything, which means she's off-limits.

That's never stopped you before.

"Ah, good, Damen." My father's voice booms through the room. "Come sit."

Her eyes meet mine and there's something in her expression

that I cannot decipher. I take my place across from my father as he whispers something to his new mistress.

He's got his new pet trained already.

Gross.

My skin crawls at the thought that my father's had his hands on this stunning woman. The old man will be sixty soon. This woman looks closer to twenty than thirty.

My brother Wystan appears from the bar and takes a seat next to me. I motion to the bartender for a glass of vodka.

"Gentleman, I'd like you to meet Lauren Bainbridge."

Lauren shifts in her seat and gives me a halfhearted smile. A wave of desire winds through my system.

"Lauren is incredibly special to me," he says, grasping her hand.

Her eyes close and her shoulders tense.

That's *odd.* She almost seems disgusted by my father, not enamored with him. Is she afraid of him?

"Lauren, say hello to my sons, Damen and Wystan," he requests.

"Hello, gentleman," she says, straightening her posture. "It's nice to meet you."

"Your accent is American English," Wystan quips.

She smiles and her fingers skim along the diamonds around her neck. "Yes, sir. Chicago"

Wystan chuckles and whispers, "I kind of like hearing her call me, *sir.*"

I refrain from rolling my eyes. "How long have you been in Vutreila?"

"Not long. But your father has been very generous and welcoming."

"I bet he has," Wystan snickers into this tumbler of vodka.

Lauren glances at my father and swallows thickly before

squeezing his hand. This has got to be an act. What is my father trying to pull?

"What brings you to our little place here in the Baltics?" I ask. "It can't be for the weather." My head nods toward the windows, where a heavy cascade of snow falls.

"I invited her." My father narrows his gaze at me. Ice slides into his stare. "I know Lauren's sister Katrina and her husband Greg. Old family friends."

I don't recall a Greg or Katrina.

Lauren speaks up, "I'd been thinking about studying abroad for a while, but I could never find the right place or program. When my sister Kat mentioned Vutreila and how much she and Greg loved it here, they phoned your dad, and he was kind enough to invite me. He insisted that I take a gap year from college and get a first-hand education of the Baltics right here in Vutreila."

Interesting.

"Did he now?" Amusement rings in my brother's voice. "Valter sent the two of us to prep school and university in England. Here I thought writing big fat donation checks was his only involvement in education."

Blush crawls up her neck. "Your father wouldn't take *no* for an answer. He's insistent."

"Well, if he had, you'd be the first." Wystan tips his glass in her direction.

Our meal arrives and my father indulges us in his usual conversation of politics and business. Throughout the evening, club members filter over to the table.

Lauren looks bored.

The night crawls by in a haze of smoke and liquor. We move from the private dining room to the club lounge, where conversation bounces off the dark paneled walls, soaring ceilings, and hardwood floors.

Lauren lingers at my father's side making effortless small talk and wooing dozens of unsavory people.

After the evening ends, Marek, my head of security, takes me back to my estate. Normally at this hour, I'd just stay at the Aldon, but I feel like I've spent way too much time there lately.

When I push through the front door, Luka lifts his head from the rug in the foyer. "Hey there, Luka." He nuzzles his head into my hands. "I missed you, too, buddy."

As Luka stands and stretches, I grab the leash off the wall and then clip it to his collar. We walk outside so he can relieve himself, and I nod to Tannil. Given the hour, I know that this is his second perimeter sweep during his shift.

"How's it going, sir?" he asks, flicking the ash from his cigarette onto the frozen ground.

"It's been a long night. And you?"

"Won some money earlier," he informs before taking a long drag. "The men really enjoy the gambling."

We renovated part of the stables years back to accommodate living quarters and a shared club space for the guards when they stay here. It keeps morale and loyalty extremely high.

"I'm glad. You can always drop your money at the casino. I'll happily take it."

He smirks. "I know you would, sir. Have a good night."

Once Luka finished sniffing around the yard, we walk back inside. I slip the leash off Luka's collar, and he trots back toward the kitchen.

The wood creaks beneath my shoes as I walk toward my study.

"Shoes off, young man." Dorel scowls at me from the hallway.

I hold my hands up in the air. "Fine. Fine. Don't shoot."

"I will if you've stained the rugs. I just had them cleaned."

Dorel's been my house manager since I bought the place. But I've known her practically all my life.

"They're off now. Happy?"

Ignoring my question, she strides back to her room, cursing under her breath the entire way.

I grab the decanter of vodka and pour a glass. Powering up my laptop, I spend a few hours combing the internet for any scrap of information about this woman. It's like she appeared out of thin air.

Lauren Bainbridge.

No social media footprint.

No university records.

Slumping into a lounge chair, I search for Lauren Bainbridge in Chicago. Nothing comes up. Bizarre doesn't even begin to cover the scenario.

Who are you, Lauren Bainbridge?

CHAPTER
nine

Damen

"I'VE GOT NOTHING." WYSTAN BARRELS INTO MY OFFICE AND helps himself to a vodka. "It's like this woman doesn't exist."

"Please come right in and help yourself."

He tosses me a smirk. "Thank you, brother. You're always the gracious host."

"So I take it your resources turned up nothing on our new American?"

It's been weeks since our dinner with the mysterious Lauren. Neither one of us has laid eyes on her since that night.

"Not a damn thing." He drops into the chair in front of my desk. "Couldn't even get Ewan to tell me anything."

"That's surprising. He's not deeply loyal to the old man."

"He's being extra cagey," he sniffs. "I offered him some money and a night here at the Aldon. Turned me down flat."

Aldon is the biggest hotel and casino in the country. Major players from all over the world come to Vutreila for a chance to win big. Others end up losing everything.

I've been in rooms listening to men and women beg and plead for their savings and possessions to be returned.

That's why it's called gambling. It's a game of chance and risk.

You play.

You pay.

"Maybe she's with the Kulinksi mafia. She said she was from Chicago."

"A Kulinksi? It's possible, but highly doubtful. Did you notice the way she flinched when Father touched her?"

He shakes his head. "No, I was too busy staring at her perky tits."

I toss him a scowl. "Of course you were."

"What are you thinking?" He leans back, crossing his ankle over his knee.

"I don't know. It's odd. She seemed uncomfortable yet answered every question with precision."

"You think he coached her?"

"Maybe. Do we know where she's staying?"

"I snooped around the country house. There's no one in any of the guest quarters. Monique is still in the penthouse. So I guess the two of them are still an item. I haven't been to the chalet yet."

The mystery continues to knot instead of unraveling.

"Do you think she has a property here? Maybe she's a dual citizen."

Wystan laughs and swallows the rest of his vodka. "I don't know. Why don't you just ask daddy dearest where she lives?"

"Something feels off about this," I tell him.

"Like what?"

"I don't know. I can't shake this feeling I got that night at dinner. I'm not so sure that she's a college student."

"Wow. You're really fixated on this mystery woman. For all

we know, she's back in the United States. Or worse, maybe the old man has her locked away somewhere."

That thought irritates me. I rise from my seat and walk toward my bar. "Fuck. He said Lauren is *incredibly special* to him. She was a little off at dinner. I bet you a million dollars she's his daughter. Which makes her our half-sister."

Wystan stands. "I think your brain is working overtime, brother. When was the last time you took a vacation? How about Greece this weekend? I can have the jet ready by five."

"It sounds awesome, but I've got too many things on my plate right now." I pour myself a drink. "There's got to be more to the story where this woman is concerned. I've never heard father mention anyone by the last name of Bainbridge."

"Why don't you invite her to dinner and get to know her?" Wystan suggests.

"First, I'd have to find her."

Wystan chuckles and downs the rest of his drink. "Well, I don't think you'll need to look much further. She's sitting at the main bar of the casino."

I follow his gaze toward the monitors in my office. Shiny blond hair drapes over her bare shoulders, leading my eye to her tits. Yes, Lauren Bainbridge looks like every man's wet dream in a strapless red dress that fits her like a damn glove.

I finish my drink and the glass hits the bar top with a thud. "I guess I'll go have a chat with the mysterious Lauren."

CHAPTER
Ten

Lauren

"IF HE TOUCHES HER, CASTRATE *HIM*."

Valter Kallas' words ring louder in my head. I look over my shoulder to see the man who drugged me sitting in the corner of the bar.

Tonight, he's playing the role of my protector.

The thought has me quietly laughing into my martini.

It's been an interesting few weeks, to say the least.

One afternoon, after being blindfolded and outfitted with earbuds, I was driven from the place where I'm staying to a place forty minutes away. Now granted, the driver could have been circling the block and then driven a short distance away. I'll never know.

That's how I ended up at Valter's country home. That day he gave me access to the library at his family estate.

"You've been here a month, Lauren, and you've managed to not be a thorn in my side. The perfect houseguest."

Houseguest. He meant hostage.

"You may use the internet. If you contact anyone, you will regret it."

Who would I contact? My sister? She might as well be dead to me. How could she put me in this hellish nightmare? Cynthia? She didn't believe in social media. No Instagram or Facebook page.

And tonight, I'm in a situation I never dreamed that I'd ever be in. I'm here to meet Kilan Dimants, the son of shipping mogul Arvid Dimants.

Over the last month, Valter has kept me busy with research and surveillance. Including monitoring Kilan's daily habits.

And as it turns out, he comes here to the Aldon every Thursday night. He has drinks at the main bar and then is escorted to a private room where he joins in a high-stakes poker game.

Tonight, I'm hoping that he invites me to join him. If I can get close and earn his trust, he'll spill valuable information, putting me one step closer to leaving this frozen ice land.

"Kilan is the black sheep of his family," Valter tells me. "His father barely tolerates him. The closest relationship they have is through his bank account. My guess is that Kilan will spill any family secrets to a beautiful young woman. Charm him."

"I'm not sleeping with him."

Valter chuckles. "That's the last thing I want you to do." His dark gaze swings to Ewan. "If he touches her, castrate him. Don't disobey me, Lauren. If you do something stupid . . . you'll find yourself sleeping in the cold."

"Excuse me, what time is it?" I ask the bartender.

"Seven-thirty, miss."

"Thanks." I order another drink as I wait for the notorious Kilan to arrive.

If it's seven-thirty here, that means it's eleven-thirty in Chicago. Right now, I'd be having lunch. Maybe at Cynthia's place. We'd be making plans for a girls' night out.

What happened to Cynthia? Is she back in Chicago? Is she trying to find me? I wonder if she's tried to contact Katrina. Or maybe Cynthia had been kidnapped . . . *trafficked* too.

I hope not.

What happened to the other women that I had been imprisoned with? Where had Bianca ended up? Was she being subjected to beatings? Rape? Torture?

These questions stir daily. Hourly. And keep me up at night.

And while I'm up at night, I try to map out where I think the chalet I'm staying in might be. I know it's somewhere outside the capital city, but in which direction? It's pointless.

When I can't sleep, I sneak around the chalet in the dim light, pretending to read a book. Actually though, I'm cataloging every window and door to memory for my future escape. It will be months from now when the weather turns warmer.

Despite the fact that Valter has been nothing but *nice* to me over the last few weeks, I still hate him.

At the end of the day, he's the monster who traded money for my life.

My thoughts turn back to my sister. Had she sat in this very bar? Had she sat here in this chair? Was this where she negotiated with Valter for my life?

As much as I hate Valter, the hate I have for my sister is a hundred times more.

I tamp down the hate that I have for Katrina. It won't do me any good.

Because I am *never* going to see her again.

It looks like my future is here in Vutreila, at least until Valter gets what he wants. At that point, I will fight for my freedom.

"Why do you think you'll be free if you go back to the United States? You're free here. More free than you would be in your precious Chicago. Here all you have to do is relax, enjoy meals that you never have to cook and cocktails that you never have to make. You even have an opportunity to earn rewards—even money. You can come and go as you please."

"I can come and go as I please with limitations."

"Those limitations are in place for your safety."

My eyes sweep around the casino bar when my gaze pins the man who's invaded my thoughts for the past month. I sat in silence, watching the tall figure move through the throng of people.

Damen Kallas.

His beauty is unfair.

The spawn of a monster wrapped in designer threads and too damn good looking for his own good.

As soon as our eyes meet, he stalks toward me, power and wealth radiating off him in waves.

With his deep blue eyes still on me, he grins. "Lauren, hi."

His voice is rich and warm, and his accent teases the corners of my mind. It hints of posh English sophistication. His brother has the same accent. Maybe they didn't grow up here?

Stop caring.

"Damen. Nice to see you again."

As far as men go, I've never seen a man in the flesh that looks like Damen. Movie star good looks right down to his severe jawline and flawless skin. Even under that suit, I can tell he has a droolworthy body.

No. Stop thinking about him like that.

"Welcome to my casino."

"*Your* casino? I was under the impression that the Aldon was your father's place?"

His jaw shifts beneath the stubble of his five o'clock shadow. "No. This place is all mine. Right down to the cocktail sticks."

I pick up my martini glass. "How nice for you."

Nice. Don't be nice to him.

He might not have been the one who paid for you. Kidnapped you. Trafficked you. But the apple doesn't fall far from the tree. All three Kallas men are probably in on the skin trade.

"Are you waiting for someone?"

"I am."

"How about I join you while you wait?" He doesn't wait for me to answer. Instead, he sits in the chair next to me and orders a glass of Stoli Elit.

I twirl the cocktail stick speared with the two olives in my drink. Absently, I watch as servers and other female staff stare at Damen. A few even say hello as they pass by.

He acknowledges their presence with a slight nod. There's no mistaking the way they look at him—pure lust.

The same way you're looking at him. Is it though? I mentally argue with myself.

"Is this your first time here at the Aldon?" A half smile pierces me over the rim of his tumbler, unleashing a storm of heat.

My nipples peak against the cups of my strapless bra. Thank goodness I can hide my body's deceitful reaction to him.

"No. I've been here a few times before tonight."

Which is true. Although every time before, I've worn a red wig at Valter's suggestion.

"I haven't seen you since my father introduced us at dinner. I thought you'd gone back home."

Home. My heart tumbles in my chest.

"No such luck."

"Speaking of luck. I'd be happy to offer you a complimentary stay here at Aldon. If you'd like. We have a salon, a wellness spa, and an ultramodern gym complete with a juice bar. Not to mention a Michelin star restaurant."

"That's generous of you, Damen. Thank you."

"Are you enjoying your stay here in Stuvica?"

I haven't really seen much of the city.

"The city is very beautiful."

"I'm happy to give you a tour from a local's point of view." He smirks, and temptation glides through every cell in my body.

"I'm sure that you're far too busy running your empire to bother with the likes of me."

"That's one of the perks of being the boss. I control my own hours. Actually, I'm glad that I ran into you. I was wondering if you'd like to have dinner with me sometime?"

Yes. But too bad you can't. You have a job to do, and that job doesn't include having dinner with Damen Kallas.

Ewan cuts a disapproving glance in my direction and shakes his head.

"What do you say, Lauren? We should have dinner and get to know one another better."

I flick my gaze to Damen, who studies me in his imperious fashion. "What part of I'm meeting someone do you not understand?"

The expression on his beautiful face hardens. "I'm sorry to have bothered you. Erik," he calls out to the bartender. "Put Miss Bainbridge's drinks on my account."

"Your father is taking care of her bill."

Panic bubbles inside me.

"Is that so?" The timbre of his voice stokes the fires on my overly heated skin. In an effort to douse the flames, I swallow down half my drink.

Kilan enters the bar, and I watch as his expensive Italian leather shoes glide over the red plush carpet.

Damen lowers his mouth to my ear. "Is that the kind of man you go for, Lauren?" The words roll like lava down my spine.

Ignoring his question, I gather my thoughts and remember why I'm here tonight.

"You should really be careful of the company you keep. Because if you're fucking my father, you shouldn't be fucking the son of his worst enemy."

My shoulders tense, and it takes everything inside me not to tell Damen to go to hell and toss my drink in his gorgeous face.

"I'm not fucking anyone, *yet.*" An inappropriate twist of lust hits my stomach. I down the rest of my martini and rise from my seat. "You know the old saying, the enemy of my enemy is my friend."

Damen's mouth curls into a wry grin. "Right. Good night, Lauren."

"Good night, Damen."

That should do it. Now Damen Kallas can add me to the list of people he hates and leave me the hell alone.

CHAPTER
eleven

Damen

THE LIQUOR BURNS ALL THE WAY DOWN MY THROAT, WARMING my insides.

Fucking Lauren Bainbridge.

Fucking her is something I've thought about every night since I've met her. My cock threatened to tear through my trousers earlier.

Back here in the confines of my office, I lean back in my leather chair, watching the monitors of my hotel and casino following her every move. Apparently, I'm not the only one.

I see at least ten men craning their necks, moving to get a glimpse of her from the end of the bar. What red-blooded man wouldn't?

Even Ewan sits across the bar, keeping a close eye on Lauren.

If she is involved with my father, she'd know that Ewan is his right-hand man. Why the hell is she openly flirting with Kilan?

Something isn't right.

Can I be all wrong about her? Wrong how exactly? And what

exactly does she mean by that statement: *The enemy of my enemy is my friend.*

All these fucking questions. Irritation claws at my nerves, setting every one of them on a fine razor's edge.

I stare at the screen, watching them huddled together at a corner table. She's leaning in toward Kilan, and he's laughing at something she said. His gray eyes latch to Lauren's chest as his index finger traces over her clavicle and up the slope of her creamy neck.

It takes everything in me not to march my ass back to the bar and snatch Lauren from Kilan's greedy stare.

What is it about this woman that has me this wound up?

You know.

Swallowing another gulp of vodka, I think about tonight's private poker game. While I won't be playing because I don't shit where I eat, I look forward to taking more of Kilan's money. And while I'm at it, I'll take Lauren from him too.

CHAPTER
Twelve

Lauren

WHAT THE HELL AM I DOING?

I'm sitting in a lavish hotel suite with Kilan, a European movie star, a tech billionaire, a Russian mobster, and Petra Gataki, the Greek hotel heiress.

They've played four hands. Kilan won the first two. Petra took the third. And now, the mobster rakes in the large pot on this latest hand.

Two hours pass by and I'm so damn bored. Kilan and I've barely been able to talk, and because I need to have my wits fully intact, I've switched to club soda.

The table agrees to a break for food and more drinks.

Goose bumps rise on my skin, and it has everything to do with the woman wearing a silky gold wrap dress who just entered the room. I know her. I'm positive that she was with me in Belize.

My eyes follow her as she saunters across the room toward the mobster.

He says something to her, and she tips her head back with a laugh. Her dark hair falls in waves down her back.

Our stares collide and her green eyes go wide.

Oh yeah. She knows me.

The realization hammers through me as I walk toward her. She whispers something to him. He tips his chin as he picks up a platter full of pierogis.

Her green eyes shift toward the other side of the room. I give her a subtle nod and walk slowly to where she stands.

She turns her head over my right shoulder. "Belize, right?"

"Yeah. Are you with that guy?"

"No. He's—" She takes a harsh breath. "He's my client tonight."

"Oh god." Disgust roils in my stomach. "So, how did you end up *here*?"

"I don't really know. After the auction, we were all given a sedative. When I woke up, I was all alone in what I thought was a hotel room. But we found out later that we're in a high rise in the city somewhere. That's where we entertain most of our clients."

"We?"

"There are two other women from Belize here. The three of us are new. Six of us live in the penthouse, and we all have our own rooms. It's not so bad as long as we obey Madam. One of the women, Clarissa, told us that she's been here for four years. She's seen many women come and go over the years."

"Where do you think they go? Home?"

She steps back. "I just love your dress."

Someone is obviously watching the two of us. I take her cue. "Thanks. I can't for the life of me remember where I got it."

"Well, it was nice chatting with you," she chirps and scoots off toward her client.

Damn it. My eyes roam the crowd. I don't know who spooked her, but I'm pissed because I have more questions. I didn't even get her name.

What if I don't see her again?

I haven't seen her here before. At least, I don't think that I have.

Across the room, I see the Russian paw at her and squeeze her ass. She plays her part perfectly. She's definitely not the frightened woman I recall from the shower stalls in Belize.

Does she like this life?

Does she like being whored out night after night?

Okay, stop. You don't know what the details of being a client mean. You haven't had sex with anyone. Maybe she got the same deal.

Maybe Valter bought her and the other two women?

Or maybe Damen bought her to entertain high-profile clients. Father and son probably participated in the same auction. A bonding moment for them.

Shaking the thoughts, I move toward Kilan. He orders another drink and flashes me a grin of pearly white teeth.

He's not special. He's just a pawn in the game. The game to get my freedom back.

The next move is crucial.

"Kilan, it's been great hanging out with you tonight, but I'm afraid I've got to be going." I slide a poker chip into his breast pocket. "This is for good luck."

"Wait," he says, grasping my wrist. "When can I see you again? Can I get your number?"

Hook, line, and sinker.

"Don't worry. I'll find you."

CHAPTER
Thirteen

Damen

I TIP MY GLASS AGAINST MY LIPS AND SIP THE PERFECTLY AGED liquor.

When I replace the glass, I lean forward and watch Lauren slip the poker chip into Kilan's pocket.

She's leaving.

Now is my chance to find out where she's staying. Time to unravel the mystery of Lauren Bainbridge.

Rising from my chair, I swipe the number on my phone screen. "I need you to bring around one of the rental cars." I slip my Prada wool coat over my shoulders and leave my office.

"Right away, sir."

My next call is to Marek. "Keep your eyes on Lauren Bainbridge. She just left the poker game in the presidential suite. I'm sending you her picture now."

"You got it, boss."

After hanging up, I bring up the security system on my phone. I take my private elevator down to the valet stand.

Holding the phone, I stare out at the inky black of night and the snow that whirls around the glow of lights.

My phone pings with a message from Marek, telling me Lauren's with Ewan and they're heading for the valet.

I pull the black Mercedes forward and wait for the two of them to exit the casino. Then it's game on.

What are you hiding, Ms. Bainbridge?

Soon, she'll find out that she can't hide anything from me.

After a thirty-six-minute drive from the Aldon, I find myself staring up at a gorgeous chalet in the middle of nowhere. The design reminds me of an English manor, but there's a contemporary element with the glass pavilion and aluminum frame.

Ewan exits the car and then escorts Lauren to the door. He inserts a card into a panel and punches in a code. The door opens, and then Lauren steps inside. After the door closes, he enters the code again.

What the fuck is going on?

That's the million-dollar question.

The only answer is that my father is up to something, and Lauren is part of whatever he's got going on.

Ewan slides into the driver's seat of his Range Rover and then maneuvers back down the long driveway. To avoid being seen, I slide lower into the leather seat.

Well, there's no way I can just walk up to the house and ring the bell. If I know anything about my father, he's got a tight security system.

And since the security panel is on the outside, I'm sure Lauren can't even open the door.

Father's had plenty of mistresses since mom died.

Locking a woman inside a house. This seems strange even for my father.

Unless. She's in danger. Which would explain why she has no social media footprint. Is she hiding? Is her name even Lauren Bainbridge?

One thing is certain, I'm not getting any answers sitting here.

CHAPTER
fourteen

Lauren

N O. No. No. No way in hell this is happening.

As I stare at the piece of paper in front of me, a cold knot tightens in my gut.

"This is the Dashiell Diamond. Arvid Dimants has it and I want it." Valter's dark gray gaze meets mine. "And you're going to get it for me."

How ironic. Dimants is Latvian for diamond.

"How am I supposed to do that?"

"The Dimants have a rare collection of jewels. Get Kilan to show you the collection, and when he keys in the code, memorize it. Rumor has it they change the code every thirty-six hours. There's no fingerprint or retina scan. It'll be like taking candy from a baby."

"I'm not a thief, Master Kallas."

"No. I suppose you're not." He snaps his fingers. "You may come in now."

I crane my neck around the room and that's when my stomach flips and my jaw drops.

Wait. One. Stupid. Damn. Minute.

Out of the shadows steps *Cynthia*. She's wearing a black pant suit, diamonds drip from her ears and wrists. Her blond hair is now jet black. She looks the same but older somehow.

"I believe that you two know one another."

"Cynthia, what the hell?"

She skewers me with a smug stare as she clips toward me in her Jimmy Choos. "It's Inga actually." Her words echo with a heavy Polish accent.

What the actual fuck?

"Do you work for him?" My arms cross over my chest.

"Yes. I'm really sorry about all this." Her black brows wing upward.

"I doubt that."

"You're right. I'm not the least bit sorry. Thanks to you, I made the biggest payday of my life." A throaty laugh rips from Inga's mouth.

"You were in on this the entire fucking time?"

Valter steps between us. "There's no time for a reunion. The two of you have a job to do. The Serpent Ball is Friday night. It's the perfect time to steal the diamond. Hundreds of suspects in question."

"What's the plan, boss?" not Cynthia, but *Inga* asks.

My nails curl into my palms. "No way in hell. I'm not working with this bitch."

Her stare turns from smug to razor sharp. "Fine. Then you can steal the diamond yourself. Good luck with that."

"Silence," Valter shouts. "The two of you will get this job done *together*."

My mind reels. Greg and Kat came to Vutreila last summer. Inga moved into my building at the beginning of July. The pieces click together like a puzzle.

Oh god.

Every time Inga and I hung out with Kat, she knew that I would be taken. Kat bailed on me for the festival, insisting "Cynthia" take her ticket. That was all part of the fucking plan.

Rage roars into my veins, shooting steel up my spine. I spent time worrying about this chick's well-being and the entire time she was the person who delivered me up to the traffickers.

"The plan is simple," Valter says as the flat-screen television on the wall lights up with a map of the Dimants's mansion. "Once Kilan shows you the diamond, located here on the second floor, you will give Inga the code, and *she* will take the diamond."

"Piece of cake, boss." Inga whips her hair over her shoulders. "Once I signal my guy on the inside, the security cameras will go down. He said that he could keep them jammed for fifteen minutes at best. Apparently, old man Dimants hasn't upgraded his system in a while."

"Can you handle the task, Lauren?" His gray eyes narrow.

"Yes, Master Kallas, I can handle the task."

Because I don't have a fucking choice.

CHAPTER
fifteen

Damen

THERE MAY BE BAD BLOOD BETWEEN THE KALLAS AND THE Dimants families, but that doesn't stop me from crashing the Serpent Ball.

I hadn't planned on being here tonight. I'd rather be anywhere else, but I'm here . . . and I don't really know why.

Call it curiosity.

Using my skills, I charm the female checking invitations and gain entry within seconds.

The instant I enter the ballroom, I clock her bathed in the dim light of the chandelier that hangs directly above, looking like an ice queen. A design of inky black branches crawl up and wrap around her long-sleeve gown.

A man next to me in a green velvet tux knocks my arm. "She's quite a beauty, isn't she?"

Blood pounds in my temples, and my jaw clenches. I don't like him looking at her. Or even the fact that he thinks about her.

Ignoring him, I walk toward Lauren.

Before I make it two steps, Brantley Cardwell, the CEO of

Rosemary Distillery, stops me. We have a business meeting set up next week.

"Didn't think I'd be seeing you before our meeting next week, Kallas."

I chuckle and reach out to take the hand he offers me. "It's nice to see you again, Cardwell."

We shake hands, and then he turns to the stunning blond at his side. "You remember my wife, Caroline?"

"Of course. Mrs. Cardwell, it's a pleasure seeing you again."

"Oh, please, call me Caroline." She wraps her arms around my neck. "I'm a hugger, and you're practically part of the family."

That makes me smile. "Next week, we'll make it official."

Brantley and his brother Weston have been wooing me over the last few months. Enticing me to carry their bourbon in at the Aldon. Next week, we'll be making Cardwell the official house brand. It will be extremely lucrative for both of us.

She takes a step back from our embrace. "Tell me that you brought a date tonight, Damen. It would be nice to chat with someone interesting rather than these stuffy elites." The last two words come out as a whisper.

My thoughts drift to Lauren.

"Not this evening. I decided to attend the event at the last minute."

Brantley's brows rise. "Could have sworn I saw you eyeing the woman in the black-and-white gown moments ago. The way you were staring at her, Caroline thought you two were an item."

I lift my glass and swallow deeply. "The night is young. Maybe we'll be an item later this evening."

Caroline laughs and shakes her head. "She's incredibly beautiful. You should definitely go for it."

"Speaking of going for it." I motion between the two of them. "I hear congratulations are in order for baby number two."

Caroline smiles and her hand covers her baby bump. "Can you believe it? We're having a boy."

"That's awesome." I toss down the rest of my drink. "Perhaps you'll name him Damen."

"Not that Damen isn't a fine name, but we've decided on something a little more—"

Whatever she was going to say gets clipped when Brantley speaks, "Traditionally Southern."

My eyes snap over Brantley's shoulder when I spot Lauren descending the main staircase. I suppress the growl of irritation when I see that she's with Kilan.

"If you'll excuse me, I see someone I need to talk to. Enjoy the rest of your evening."

That someone is Lauren.

CHAPTER
sixteen

Damen

I WATCH IN TOTAL FASCINATION AS LAUREN TALKS TO KILAN.

Laughing at what—his stupid jokes.

Hanging on his every word.

Playing the part of the enamored companion almost perfectly. Every time he touches her, she has the same reaction that she did to my father's touch.

The wince is ever so subtle, but I notice. I swallow down the alcohol in my glass in the hopes of smashing the heat coursing through my veins.

She excuses herself and I follow her as she rounds the end of the bar. Lauren stops and spins around the darkened foyer. She looks up the staircase and then back toward the hallway.

Lauren stops one of the staff and he points down the hallway. She thanks him and begins walking down a small corridor.

Bathroom.

Lauren pushes the door open and disappears inside.

A few minutes later, a woman with a short red bob wearing

a black pantsuit emerges. Thirty seconds after that, Lauren steps out. When she lifts her head, she stumbles backward.

Straightening her shoulders, she regains her footing and walks back toward the Dimants'ss family hall. We pass under the archway and step into the black of the room.

Spinning around, her dark gaze locks on my face. "What are you doing here, Damen?" she snaps.

"It's one of the biggest social fundraisers of the year. No secret as to why you're here. Having fun with Kilan?"

"What's your deal?" Her blue gaze turns scorching hot.

"*My deal*? I should ask you that very question. My guess is you've got a lot of deals going here."

Lauren rolls her eyes and steps around me. "You don't know a damn thing."

I reach out and grasp her wrist, hauling her closer. To anyone else, we look like two people carrying on a conversation over the loud noise of music.

"Let me go," she hisses, and her brows dig deeper. "I'm leaving."

"You're not leaving because I have a few questions for you. For starters, why are you pretending with Kilan Dimants?"

"I'm not pretending anything with Kilan."

"Your body betrays you." My jaw flexes and I feel the tendons in my neck tighten. "So I'll ask you once more—why are you pretending to have any kind of interest in Kilan?"

Her eyes narrow and she smacks her clutch against my chest. "I don't owe you any answers. So don't ask me questions."

"I'll ask you as many damn questions as I want." My grip tightens on her wrist. "Who are you?"

She tries to wiggle free from my hold. "Let. Me. Go."

I shake my head and pull her further into the dark. "Why did my father really bring you here?" The words roll off my tongue with a sharp bite.

Before she can answer, the beating of Kilan's slow clap draws the attention of the partygoers.

"This is a sight. Damen Kallas here in Dimants Manor. I should've hired tighter security."

"With what money, Dimants? You lost it at my casino last week."

Kilan's smug smile turns into a scowl and then he lunges at me. "You're an asshole, Kallas."

"Yep, but at least I'm a rich asshole, and that's more than I can say for you."

Kilan grips the lapels of my tux and my hands smack over his wrists. He sneers. "Fuck you. Get out of my house."

"Don't you mean daddy's house?" I shove Kilan off and straighten my jacket.

Security rushes in and I realize my time here is up.

I take a bow. "Ladies and gentlemen, I'm sorry for the interruption of the evening. I'd like to make it up to you. Come to the Aldon this weekend and just present your Serpent Ball invitation for a five hundred dollar voucher."

Applause of appreciation filters around the room.

Check and mate, Kilan.

Lauren stares at me for a beat and a second later, a small smile tugs at her lips.

CHAPTER
seventeen

Lauren

"**W**HY DID MY FATHER REALLY BRING YOU HERE?"
Those words, compounded with Damen's anger toward me, have me wondering if he's not a trafficking bastard like his father. Maybe Damen Kallas is a different kind of bastard?

Is it possible that Damen doesn't know what a monster his father is? Not possible. Valter is head of the Kallas crime family. They're all in on crimes. To what extent, I have no idea.

It's been twenty minutes since I gave Inga the code to the jewelry case that holds the precious diamond Valter wants. My job is to stay until the party ends.

Looks like the party is coming to a quick end. This gives me a small window of opportunity.

More security guards filter into the ballroom, attempting to restore calm.

This diversion could be the perfect opportunity to escape. Escape where?

It's been snowing all night. I'd die of hypothermia before

getting anywhere that wasn't under Valter's rule. I could hide here until morning and then talk Kilan into helping me.

I caught Kilan in the library after dinner with one of the blond bartenders. He didn't see me, but I watched him back her into the corner, lift her legs around his waist, and fuck her.

I didn't mean to watch. I've never seen anything so erotic, so raw in my entire life. For the briefest of moments, I allowed myself the tiniest fantasy that I could be that uninhibited with someone.

Her head bowed back, and his mouth opened, pouring out a guttural groan that I've never heard before.

After they finished, he came back to the bar. Her scent was all over him, and I pretended not to notice.

Gazing around the room, I search for Damen. The man I thought about the entire time Kilan and the blond pawed at one another like beasts.

While Kilan is busy calming his guests and urging them to stay, I blend into the sea of party people. Ewan is still nowhere to be found. Neither is Inga.

I leap and don't bother with the coat check; I just ride the wave toward freedom. Or at least the cresting wave toward freedom.

Once outside, I spot Damen at the valet stand. Security stands in close proximity. They could be on Valter's payroll, for all I know.

Fuck. Fuck.

My heart hammers in my chest. Think, Lauren.

When the sleek black Audi A7 rolls to a stop, Damen steps forward.

It's now or never.

I move through the crowd and slip my arm around his. "Hello, my friend. Can you give me a lift home?"

Damen's cool steel stare bores into me. "Of course. Get in."

CHAPTER
eighteen

Damen

A S SOON AS WE SPEED AWAY FROM THE DIMANTS'S MANOR, A blood-curdling scream rips from Lauren's mouth. Her entire body shakes as she fumbles with the buttons on the passenger door panel.

"What are you doing?"

"I did it. Oh my god. He's going to find me. He's going to kill me."

"Lauren. Who are you talking about? Who's going to kill you?" My hands grip the steering wheel tight.

"Can you roll the window down, *please*?"

"Are you okay?" I ask before pressing the button for the window.

Her head hits the headrest, and she gulps in the night air. "I don't know."

She wraps her arms around herself, and I notice her breaths coming on stronger. I hope she's not going to be sick.

The car cuts through the black of night, racing down the road toward Stuvica. Drawing in a deep breath, I focus on the snowy road glittering in the headlights.

"What do you need?"

She laughs and it sounds like she's crying. "I don't know anymore, honestly. Just take me away from here."

"Are you in some kind of trouble?" I glance at her. "Did Kilan hurt you? I noticed Ewan wasn't at the party with you. Isn't my father keeping tabs on you?" I keep pressing, hoping she'll give me something.

I steer the car around a soft left bend toward downtown Stuvica. "Last chance to tell me exactly what you need, because the turn that leads to the house you're staying in is about three blocks up on the right."

The car speeds closer and closer to the turn.

"Lauren, it's decision time. Am I turning or not?"

She shakes her head, drawing in a deep breath. "No. I don't want to go there. Ever."

My foot hits the gas, and we zip past the turn and head for the Aldon. Lauren casts her gaze out the window. I feel her tensing beside me even though she's here of her own volition.

"Wait, how did you know about that house?"

My grip tightens on the steering wheel. "You think I don't know what's happening in my own city? I own this town, sweetheart. I have eyes and ears everywhere."

And so does my father.

She crosses her arms over her chest. "I think this town belongs to your father and since you're your father's son—I'm pretty sure that means he owns you too."

"No one owns me. Not even my father."

It's mostly true. The relationships between fathers and sons are often complicated.

Why is my father so attached to this woman? If there's

anything I know about my father, it's his taste for useful things and people.

Obviously, she is of interest to him. The thing I can't wrap my head around is her loyalty to him. But why? None of it can be good.

"Where *are* you taking me?"

"To my place at the Aldon, where you and I will have a little chat."

Her shoulders sag and the visible unease thaws from her body. "I suppose I owe you that much since I'm basically a stowaway."

The glow from the dash casts just enough light for me to take in her profile—chin, lips, cheekbones—she is beautiful madness, and you can see it in her eyes.

I pull into the private garage at the Aldon and park in my regular spot near the elevator. Lauren doesn't wait for me to open the door. She eyes the exit and then her gaze swings back to me.

"This way," I say, jutting my chin toward the elevator.

Gathering up the sides of her gown, she walks around the front of my car.

I slide my card into the panel and then punch in the code. My phone buzzes and I key in the five-digit code. Two-factor authentication.

The elevator door opens, and I motion for her to step inside. We ride up to my floor in silence and my mind races trying to figure out why she's here.

The doors open into the foyer of my penthouse. As we step inside, I watch in complete fascination as Lauren stares up at the chandelier, and then her eyes sweep to the artwork I have lining the walls.

I shrug out of my jacket and toss it onto the cherry-colored leather chair in the living room. Lauren walks through the living room and stands in front of the floor-to-ceiling windows overlooking the Baltic Sea.

"You can see everything from up here. Your tower of black ice. It's kind of beautiful," she says, smoothing her palm over the dark stone of the kitchen island.

Tower of black ice?

"Have a seat."

Lauren glances at the plush leather sofa near the fireplace and squeezes her eyes shut like she's trying to gather her thoughts.

My body buzzes with energy. Too much. It hasn't been that long since I've been with a woman.

Her eyes crack open when I toss a few ice cubes into a tumbler.

"Would you like a drink?"

"No."

She's turning down a glass of ten-thousand-dollar vodka. *Hmm.*

"How about we start at the beginning?" I pour a generous count of vodka into the glass.

"If I tell you my story, I could be risking my life." She walks toward my desk and picks up a pen and notepad. She scribbles something and then flashes it up to me.

Is this place safe?

I nod. "My hotel has the latest technology. Security is updated routinely, and they sweep for bugs every six hours. I assure you, this place is safe. Are you in trouble?"

"Are you working with your father?" The words rush out of her mouth. Fear dances in her blue eyes.

"In what regard? Here at the Aldon?"

"In any capacity, legal or illegal." Her voice trembles as she speaks.

"I take people's money for a living. I don't care where it comes from. Gambling is completely legal. What people do outside these walls is none of my concern."

Liar. You've been concerned with *her* for the last weeks.

Her brows snap up and she skulks toward me. "Well, maybe you should care. Maybe you should know a little bit more about the men and women who sit at your gambling tables. And the women in the glittery dresses who float around on the arms of your high rollers. You should definitely care about the money that sits in your father's fucking bank. Why did I think that I could trust you?"

"Sit back down. We're not done here."

She folds her arms against her chest. "I'm so tired of people telling me what to do. That's all it's been since I came to this frozen tundra and now in this ice tower."

"You're not leaving *this* ice tower until I have answers."

"What if I refuse?"

"Test me and you'll find out what it's like for the palm of my hand to crack your bare ass. Sit down and answer the question. I won't ask you again."

CHAPTER
nineteen

Lauren

THE DIRTY THOUGHT SHOULD NOT EXCITE ME OR TEMPT ME because of the abuse I endured.

The idea should repulse me. It should not turn me on.

But oh holy Moses, the thought of Damen's hands on me sends wetness damping my panties.

It's only because of what I saw earlier between Kilan and the blonde.

Liar. You want *him* to touch you.

My breath catches in my throat when his hardened expression turns into a wicked grin. His stormy blue eyes threaten to expose my secrets.

If he unlocks my hidden desire, would he actually do it?

Damen takes a sip of his drink, sending a shiver up my spine as he continues to stare. "Why should I care about the money in my father's bank account?"

"As if you don't already know." I challenge him.

He prowls toward me. "Pretend that I don't and tell me."

I swallow thickly. "It's dirty money."

A sardonic laugh leaves his throat. "There you go. I already knew that. Tell me something I don't know, and maybe I'll reward you with some of our *dirty* money. Is that why you're here, Lauren Bainbridge, to get your hands on some money?"

"You would think that about me. You're so fucking arrogant."

"I don't know what to think, Lauren. You show up here out of the blue on my father's arm. Then you're with Kilan and now you're here with me. How many billionaires are you trying to seduce at once time?"

"I'm not trying to seduce anyone. I would rather be anywhere but here. But it wasn't my choice."

He steps closer. "I don't believe you. What's your fucking game?"

"My *life* isn't a game. But you people . . . you dirty rich assholes with all your fucking possessions and glitz. You think you can buy everything and everyone." I pry the glass from his hand and swallow down the contents.

Anguish and the heated fire that lives in my soul spurs me on.

"With a snap of your fingers, money appears, and people disappear." *Snap.* "People appear and money disappears."

His expression twists and a dark conclusion paints his face. "Help me understand, Lauren. I hope to hell that you're not telling me some goddamn lie."

My fingers tighten on the glass. Memories of inky, musty hell assault me.

Drugged. Taken. Beaten. Sold.

Stiffening my spine, I look Damen square in his eyes. "I didn't just appear out of thin air. I had a life. I belonged somewhere. My life was stolen, and that's why I'm here."

CHAPTER
Twenty

Damen

S HE WAS TAKEN. KIDNAPPED. THAT'S WHAT SHE'S TELLING ME.
I know what lies and deceit smell like. I've seen the look on dozens of faces.

I've seen a lot of shit in my past. I've done my share of lying and dirty deeds. But the thought of owning a person? A human soul?

"*. . . the women in the glittery dresses who float around on the arms of your high rollers.*"

I'm not totally oblivious. I know that prostitution exists. And if I could, I would extinguish it from the streets of Vutreila.

Lauren isn't a prostitute. She didn't have a choice, just like Zofia.

Tightness grips my throat.

I never give the people who visit the Aldon a second thought. I don't care where they come from. Don't care how long they stay as long as they spend their money here.

If they have the money, I'll give them anything they want.

Even rooms by the hour will cost you double the nightly rate. But they pay it, and I don't ask questions.

If they gamble away their life savings. Not my problem.

Lost your kids' university tuition. Don't care. You're a shitty parent who should have made better choices.

Money is money. Business is business. My business is money.

Apparently, my father's business dealings include buying women. A heavy knot settles in my gut.

Lauren tugs at her hair. One by one, tiny fragments pop off and sail onto the white rug beneath our feet.

Her long blond hair spills free from the pins, and the strands swirl around her shoulders.

Fuck, she's gorgeous.

Tears roll down Lauren's cheeks, and her sobs morph into full body shaking cries.

"Shit. Lauren. Try to calm down. You need to breathe." I hand her a glass of water. "Here, drink this."

She curls her shaking fingers around the glass and gulps it down. "Thanks."

"Are you okay?"

Her blue eyes, wet with tears, blink up at me. "That depends on what you're going to do with me now that you know my secret."

CHAPTER
twenty-one

Lauren

M Y HEART HAMMERS HARDER AS I STARE AT THE RIGID EXPRESSION on his beautiful face.

"What are you going to do with me?" I repeat the question.

He doesn't answer until I meet his dark gaze. "Nothing."

A shiver rolls down my spine. How can one word affect me this much? But it's not just the empty word. It's *him.*

"I just bared my soul to you and you're going to do nothing to help me?"

Damen turns his body to face me. "Firstly, you didn't bare your soul to me. Save the drama. Secondly, You didn't ask for my help."

Dramatic. *Pfft.* I think I've earned the right to be a little dramatic.

"You want me to *beg* for your help? Seriously? You really are a dirty asshole."

"I may be dirty, and I might be an asshole—" he pauses for

dramatic effect, making me want to punch him. "But I *can* help you. All you have to do is ask."

"What's the catch?"

Laughing, he lifts a shoulder. "I deal in favors. I do a favor for you. You do something for me."

"What do you want me to do for you?"

He studies me thoughtfully. "I'm not sure yet. In the meantime, I'm going to need more information from you."

"Like what?"

Before he can answer, there's a pounding at the door.

"Someone better be dying," Damen growls under his breath. He walks over to the door and a man dressed in all black enters. He's as tall as Damen and his jet-black hair is slicked back.

The man's gaze swings to me. "We have a situation."

Damen looks over his shoulder at me. "It's fine. You can speak. She's not going to say anything."

He's buying my silence and I'll find out the cost soon enough. I suppose that's a good tactic.

"Earlier tonight, an item was stolen from the Dimants's estate."

"What item?"

"The Dashiell Diamond, sir."

A tiny gasp slips past my lips and my shoulders tense. Dread coils around my spine.

Calm down. *You* didn't steal the diamond.

"And all the guests are now suspects in the crime, I presume."

He nods. "You're wanted for questioning. Detective Zabek is waiting in the private dining lounge on the mezzanine level."

There's a detective here? On the mezzanine level. I should bolt out of this suite and run screaming all the way.

Damen sneers. "That's what I get for being persona non grata. But Zabek will have to wait until tomorrow because I'm busy entertaining a guest."

"Yes, sir. I'll inform Detective Zabek."

"I'm sure that Zabek will gladly move me to the bottom of the list. Be sure to let him know that I'm happy to keep his extra-curricular activities a secret. It'd be a shame if his wife found out."

Damen's words smash into my heart with a powerful blow. The flicker of hope that the detective would help me snuffs out and turns to ash. His loyalty will always lie with Damen.

The man backs out of the penthouse, clutching the doorknob.

"You must know a lot of secrets," I tell him.

Damen closes the space between us and reaches for me. His fingers brush back the errant strands of hair on my face and I flinch. He pauses, his indigo gaze penetrating mine.

"Are you afraid of me?"

"Isn't that what you want? For me to be afraid of you."

His gaze intensifies and he drops his hand to my shoulder, caressing the tight bundle of muscles. I've never been so power-fully drawn to a man like Damen Kallas.

He's a tangled icy web of danger and temptation luring me in like prey to the predator.

Too late. You're here in his ice tower. He's already captured you.

It's what you wanted. Him to be your captor instead of his father.

"You should be afraid. Afraid of what I can take from you."

My mouth goes dry, and I try frantically to come up with some kind of response. I can't let him think that I'm afraid of him.

"What if I take from you instead?"

CHAPTER
twenty-two

Damen

WHAT IF I TAKE FROM YOU INSTEAD? She has no idea the meaning of those words.

I take a step closer to her, getting my fill of vanilla and jasmine. "What could you possibly take from me, Lauren Bainbridge?"

Fuck. She smells amazing.

Her breathing is unsteady, and I don't know if it's from nerves or frustration. Or perhaps it's arousal.

A million dollars says if I dip my hand into her panties, I will find her completely wet. Heat licks along my spine at the mere thought. The pressure in my tuxedo pants is excruciating.

"I could steal all your secrets. Take something precious from you while you sleep soundly in your bed."

"Is that where you'd like to be, sweetheart? In my bed?"

The thought of my cock deep inside her thrills me. I tamp down the thrill and refocus.

Beautiful women come to this hotel from all over the world and they constantly throw themselves at me. Married. Single.

Doesn't bother me. Doesn't stop me from stealing their pleasure. Their secrets. I take it all without a single hint of regret.

But not a single one of them affects me in the way Lauren does.

Her eyes flash with a dazzling, lethal heat. "My name isn't Lauren Bainbridge."

I brush my fingertips across her collarbone. "What is your name?"

The feel of her skin sears against mine.

Stop touching her.

"I have conditions."

My gaze narrows and my hands wrap into her hair, tugging to arch her neck. "You're already bargaining with me. You must have some fascinating information."

Her self-confidence is fucking hot. The fact that she thinks she can negotiate with me drives my lust by the second. If I'm not careful, I'll lose control of this situation.

Get your hands off her and step back.

She locks eyes with me, distracting me once again with her beauty.

"Your name—" I force myself away from her. "Keep your name. For now." I spear a hand through my hair and take a deep breath, reigning in the calm I need. I've spent years tamping down my emotions because of who my father is. This situation is no different.

"I have something you'll want even more than my name."

I lift a brow. That's quite an assumption. "I'm all ears, Lauren. You get one condition. Make it count."

"Keep me in your protection. Let me stay here with you."

Protection. That's what she needs.

"Did my father hurt you?"

She shakes her head. "No. He hasn't touched me. But he's made threats about the things he'll do to me if I don't obey him."

Goddamn it.

Going up against my father. This woman is going to be the death of me.

The condition is a risk. Good thing I deal in risks, and lucky for me, I get to see the hand she's dealing before I agree.

"What do you have to offer me?"

"I know who stole the Dashiell Diamond."

My brows rise. "That's excellent information."

"It was your father."

Fucking hell.

CHAPTER
twenty-three

Lauren

THE HEAT BURNING THROUGH MY VEINS IS UNBEARABLE.
He had his hands on me for a few minutes, but the sexual tension hasn't vanished. In fact, I'd say it's flourished.

Damen looks at me like I've given him something more valuable than the Dashiell Diamond. Which, for the record, is worth exactly $38 million.

With a rough tug, he yanks me against him until every part of me is pressed against the solid muscle hidden beneath his tux. His hands slide down to palm my ass.

Damen's mouth hovers inches from mine. His piercing blue gaze spears through me, stabbing all the way to my heart, making it pump faster, threatening to beat out of my chest.

"I know that I shouldn't, but fuck, all I want is to kiss you."

The whisper of his confession hits me like a tsunami. My stomach tangles with the frosty black branches that decorate my gown at the thought of kissing him. And thoughts of kissing him lead back to earlier and the erotic moment I watched unfold in the library of the Dimants's manor.

His lips hover over mine, the yearning in my body rages.

"I haven't been touched . . . *kissed* . . ."

Secret. My virginity is a secret for now. Information and my body are the two most valuable possessions I have at my disposal. It may be a bargaining chip in the future. The thought sickens me.

Clearing my throat. "What I mean is, I haven't had a welcoming touch in a long time."

His mouth crashes down on mine, kissing me, rendering me senseless and breathless all at once. My nails dig into his neck as I try to hold my balance when he grips my ass tighter.

My panties are officially soaked. Never. Not once have I ever had this kind of reaction to a kiss.

"I shouldn't have my hands on you, *Lauren.*" My name comes out in a low growl.

My hands thread through his dark hair, pulling him closer, silently begging him to kiss me harder. When his tongue meets mine, it's toe-curling, hot lust.

The touch of his lips against mine sets fire to every part of me. Maybe even my soul.

Without warning, Damen's hands fall away from me, and he strides toward the chair where his jacket lays neatly draped over the back.

Oh my god. Is he getting a condom?

Nope.

He tugs on his jacket and then hits a button on his phone. Seconds later, the man in black enters the suite.

"Get Ms. Bainbridge anything she wants or needs. Food, drink, and then have Clara bring a change of clothes and something for her to sleep in."

"Of course, sir," the man replies.

Damen pauses, staring at me strangely. My mouth drops open

when he picks up his keys. My chest rises and falls as he puts more distance between us.

He's leaving. Leaving me here alone?

"Where are you going?"

"To have a conversation," he replies gruffly.

Before Damen disappears out the door, he whispers something to the man, and he nods.

Did I make him angry?

Who is he going to talk with?

And what did he say to the man in black?

CHAPTER
Twenty-four

Damen

MY PATIENCE FLEW OUT OF THE WINDOW WHEN LAUREN'S BLUE gaze flitted over my chest and rested on the tie around my neck.

It was too close.

Had to have her. A taste.

As we stood in the room, bathed in shadows of light cast from the chandeliers above and the roaring fireplace, studying one another, lust howled through me.

She kissed you back. Wanted you just as much.

Did she?

Does she?

I need to concentrate on something other than how she felt against me. Focus on something other than how much I want to shove her to her knees and watch her take my cock between her sweet pink lips.

Thrust after thrust, plowing between her plump lips, fucking her gorgeous face.

A dirty thought slips through my mind. Has she ever been properly fucked?

I slam the steering wheel with my palm.

Don't apologize for your thoughts.

She's in complete control of you. And you proved it to her. Now she knows that you have a weakness. I need to shut my reaction to her down.

My car rolls to a stop outside my father's estate. Breathing deeply, I realize that what I'm about to do will undoubtedly put a target on my back. Or a knife. Or a bullet.

A target for a woman I barely know. A woman who was brought here against her will.

She doesn't belong here.

She doesn't belong in this world.

So I can't keep her.

For now, I'm going to protect her.

I've never had a reason to go against my father's rule. But even I have lines that I don't cross. Our mother would be ashamed to know that he's kidnapping women and selling them into sex slavery.

I glance in the rearview mirror, straightening my tie, and I notice red marks on my neck. I'd obviously taken her by surprise with the kiss.

Security nods as I pass by and open the front door. The house is swathed in darkness and silence.

"I've been expecting you," my father says from his shadowy position in his favorite leather chair.

"So you know why I've come here tonight?"

He laughs and snaps the book he's reading closed. "You forget I have eyes and ears everywhere."

"No. I know that you do."

And I do too.

He stands and walks toward the sideboard where multiple glass decanters sit holding liquor. "Would you like a drink?"

I shrug. "Sure, as long as that's vodka and not poison."

A sneering smile crosses his lips as he plucks the glass stopper from the decanter. "You think so little of me, Damen. You always have."

"I have my reasons."

He hands me the glass. "Why don't you and I get right to the reason you're here tonight—Lauren."

My temper flares. I hate that he says her name. How dare he speak it? She is beauty and light. He's ugliness and blackness.

"Yes." I wash down my anger with the vodka. "She's in my protection now."

He chuckles. "Is she? Are you sure about that?"

I nod. "Yes. Absolutely."

"We'll see about that."

His insinuating threat irritates me. "If you lay a hand on her or come near her, I'll put bullet in your skull and toss your body into the sea."

"You stand in my home and threaten to murder me?"

"Not a threat. A promise."

He smirks and tosses back his drink. "Fine. You can have her." He waves a hand over his head. "She was a means to an end anyway."

My brows rise. "How's that exactly?"

"She served her purpose." He lifts a cigar from the three-finger case.

"Are you suggesting that she helped you steal the Dashiell Diamond?"

He cuts the end of the cigar, holding my gaze. "I'm not suggesting or admitting anything, son."

"You got what you wanted and in exchange for my silence

regarding the diamond and the fact that you bought her, you're going to leave Lauren the hell alone."

"She told you that I bought her?" He feigns surprise.

"We agreed that prostitution and trafficking weren't in our best interest for the business. You knew how mother felt about that, and you're doing it anyway. Breaking her heart even in death."

Our mother, Zofia, had been given to our father when she was only fifteen. She was the daughter of our grandfather's enemy and the payment for an old family debt.

Upon her death, she asked our father for many things. One, that Wystan and I would never inherit the family business.

As it stands, this request has been denied.

Two, that we would always have the protection of the Kallas family.

So far, neither one of us felt the need to sleep with one eye open or with all the lights on.

Three, that the Kallas family would get out of the prostitution business upon her death.

How do you refuse a dying woman's wish? *Money.*

Money is the only reason.

Annoyance and anger rage inside me like an inferno, threatening to melt my icy exterior.

"Like I said at dinner, Lauren's a friend of the family, and they owed me a debt. That debt is now paid."

My teeth grind. "Must have been some debt."

"Tell me something, Damen." His eyes settle on the red marks on my neck. "Do you plan to fuck your new pet?"

"That's none of your goddamn business."

"She's still my possession until you leave this house, so I'll ask as many questions that I want. Or you can make this easier on both of us, and you can buy her from me. Make me an offer."

His bravado sends anger funneling through my veins. I stroke the ridges of the glass, counting the peaks and valleys to keep my-self from crushing it to dust. "Lauren is a person not a possession."

"I'd planned to fuck her myself, but then I realized I could sell her body. There's lots of value in a virgin. But then again, there's nothing like fucking a tight virgin hole."

She's a virgin. *Christ.*

He pours more liquor into his tumbler. "She does have an-other value . . ." He pauses for dramatic effect, and it pisses me off. "A photographic memory."

I say nothing.

"A real businessman would sell her or use her assets."

"Not everything in the world is a business transaction. Not only that but have you forgotten your promise to our mother? Have your forgotten your promise to your dying wife?"

He levels his hardened stare at me. "You can show yourself out now."

With fucking pleasure.

"I will think about using her assets though. A photographic memory may come in handy in a casino. Don't you think?"

A wolfish smile turns up his mouth. "Yes."

Tonight may be the last one I sleep with the lights off.

CHAPTER
twenty-five

Lauren

MINUTES BLEED INTO HOURS.

Where had Damen gone?

Would he be back here tonight?

It's almost two in the morning and I can still feel Damen's lips on mine.

"I know that I shouldn't, but I want to kiss you."

I allow myself the tiny fantasy of romance, passion, all things forbidden with Damen.

His kiss.

His touch.

Is the best thing that's happened to me since I arrived in this place.

He isn't a sweet man, Lauren. Look who his father is. What his father did to you.

Is Damen capable of the same kind of evil?

My eyes dart to the empty dishes sitting on the island. I'd asked for a carrot cake and a glass of milk. Two things I'd been craving since . . . well, the kidnapping in Isla Mujeres.

The food tasted so incredible, easily bringing me comfort.

Sleep hadn't been easy over the last weeks. I trudged from the living room to the bedroom and climbed under the covers, succumbing to sleep.

"Get your ass in the air."

"Finger that pretty pussy." The rough voice cuts through the dark. "Do you wish that it was my cock pounding into you over and over?"

I shoot straight up, clasping the silky sheet to my chest. "Damen?"

My eyes blink back the heavy fog of sleep. Is someone there? The room is completely black.

Sweat coats my skin, and my heart hammers in my chest as my eyes dart around the dark bedroom. *Damen's bedroom.*

There's no one here. It's only a dream. A dream that didn't turn into a nightmare for the first time in weeks.

A dream that turned into something wicked.

The left side of the bed is untouched. Did Damen not sleep here?

Why would he sleep beside you?

Pushing back the covers, I settle my feet onto the charcoal-colored rug. Stretching my arms over my head, I slowly take in the room.

It has the same dark wood floors as the living room, but the walls are glossy black, and the bedding is a smoky black. Totally opposite to my white and pink bedroom back home in Chicago.

There's a giant chrome, freestanding mirror on the opposite wall. Everything is dark and masculine and opulent.

It even smells like him. All I have to do is breathe in the hints of spice, wood, and vanilla. All of it is perfectly divine, like Damen.

The urge to pee interrupts my examination, and I glance around the room, spying a door that I hope leads to the bathroom.

I push it open and find a luxurious ensuite. A black free-standing tub sits in the middle. Beyond that is a large rain shower. The tile and the wood floor are the same colors as the rug in the bedroom.

Custom.

Once I've made quick work of my usual morning routine, I step into the living room. Damen is nowhere to be found.

"Ms. Bainbridge, good morning." The greeting comes from the man in black. He's sitting at the writing desk with his eyes focused on his iPad screen.

"Good morning. I'm sorry. What's your name?"

He gives me a tiny smile. "Marek."

"Marek. Can you tell me where I can find Mr. Kallas?"

"Mr. Kallas will return shortly. But he did say that you should order breakfast and he'll join you as soon as he can." He hands me a menu.

"Okay." My mouth waters as I read over the menu. "Everything looks so yummy. How about French toast, bacon, and fresh berries? Coffee too."

"Very well, Miss Bainbridge." Marek takes the menu.

I cringe at the name given to me by my captor.

"It's actually Miss Sanders, not Miss Bainbridge. Lauren Sanders."

He nods. "I'll alert the staff of the change, Miss Sanders." He picks up the phone and places the breakfast order.

I take a seat at the island, and the reality of my situation slams into me with force. *I'm free.*

I can go home to Chicago and back to my life. Back to my job.

A job that kept you isolated and lonely.

I'm isolated here, but not lonely.

You were isolated and lonely at the manor . . . *his* manor.

Wake up, woman. You don't belong here.

Do I belong in Chicago? With a family who sold me.

You'll be going home a different woman. Not so naïve anymore, and you're an accessory to a crime.

You're a jewel thief. A con artist and possibly a temptress.

He made me all those things. I had no choice.

I rise from the seat at the island and walk toward the windows. Would I even be able to go back to my old life?

How would I handle Kat and Greg?

You won't. Remember?

There's nothing really for me in Chicago. I should go back, clear out my apartment, move anywhere I want, and start over.

I catch a glimpse of myself in the mirror, not completely recognizing the woman staring back at me.

What do you really want?

That's the million-dollar question. Isn't it? More like the 3.2 million-dollar question.

This experience has taught me a lot of things. The most important lesson, though—trust no one.

But you trusted Damen enough to leave the party and beg him for protection. Do I trust *him*?

He could be out there negotiating with his father, for all I know. Damen could be bargaining with his father for my life.

"I take people's money for a living. I don't care where it comes from. What people do outside these walls is none of my concern."

The sound of chimes pulls me from my thoughts.

"Your breakfast is here, Ms. Sanders," Marek tells me as a woman wearing a black pencil skirt and a white blouse pushes a dining cart inside the suite.

Marek returns to his seat at the desk and taps his finger on the screen.

"Miss Sanders," the woman says my name with an elegant French rasp. "Can I get you anything else?"

I step up to the table, inspecting the spread. "This looks delish. I don't need anything else. Thank you."

She bows to me and then exits Damen's penthouse. As I sit and eat my breakfast, soft music pipes through the sound system. This feels normal. *Normal-ish.*

For the first time in a long time, I allow myself to relax. Snow falls from the sky as snowflakes ping off the windows. It seems to grow heavier with each bite I take.

The doorbell chimes again, and Marek glances at the tiny screen to his left. He gets up and walks to the door. Is Damen back?

No, dummy. It's his place. He wouldn't ring the bell.

Wystan, Damen's brother, steps inside the suite. "Well, well, well. We meet again, Lauren."

"What are you doing here?"

He stands over me and swipes a strawberry from the bowl. "Marek has a meeting, so my brother sent me here to look after you until he gets back."

Did Damen leave the city? The country?

My heart pounds against my ribcage. "Back from where?"

His big body drops into the chair next to mine. "I don't know. I didn't ask. All I know is that our father is a bigger asshole than I realized. He really had you kidnapped?" Wystan leans back and shakes his head. "Completely fucked up."

I nod. "You have no idea."

And while I have no idea where Damen is or what he's doing. Being here with Wystan puts me more at ease.

When I first met them at dinner, it was easy to see that they were close. I thought I had that same closeness with Kat. I was so wrong about that.

My thoughts hop from one memory to another.

I clear my throat. "Technically. Your father didn't kidnap me. My sister had me kidnapped."

"Yeah, I heard a little something about that. I'm sorry that all this has happened to you. But I assure you that you are safe here."

My eyes narrow. "You'll excuse me if I'm not totally convinced that's true."

He leans forward. "Hey. I get it. But Damen's a good guy."

I laugh. "Um. I know you guys have some questionable business practices. You're not entirely innocent." I point my fork at him. "I saw the kind of people milling around in the le Rideau Bordeaux."

Wystan cocks a brow. "Guilty as charged. So we dabble with some not so nice people. It's a hazard of our environment. It's true our father is the king of this place. Eyes and ears everywhere, but Damen and I have learned from the master, and you know what they say, the student becomes the teacher."

I swallow thickly. "Yeah. I suppose there's some truth in that."

"I heard you stole the Dashiell Diamond." He winks and pops a grape into his mouth.

"I didn't steal it. Inga did."

"Who the fuck is Inga?"

My brows crinkle. "You don't know her? It seems like you would know all the people who work for your father. Do his dirty work." I give Wystan a knowing glance.

"Guilty as charged. The Kallas family has a lot of 'helpers' and now, you're one of them. Admit it. You probably got a little rush from helping this Inga person."

I shake my head and pick up my coffee mug. "They forced me to do it. But yeah, maybe it was a little . . . thrilling. *Maybe*."

A slow grin spreads across his face. "I thought so. Tell me something."

I take a drink of coffee. "What?"

"If you're not a college student taking a gap year, who are you?"

Leaning back in the chair, I take a long breath. "Lauren

Sanders. I'm twenty-four, and I'm a virtual concierge. Well, I was, but now I'm in limbo. I don't even have my driver's license or my passport. It's like I don't exist."

Wystan pours himself a cup of coffee. "Except here, you are existing. Do you want to be a virtual concierge?"

I lift a shoulder. "I don't know how to answer that because I'm not going back to Chicago. They've probably already replaced me. If I go back home, it'll be to get my stuff."

Wystan studies me over the rim of his mug. "If you don't want to go back to Chicago, we can hire someone to pack your apartment and ship your things here. Hell, we can send a private jet. That's if you want to stay here."

I cock a brow. "Why would you do that for me?"

He shrugs. "Because we have the resources to do that for you. And I guess in a way we should because of what our father did to you."

"Are you going to do that for every woman your father trafficked?"

His brows knit in confusion. "What do you mean?"

My hands wrap around my warm mug. "Do you really think I'm the only one your father's done this to?"

Wystan reaches up and scratches the back of his head. "Are you saying there are more women?"

I nod. "Yeah. Dozens. I bumped into a women who was taken at the same time as me here in the hotel. I think your father might be running an escort ring for the high rollers."

"From what Damen said, it sounded like you were the only one."

I roll my eyes. "Pfft. Like Valter's going to admit his crimes. It won't surprise me if your father uses your club and the Aldon for shady shit."

His deep brown eyes bore into mine. "You're serious."

"As a heart attack."

CHAPTER
twenty-six

Damen

I LEAN BACK IN MY CHAIR STUDYING THE VIDEO OF LAUREN THE night she met Kilan Dimants at my bar.

So your real name is Lauren Sanders.

Lauren Sanders.

Even though I had to shell out a fuckton of money, it was worth it. Turns out Ewan does have a price, and he doesn't seem to like the idea of selling people. Who knew Ewan had a soft spot?

"Maybe you should know a little bit more about the men and women who sit at your gambling tables. And the women in the glittery dresses who float around on the arms of your high rollers."

Thanks to this information, I have been able to piece together a timeline. Turns out Lauren's sister and brother-in-law had stayed at the Aldon in our Elite Suite.

Even more interesting, my father has been running his own private underground, high-stakes games for years. He sends them a VIP invite and charms them with a cocktail reception after they've been on a massive losing streak.

The location of my father's games has changed throughout the years. A secret passcode is hand-delivered an hour before each game. On some level, I envy my father's brilliance, wishing that I had thought of the idea myself.

Gregory Woodward was targeted after losing a hundred and fifty thousand dollars here at the Aldon. A debt that he paid.

However, the private poker game is an entirely different story.

My father's ruthless idea cost Woodward three and a half million dollars. And cost Lauren her freedom. Her trust. Her faith in her family. I imagine that she will never truly recover from this horrible ordeal.

I've learned a lot about my father in the past eight hours. Too much of it has been right here under my nose for years. How could I have been so blind?

Marek walks into my office with Jonas, another member of my security team. "I've got some information, and you're not going to like it."

I spear a hand through my dark hair. A lash of heat licks my chest. "What is it?"

"We were able to follow the money. Turns out your father has a shell corporation set up in the Caribbean. We believe that's where he's funneling his trafficking money. He's been doing this for over a decade."

"Jesus Christ. There's just never enough money for this guy."

They continue to fill me on their discovery, including a video of Kat and Greg making a deal with my father's second in command, Hillar.

"Mr. and Mrs. Woodward," Hillar greets them. "Pleasure to see you. I've been made aware of your situation. Now it's just a matter of the deposit."

"A deposit?" Greg asks.

"It is customary for us to ensure certain protocols and that all goes well with the transfer."

Kat smiles. "How much?"

"Twenty percent. Seven hundred thousand dollars. Boss gives you a big discount because he knows that the merchandise is . . . untouched. Will fetch a high price at auction."

Kat's eyes close, seemingly disgusted by the thought.

"Are you sure there is no other way?" Greg asks. "I can offer the entire amount when I get my bonus at the end of the year."

Kat gasps and grabs his arm. "Greg, no. That's the girls' college fund."

Repulsion hits my stomach and I stop the video. For a split second, I thought these two were redeemable.

Lauren shouldn't have been forced into this situation.

None of them should.

No one should.

At least I can protect Lauren. For now.

Send her home and be done with it.

Or you can keep her close and find a way to take everything from your father. Crush his empire. Steal his control. Take his power.

And unravel his trafficking ring.

That could take an eternity.

An eternity that keeps Lauren here with you.

It has to be her decision.

My cellphone buzzes and a text from my brother appears on the screen.

Wystan: Front desk called and said Detective Zabek is here looking for you and Lauren might be having a slight panic attack.

Me: I'll be right there. Get Lauren out of the Aldon. Take her to your club or your place. Hell, take her out to lunch. But do not take your eyes off her.

Wystan: I can do that.

I power down my laptop and then grab my keys.

Marek looks up at me from the table in the corner of the room. "What's going on?"

"Personal matter. Update with anything else you find on my father and this trafficking ring."

When I make it to the mezzanine level, Wystan texts me to let me know he and Lauren are headed to his place.

"Detective Zabek," I greet him as I approach the table in the private dining lounge.

"Mr. Kallas." He stands to shake my hand. "You know why I'm here."

"I have no idea," I lie. "But I'm happy to help."

"Listen," he says, leaning in. "I'm only here for appearances. If you took the diamond. I don't care. Dimants has been a thorn in my side for years. I can't say I didn't enjoy his little meltdown over the loss of the diamond."

My shoulders relax and I take a seat across from him. "Then what can I do for you?"

"My son turns eighteen this month, and I want him to have one of your girls," he whispers.

"One of my girls?"

He smirks. "I see. Look, I'm sure this isn't customary, but given that we're keeping each other's secrets, I thought I'd ask you for a personal favor."

Customary? My girls? What the fuck is going on?

"I know I should go through Em, but this is my son," he says, his voice shaking slightly. "Man to man, you remember what it's like your first time. My son, he's eighteen and has never been with a woman. In this day and age, it's almost unheard of. I want him to be with someone close to his age. She should be experienced and, of course, clean."

Jesus Christ. Em? Who the hell is Em?

He slides a black keycard toward me with a gold number stamped on it. "You'll see that my account is completely in order."

What the fuck am I supposed to do with this card? I have way too many questions and not enough answers.

"I trust you, Zabek." I slide the card back to him. "I don't have anything to do with the booking of the women. But we should go see Em right now and get all of this squared away."

Before he can answer me, his phone buzzes. "I've got to take this. It's urgent, but I'll be in contact soon."

When he walks out of the lounge, I dial Wystan. "Hey, you can bring Lauren back here. It was a false alarm. We've got another problem on our hands."

"Okay, we're on our way. Is the problem one of the paternal variety?"

"Unfortunately, yes."

As I end the call with my brother, Lauren's words come back to haunt me.

Maybe you should know a little bit more about the men and women who sit at your gambling tables. And the women in the glittery dresses who float around on the arms of your high rollers."

My girls. As Zabek had said. And who the hell is Em?

When I make it back to my office, I pull up the employee records and search for this Em woman Zabek mentioned. It takes a while because I have several employees whose names begin with the letter *E*. I've got three employees: Emilia, Emma, and Emelina. Two are in housekeeping, and the other is a bartender. This seems like a stretch.

Frustrated, my fist pounds against the desk. I need to talk

to Wystan and Lauren. I grab my laptop and head for my private elevator.

Is my father running a prostitution ring out of my hotel? If it is true, how has he been able to do it right under my nose?

Things are getting messy. I need to come up with a plan to keep Lauren safe and help these women without getting myself, Wystan, or Lauren killed in the process.

CHAPTER
twenty-seven

Lauren

DAMEN WALKS THROUGH THE DOORS AND RELIEF WASHES through me.

He looks like he hasn't slept at all.

"How are things with the good detective?" Wystan asks.

Damen shrugs out of his coat and tosses it onto the chair. "He's good, and you're safe for now, Lauren." He pours himself a drink. "He doesn't care about the diamond."

Wystan stands and then walks over to the bar. "Then what does he care about?"

Damen tosses down his drink and then pours another before motioning to me. His unspoken way of asking me if I'd like a drink.

I nod and scoot forward from my place on the couch. With drinks in hand, the two men join me in the living room. Damen hands me a glass of red wine and I smile.

"He wants his soon-to-be eighteen-year-old son to have his first experience with one of my women," Damen inches out.

"One of your women," Wystan repeats. "What the hell does

that mean? And is this a first experience with a woman in general or an—escort?"

Heat flames my face and down my neck. I know Wystan doesn't mean to refer to these trafficked women as hookers. But it's what they've become. Used and paid for sex.

"I didn't get into specifics." Damen informs us about his conversation with Detective Zabek. Everything from some woman named Em to a black keycard.

Shaking my head, I rise from the couch. "Your dad is running an escort service, but I don't think the women are *here*. The girl that was in Belize with me, the one I spoke to the night I was with Kilan . . . um, not important, remember I told you she said something about a high-rise?"

"Yes, I remember." Irritation paints Damen's face.

"So let's say that our father is running this escort ring from some high-rise here in the city," Wystan states. "What can we do about it? We don't know where this place is located. Not to mention, Zabek thinks that you're running the entire thing. And I, for one, don't trust him. We don't know who our father has in his pocket."

Before Damen can respond, Marek walks in and whispers something to him. I can't make it out because Marek is speaking a language that I don't understand.

"Where is he now?"

"We have him in a holding cell."

They continue the conversation in this unfamiliar language. It's not Russian and it's not Polish. Valter had lied to Damen and Wystan that first night at dinner when he told them that I knew more about this country than either one of them. I don't know what possessed Valter to do that. My guess is to irritate the two men.

Damen swings his gaze to me. "Wystan and I have some business to take care of. I'll be back soon."

I didn't know what to say. Was it Valter in the holding cell? Maybe Kilan?

Uneasiness climbs into my body and settles in my chest. My guess is that someone stole from Damen and now they will be punished for that crime.

Maybe even killed.

It's been three days since I've seen Damen.

The only people I've talked to are Marek, Jonas, Clara, and the woman who delivers my food, Teresa. I've been allowed to go to the gym, the pool, and the spa, not without a bodyguard, but I've spent a majority of my time locked inside this penthouse.

"Is there a business center here?" I ask Marek when he stops by to do the security sweep.

"Yes. Why?"

"I'd like to use the internet. I'm bored with watching movies."

Saying nothing, he shakes his head and continues on with this work.

Within an hour, an iPad, laptop, and cellphone appear on the kitchen table. Along with a note that says: *Download books. Play Candy Crush or Solitaire. Surf the web and do some online shopping. My number is programmed so is Wystan's. I've installed software on the phone that prevents robocalls.*

Shaking my head, I smile. He forgets that I don't have any money.

I scoop up the phone and type out a message to him. Seconds later, I get a reply.

Damen: You can use my credit cards until we can get you your own.

Me: Does that mean I can finally get a job here?

Damen: I'm open to a discussion.

Sighing, I set the phone down and power up the laptop.

I think about logging onto my social media accounts. What's changed since I've been . . . gone?

Hours pass and I eat another meal alone. I realize that I'm just as trapped here as I was at Valter's manor. The only thing that's different is that I'm living with less fear.

While there's a lot to be said for solitude, I've had enough to last me a lifetime. I try to read a book that I downloaded, but my mind is pinging like a pinball machine.

I try meditation. I try yoga. I try taking a nap.

Nothing works.

So I do the one thing I probably shouldn't—I look up my sister's social media accounts. My heart hammers in my chest when I click on her Instagram. The most recent picture is one of my sister, Greg, and the girls in Aspen. They went skiing over the girls' fall break.

How nice for them.

I don't get very far. The box asking if I want to login in or create an account pops up. I try again, this time on Greg's account. There's a shared item from the Missing Persons Facility. A graphic with information and my picture.

Please share this missing person profile as much as possible. Sanders has been missing since October 4th. Any tips or information to help determine where Lauren may be or what happened to her is greatly appreciated.

There's a link and phone number. I have a mixed flood of emotions. I could call and say that I'm alive. That would surprise the fuck out of Kat and Greg.

From an incognito window, I search the internet for my name and attach the words: missing, dead, obituary. There's a group on Facebook: Lauren Sanders Missing. I can't access it without joining. Should I create a fake account to join the group?

After a while, reality hits me—the worst torture, and I did it to myself.

Stop thinking about them. Stop thinking about your old life.

My new life doesn't feel like I'm living.

But I suppose I should be grateful that I'm alive at all.

As I step out of the shower and into the bedroom, I'm scared half to death when I see Damen sitting in the corner chair.

"Jesus Christ, Damen," I breathe out. "Do you always sit in the shadows like that?"

The flames of the fireplace hiss and crackle as Damen stands. "I'm sorry. I didn't mean to scare you. I'm also sorry that you've been bored here. I know it can't be easy being locked up with no real connection to the outside world."

Dislike of the situation or not, I'm glad to see Damen. Dressed in all black, with the sleeves of his button-down shirt pushed up to his elbows, he looks sexy as hell. His shirt clings to his muscles in all the right places, his perfectly chiseled jawline is covered in a slight five o'clock shadow, and even from here, I can smell the intoxicating scent of his cologne.

"Where have you been? I haven't seen you in days."

A slow smile spreads across his face. "I've been busy. Working. Were you worried about me?"

"Worried? About you? Only in a sense that I wonder if you ever sleep," I ask before stepping back into the bathroom and sliding on a pair of cotton underwear and a bra.

"I do."

"Good. So, what are you doing here?"

"Well. I thought that we might take a little trip."

I cock a brow. "A trip?"

"Yeah. I have a place in the country. I had the idea that we could spend the weekend there. If you want to."

"You have a place in the country?"

"I do. It's nice and secluded. Plenty of privacy. I thought it would be a good change of scenery."

"What about your work?"

He shakes his head and scoops up his coat from the bench at the foot of the bed. "I have an office I can work from if I need to. So what do you say?"

"I say that sounds wonderful." I can barely keep the excitement out of my voice.

"Great. I'll be back in an hour. In the meantime, Clara is coming up to help you pack." He calls over his shoulder as he passes through the doorway.

"You know that I'm a big girl and can pack myself."

He circles back and stands in the doorway. "Yes. I know. But she's bringing more clothes for you to try on. A friend of mine and business partner is coming to dinner tonight and bringing his wife. I think you'll like them."

I try to hide my surprise. Damen wants me to meet his friends. He wants me to mingle with people and be a part of his life.

"You want me to have dinner with your friends? I can't have dinner with your friends."

"And why not?"

"I'm sure they'll ask questions about why I'm here. What I'm doing at your place in the country."

"Tell them whatever you like," he says, looking into my eyes. "And as to why you're at my house. It's simple. You're my guest and I invited you."

I swallow the lump forming in my throat and tamp down the dizziness fogging my brain. Having dinner with friends is so normal . . . it's something that feels normal. Normal is good.

"Okay. I'll go. But you can't keep buying me clothes and letting me stay here rent-free," I tell him. "There's got to be something that I can do with my time. Like, get a job."

"You're forgetting that you're here because you asked me for help. In exchange, you told me that my father stole the Dashiell Diamond. That makes us even. Think of the clothes, food, and shelter all part of our deal." He slips his coat on over his broad shoulders. "I can't very well let you walk around naked and starving."

"Right. This work that you've been doing. Does it have anything to do with me?"

"Some of it, yes. How about we talk on the drive? I'll tell you anything you want, but right now, I've got to get to a meeting. See you soon, okay?"

I smile weakly and watch as Damen walks out the door.

Even now, locked away safely in this world, Damen's world, everything still feels uncertain. Will this ever end? Will I ever be truly safe?

I could go home to Chicago and press charges against Kat. But then the girls would grow up without their mother. That's clearly not an option.

Trudging back to the bathroom, I stare at my reflection in the black framed mirror.

"Well, at least you're getting out of here for a little while."

CHAPTER
twenty-eight

Damen

THE MEETING DRAGS ON.

I stare at the two men who've been arguing for the past forty minutes about their grievances with their private poker game.

"He cheated," Ludwik Korecki, a Polish businessman, yells. "I'm telling you, Mr. Kallas. This man is a liar."

The other man, Ivan Popov, a Russian billionaire, leans back in the chair, laughing. "I don't cheat. You're a shitty poker player."

The men continue to argue, and, in my boredom, my gaze wanders to the monitor on my computer screen. I see no cheating. Just a man who's very bad at reading the room.

"Korecki, you *are* a shitty poker player."

The men jerk their heads in my direction.

"And I love that about you because the more money you lose here makes me a very rich man. Popov, you're a lot of things, but you're not a liar."

Fuming with anger, Korecki stands. "But—"

"But nothing. Do you want to see your wife and kids again?

Because if you continue to waste my time with these false claims of cheating, I will put a bullet in your brain, and your family will get a sympathy card from me."

His mouth snaps shut, and he drops back into the chair.

"Ivan, would you like your usual table tonight?"

He nods. "Thank you, Damen. As always, I appreciate your hospitality."

"Good. Then we're done here. And Korecki, at least try to learn the game. A little effort goes a long way."

His nostrils flare, but he offers me a roguish smile before walking out of my office.

The last man caught cheating left this place with a broken nose and a missing pinkie finger.

I didn't feel the need to ban him from the Aldon. I'll happily take more of his money. But if he steals from me, I won't hesitate to remove another finger. But I can't take all his fingers. He needs them to play at my tables. I may consider removing his teeth or his toes if the issue persists.

My phone buzzes, reminding me that tonight is the scheduled Kallas family dinner. Since my father broke his promise to my mother, I decided to break one of my own.

Family dinners became a Friday evening tradition when Wystan and I would return home from boarding school. They continued through our university years.

When our mother died, it had been Father's idea to continue in her memory. At first, the meals were at our father's chalet. Sometimes he'd move them to his penthouse. But when he started spending time with Monique, they became a rarity.

And then, a few months ago, Valter requested we meet for dinner again. So the Kallas family dinner tradition is just an excuse for our father to do business and show the underworld he's still a family man.

Family has always been important to the Kallas dynasty.

Since I wasn't going to get any answers from my father, I went to someone else—Gregory Woodward.

Seventy-two Hours Earlier

He's thirty minutes late.

If I was pissed before, I'm furious now.

Situated on the top floor of a shiny, towering building in Chicago, the model condo is a neutral hue of colors. The floor-to-ceiling windows cast dim shadows throughout the space. The views of the lake and city are quite stunning.

The moment I learned that Lauren's sister had been the one who sold her to my father, I bought this newly constructed residential building. The paperwork had been finalized before we landed.

On the drive from the private airport, I confirmed my meeting with Gregory Woodward. Which brings us to this moment.

Woodward is the managing partner of a venture capital group. I'm playing the part of an entrepreneur who needs to make my dreams happen, and he is the man to help me achieve that goal.

Wystan alerts me that Woodward is on his way up through the private elevator. In about thirty seconds, every security camera and feature will go down for routine maintenance, except for this unit.

As a gift from the new owner, all staff from security to the front door has a paid four-day weekend. Within the hour, I'll put my own men on the job through Monday morning.

The elevator doors open and Woodward steps into the entryway. He looks like the kind of man you would expect to work in finance.

First, the impeccably tailored navy Armani suit paired with the matching tie. The accessories a pair of shiny silver Cartier cufflinks that were probably a gift from his wife. It's all part of the grift, and it works, mostly. But it's his twenty-dollar haircut that gives him away, which makes him look like every other flunky in a corporate job.

Wystan greets him and asks for his cellphone and then takes his coat. When Woodward questions, my brother gives him a speech about my customary business practices for meetings regarding electronic devices and how it would be rude to refuse my request.

Displeasure flashes on his face, but he complies.

"Mr. Arthelais," he says, extending his hand to mine. "I'm sorry I'm late. I should've known better than to take Fullerton this time of day. Shall we get down to business? I know you're a busy man."

Nodding in response, I gesture for him to take a seat at the dining room table.

"So tell me about your business? You mentioned something about information technology and safeguarding data." He clicks open his expensive briefcase.

"My business is Lauren Sanders. I believe you know her?"

"I'm sorry, are you a detective? Because we've been working with Detective Fleming since Lauren's disappearance in Mexico."

I take a seat across from him. "Yes, I know."

"Has Lauren been found?" He swallows.

Grabbing the neck of the vodka bottle I'd set out earlier, I pour myself a shot and toss it back. "That depends," I say, and his face immediately pales.

"Depends on what?"

I tap my fingers against the table. "On how you answer the next question. And I'll know if you're lying."

He glares at me. "Who the fuck are you?"

"I told you, I'm Saint Arthelais."

"What do you know about Lauren?"

I slam my hand against the table. "I'm the one asking the questions here. Not you."

His shoulders tense and he holds up his hands. "Fine. *Fine.*"

"Did you and your wife arrange for Lauren to be kidnapped to clear a debt?"

He gasps and falters in his attempt to stand. Wystan grips his shoulders from behind, steadying him back into the chair.

"This is the part where you choose your answer very carefully," I warn.

While I wait for him to answer, I pull a lighter from the inside of my jacket pocket and set it on the table between us. There's a cigar box next to the decanter of vodka. I lean across and pluck one of the rare cigars from the box.

"Yes." He hangs his head. "I lost a lot of money, and I never would've done it, but Kat, my wife, made me. I didn't have a choice."

I lean closer to him. "You had a choice. But you knowingly put your sister-in-law in grave fucking danger. Do you know what happens to women when they are kidnapped? Taken? When they're sold?" My voice rises with every word that inches out.

He shakes in his designer threads. "I-I was assured that they would knock her out like when they give you laughing gas at the dentist, and then she'd wake up and not remember anything. I was told that she would have a good life. They guaranteed us that they'd give her a job and a place to stay."

Jesus Christ. This man is a millionaire, and he is as dumb as a box of rocks.

"I'm usually civil about these matters," I say, rising from my chair. "But in your case, I'm going to make an exception."

His eyes are wide, and he looks scared shitless. "Please don't kill me. I have a family. I have kids."

This motherfucker should be scared, but I'm a gentleman, and he's only getting a taste of my wrath. I can only imagine the fear that Lauren felt while they held her captive in Belize and then again with my father.

This fucker is lucky I don't chop off his cock and send it to his wife in a box. But I won't kill him. Instead, I'll let him suffer a little longer. He'll sit in the darkness and fear just like Lauren did.

"I'm not going to waste a bullet on you."

When Woodward swings his gaze to Wystan, his eyes go wider. At six foot four, my brother is an imposing figure with a well-built physique. I wouldn't want to be on the receiving end of Wystan's fury.

"Is *he* going to kill me?" His voice shakes.

"That depends." I clip the end of the cigar and then light it.

"On what?"

"How you answer this *next* question." I take a few puffs, and the rings of smoke billow up into the air.

"I'll tell you anything you want to know. Just please don't kill me."

Wystan hands me the portfolio that I've been through five times. "Does your wife know that you've got a mistress?"

His face scrunches up. "*No.* Please don't tell her. I'll break it off, I swear."

I flip through the contents and then slide a few black-and-white photos in front of him. "I bet Kat doesn't know about your Tinder profile either. You've been a very busy man, *Conner Anderson*. Lots of women. Far less beautiful than your Kat. And much younger." I flash the photo of a young woman named Claudia in his face. "Do you know that she's not even eighteen?"

Paling, he looks away from the picture. "I didn't know. Her profile says that she's twenty-one. She looks older."

"You think a judge will care? Or your wife?"

Wystan yanks him up from the chair. "Strip."

On unsteady legs, Gregory's gaze pings between the two of us. "What? Why?"

My brother's grip tightens. "You don't get to ask the questions. I. Told. You. To. Strip."

I walk toward a door that opens to the terrace and unlock it. When I push the door open, a stiff wind wades in, bringing along the icy chill of winter.

"I won't strip. Tell me what you're going to do to me."

"How about you just take off your jacket?" I suggest, and Wystan tugs on the sleeve.

Gregory slips the jacket over his shoulders as I unlock the window in the living room and pop it open. More frigid air sweeps inside.

"Now your dress shirt. And I won't tell you twice."

When I cross back, I flick the ash from my cigar onto the terrace. Gregory works the buttons on his white dress shirt, and I pop another window open.

"Is Lauren alive? Can you at least tell me that?"

Taking a long drag from my cigar, I glare at Gregory. "I'm surprised that you care." I pop open the last window in the dining room.

"My wife would want to know," he admits. "The man I lost my money to said he would take my daughters if I didn't pay. They're only eight and six years old. I offered installments over time, but he refused. I told him I could pay him back in five months. He still refused."

The temperature in the condo is bitterly cold. It doesn't bother me or Wystan. The two of us are used to the frigid Baltic temperatures. Stripped to only his boxers and socks, Gregory seems less accustomed to the wintry weather. Which I find fascinating given that he's lived in the Windy City for the past fifteen years.

"You shouldn't gamble away money you don't have, Gregory."
I approach him slowly.

He shivers against the hold Wystan has on him. "I know that
now. What do you want? Do you want money? I can pay back the
debt, and Lauren can come back home."

Gregory and Kat have been extremely busy since they returned from Vutreila. When news broke of Lauren's disappearance, his business tripled. They went from wealthy to millionaires
practically overnight. Gregory has formed an exploratory com-
mittee to run for mayor of Chicago.

In the wake of Lauren's disappearance, management offered Kat a position at work that required far less travel. Her
boss thought it would be good if Kat wasn't away from her kids
as much.

"I don't want your money. As far as Lauren goes," I say before flicking the ash from my cigar onto the floor, "she's none of
your concern."

Wystan shoves Gregory into the suede chair. I pick up the
iPad sitting on the table and bring up the video of Greg and Kat
making a deal with Hillar.

"Fuck," Greg whispers.

A mixture of shock and pain passes over Greg's face as he
watches the video. The video of him and his wife plotting and
paying for a kidnapping. As the video nears the end, he turns away,
but Wystan pushes his head back toward the screen.

"What's the matter, Greg?" Wystan hisses in his ear. "Must
feel pretty dirty seeing this from another angle. The angle of
your colleagues, friends, and family. Not to mention your potential voters. I've got a feeling they wouldn't like you too much
after seeing this."

"Good. Very good," Hillar announces. *"Boss thanks you for your
business. You will be contacted by our associate in a week. Then the plan
will be set in motion."*

"Who are you people?"

"No one you need to concern yourself with," Wystan answers and quickly pulls a zip tie around Greg's wrists.

"What are you doing? Please. I'm begging you."

"Begging won't help you," I tell him as I snuff out my cigar on his biceps.

"Fuuuuccckkkk," he yelps. "Are you fucking crazy?"

"No. If you ask me one more question . . ." I pick up the gun that's wedged behind the flower arrangement and nudge it under his chin. "You'll leave this place rolled up in that rug. I'll have your dead body on a plane to Vutreila and dump your body in the forest where the gray wolves and brown bears can feast on your flesh and bones. Do you understand me?"

He nods and his face pales again.

"You're going to stay here and think about the choices you've made. You will not tell anyone about our meeting. If you tell your wife, I will know. If you shut these windows, I will know."

"I'll freeze to death."

"There's a blanket hidden somewhere in this condo. You'll find it."

Wystan binds his ankles to the chair. I pull a box cutter from my coat and toss it onto the sofa.

"There's vodka and I'm sure you can drink the tap water."

Wystan brings me a laptop. "I've taken the liberty of emailing your wife and colleagues. You're on an extended holiday. Kat thinks that you're at a meditation retreat on a journey of self-discovery. Something that she's asked you to do for a long time." The screen comes to life. "You're going to email Detective Fleming and tell her that Lauren has contacted you to let you know that she's alive and well. You will inform the detective that her services are no longer needed. You'll have the recovery called off and say that your family requests privacy at this time. The only public statement will be that Lauren has been found safe. There will be no further investigation. You're going to make a sizable donation to the Chicago police department as a thank you for their efforts."

He nods. "I know I'm not supposed to ask questions, but I need some clarification."

My eyes narrow and I place the barrel of the gun to his forehead. "You're testing my patience, Mr. Woodward. How can I make this any simpler for a smart guy like you?"

"I'm . . . What am I supposed to do when the police push back? Won't they want proof of life?"

"That isn't my problem. Furthermore, you'll find a way to expedite replacements for Lauren's passport and driver's license. In addition to getting her bank card and credit cards replaced. You'll find an address in the contacts folder. Make sure those items are mailed there." I open the file folder. "This is a checklist of all the things you're going to accomplish before you leave this place. You'll be rewarded for each item you check off the list."

"Rewarded," he repeats.

"Yes. Check an item off, and you'll get a piece of clothing or two back. Maybe a window will close. Soon you can have food, a shower, and a roaring fireplace." I place the barrel of the gun under his chin, forcing his eyes to mine. "I'm a gentleman, after all. Men like you and me, we deal in favors and incentives. You do something for me. I do something for you."

He blinks back his frustration. "Detective Fleming will want to meet with me in person. She won't be satisfied with an email."

"Not my problem. I have complete faith that you'll get it all sorted out. Just remember, I'll know if you try to contact anyone. If you fail me, your wife will know all about your extracurricular activities, and I'll make sure Claudia's parents know you've been fucking their teenage daughter. Are we clear?"

He nods, and I put the gun away. I pat his shoulder, giving it a tight squeeze.

"Goodbye, Mr. Woodward."

Saying nothing, he returns his focus to the laptop in front of him. I'm certain I hear a "fuck you" under his breath.

We exit the main room. Two of my men, Olev and Riks, sit at a small table in the entryway. I hand Riks a burner phone.

"Use this to contact me with any problems. One of you sits in there with him at all times. Call Tannil at the front desk when you need to take breaks. Don't let Woodward kill himself."

"You got it, boss."

When the instructions are completed, Wystan and I step into the private elevator.

"Do you think he'll get everything done or freeze to death?"

I chuckle. "He's motivated. Trust me."

CHAPTER
twenty-nine

Lauren

AS THE CAR TURNS UP THE SNOWY, TREE-LINED, PRIVATE DRIVE, I somehow manage to tuck away my nerves. Or maybe it's the Champagne working its way through my system. *How big is this place?*

A break in the dense forest reveals a huge . . . house isn't a sufficient word. If his penthouse at the Aldon is his ice castle, this place is his ice fortress.

"This place is massive," I say. "You live here all by yourself?"

He nods. "Yes. I like having something very few people know about."

And I thought Greg and Kat's place in Lincoln Park was big. They have seven bathrooms. I wonder how many this place has.

I've been around wealth, and wealthy people. Mostly lingering on the outside, looking adjacently. But this place is something otherworldly.

Our driver, Kacper, opens the trunk and Damen helps unload our luggage. My eyes sweep around the property. Despite the house being lit up like a Christmas tree, it's hard to see anything in the black of night. Men dressed in ink black suits and over-sized coats, with earpieces, are situated around the property. I'm sure their guns are holstered beneath their coats.

A woman in an elegant black sheath dress stands at the top of the stairs next to the opulent door. Her blond hair is pinned neatly in a low chignon, and I don't miss the way her light eyes inspect every inch of me.

"Ah, Dorel, hello," Damen says. "I'd like to introduce you to Lauren Sanders. Dorel is the head of my household. If you need anything at all, she'll take care of you."

Dorel nods and smiles. "Welcome, Miss Sanders."

"Nice to meet you, and please call me Lauren."

Saying nothing, Dorel turns and walks inside. Damen's hand lands on the small of my back, guiding me up the stairs.

As we make our way inside, I take in the surroundings. The décor is supremely modern and grand, with sophisticated lighting, sweeping ceilings, and rich wood floors.

Inviting cozy leather couches, faux fur throws, and a deep color scheme of dark shades adds nobility and luxury.

"In case I didn't mention before, you look beautiful," Damen says as he helps me with my coat.

I feel the blush creep up my neck. "You mentioned something earlier. Thank you. You don't look so bad yourself."

I changed my outfit ten times. I know because Clara counted. Finally, I settled on the three-quarter length sleeve, gray Dior cocktail dress for tonight's dinner.

"Please have Lauren's luggage taken to the guest room next to mine," Damen mentions to the man who opened the door for us.

"Right away, sir."

Before I can get a word out, a large black and white dog charges at the three of us. A man with dark hair chases after the large beast, yelling, *"Peatus. Peatus."*

The dog, which I believe is a Siberian Husky, runs toward

Damen and comes to a screeching halt when he says, "Luka istuda."

Damen pats his head. "Tubli poiss. Good boy. Very good, Luka."

I look up at him. "Is Luka *your* dog?"

"Yes. We haven't seen each other much. As you can tell."

I smile at the sight of Damen kneeling in front of this beautiful dog and showing him an enormous amount of affection.

"Can I pet him?"

"Of course." Damen stands and then walks toward the enormous fireplace, where Dorel waits for him with a clipboard in hand.

The two of them carry on a conversation while I get to know Luka. "You *are* a very handsome boy."

Damen's demeanor seems to have changed a bit. Maybe I'm imagining it. While his presence is just as commanding, he does seem a bit more relaxed. A butler offers me a glass of Champagne when I step into the living room.

"English only tonight, please," Dorel announces to the staff. "We have American guests."

Guests? Damen's friends are American?

Damen tugs my elbow. "Let me show you around before our guests arrive."

"Your home is really beautiful," I tell him as we walk up the stairs. "Is this where you've been the past few days?"

"No. I was out of town on business."

I roll my eyes. "Yes. I know you had business to take care of, but since you said the business was about me. Can you tell me about it, please?"

When my feet hit the top of the stairs, my mouth drops, and a tiny gasp falls from my lips. "Wow."

Floor-to-ceiling glass. Two double doors on either side of

the room lead out to a terrace. Snow-capped pine trees outline the horizon for miles.

The room itself is gorgeous, with a seating area of two couches and various hutches and tables. There's a roaring fireplace, and low lighting and candles illuminate the space.

"Oh my god. You have a pool *and* a hot tub? Do you ever get to use them?"

He laughs. "Yeah. There's an indoor pool too."

"Of course there is."

"You're welcome to use the pool and the hot tub."

"I don't think I packed a swimsuit."

Damen smiles. "I'd be surprised if Clara didn't tuck one inside your suitcase."

"Guess I'll find out once I unpack."

"The staff has already unpacked your belongings," he says and tips his head toward the hallway. "The bedrooms are this way."

This dreamy hideaway is everything you could wish for in a mountain retreat. Wood and timber construction, amazing snow-capped mountain vistas, and cozy, comfortable furnishings. Everything about the style and design of this home invites relaxation, both indoors and out. I could totally vacation here.

The bedroom Damen's staff set me up in is gorgeous. It's really a suite of rooms with two bathrooms—a full and a half, a giant walk-in closet, a bedroom, and a sitting room. The entire ceiling in the master bathroom is made of glass. I can watch it snow while I take a shower.

What am I doing here?

"Okay. So tell me about this dinner tonight. Why am I here?"

Damen chuckles. "I thought I already covered this earlier?"

"I'm the one asking questions. And while I have your undivided attention, let's circle back to my earlier question about where you've been, and I'd really like to know how it involves me. You promised you'd answer any questions on the drive out here."

"You didn't ask me any questions on the drive," he points out.

"*Pfft*. Fine. You can answer me now though, before your guests arrive."

He stands by the fireplace in the bedroom. Dark eyes, broad shoulders, and smooth black lines. Damen fills out a suit better than any man I've ever seen.

"It might be a longer conversation than a few minutes."

I walk into the bathroom and brush out my hair. "Is your dad looking for me?"

"I don't know. He said the debt had been paid."

"Is what Valter said about Kat and Greg true? Did they have me kidnapped?"

His concentrated gaze holds mine. Every second he remains silent, the longer my heartbeats stretch until it's a drum thumping in my ear.

"I'm sorry to say this, but yes, I have video proof."

The confirmation spreads through me like acid. A part of me wished Valter had been lying. That he'd only said that it was my sister's doing to hurt me.

My own sister. All the breath in my lungs evaporates. Tears gather at the back of my throat. It's a weight that I thought I could bear.

"Why would she do this to me?" I wonder aloud as I walk out of the bathroom.

The one person I thought I knew most in this world. Swallowing the bitter, jagged reality, along with the things I knew about Kat. I knew that she couldn't ride a bike without training wheels until she was ten. She hated eating raw veggies. But she'd eat cooked ones all day long. Kat hated pickles, but she loved Cubano sandwiches.

And at night, after our father would take his alcohol-fueled hatred out on the two of us, it was Kat who came into my room and nursed my cuts and scrapes. Not our mother.

My fingers rub at the strand of pearls around my neck as I stare out the windows into the black of night.

I have no family. No mother. No father. No sister. I will never see Cora and Thea again.

At least with Kat and Greg, I thought I was a part of something—a family.

Who am I without them?

Two warm hands glide over my shoulders. *Damen.*

"I'm sorry. I'm so damn sorry for all you've been through," he whispers into my hair.

I turn to face him. "There's nothing for you to apologize for. I appreciate your honesty."

"Of course. Are you okay?"

"No. Not really. But I will be and I'm going to put this in a little box until I can deal with it." I square my shoulders and smile. "I can't wait to meet your friends. How about we go have a nice evening?"

He holds my gaze for a second and then nods. "That sounds like a plan to me. You totally got this."

"You sound so young saying that." I laugh.

"I am young," he deadpans.

Damen takes my hand as we walk across the room and then releases me as we descend the staircase.

"Mr. and Mrs. Cardwell's car just passed through the gates," Dorel tells Damen.

The two discuss the final details for the evening and I'm handed a glass of Champagne.

When the front doors open, Damen takes my hand and leads me toward the entryway. My heart skitters in my chest when I recognize the blond woman wearing a long-sleeved, glittering, blush-colored dress with a plunging neckline.

Caroline Cardwell. I've got nearly every item from her Athleisure line. I read an article about her designs on Instagram.

She started with a few pieces, but when a monthly subscription box sent out one of her designs, Caroline exploded onto the athletic fashion scene.

I could wrap my hands around Damen's neck and strangle him for not telling me. Caroline is married to Brant Cardwell. His family owns Cardwell Bourbon. It's the best bourbon on the planet. Greg has every one of their flavors. Cardwell is a staple at Kat and Greg's.

"It's such a pleasure to meet you, Lauren. Although I admit, I've seen you before. So forgive me if I'm surprised."

My brows crinkle. "What do you mean?"

"My husband and I were at the Serpent Ball, and we could've sworn that you and Damen were a couple that night. He said you weren't, but I guess he asked you out, seeing as you're standing here tonight."

"You don't say?" My gaze swings to Damen, and I can't help but laugh. "I think you and I are going to be great friends, Caroline."

"Hi, Lauren," Brant wraps his arm around his wife's waist. "It's really nice to meet you."

"Great meeting you as well," I say.

Dorel whispers something to Damen, and then he directs us to the dining room. Surprise hits me when Damen doesn't sit at the head of the table but rather next to me and across from Brant.

The table sits twelve, but the four of us are situated on one end of the long wooden table.

Caroline compliments Damen's home and thanks him for inviting the two of them to dinner.

"It's more than dinner, if you like," Damen asserts. "As I said earlier, you're welcome to stay the night. And if you can't, you just let me know and you're welcome to holiday here any time."

"Thank you for the kind offer," Brant says. "I think we'll be going back to the hotel tonight. We're leaving tomorrow."

"Yep. Thanksgiving is next week and with the Cardwell's every holiday is a production." Caroline playfully rolls her eyes.

Brant laughs. "Thank god we have a professional chef and baker in our family."

A bottle of Champagne is brought to Damen by one of his staff and once he approves it, he pours everyone but Caroline a glass. She gets a glass of sparkling water.

"Thank you, Bendek," Damen says. "Please bring Brant and me a glass of bourbon. Cardwell."

"Of course, sir," he replies.

"Lauren, are you American or Canadian?" Caroline asks. "I can't quite tell from your accent."

Her question is such a familiar one. "No worries, I get that a lot. I'm from Chicago," I tell her before taking a sip of my Champagne.

"I just love Chicago. The museums, the food, and the shopping. Will you be going home for Thanksgiving to celebrate with your family, Lauren?"

Anxiety bubbles up, and I don't want to lie to her, but I panic when the words rush out of my mouth. "I'm staying here, and I thought I might treat Damen to a traditional American Thanksgiving." I eye him over the rim of my glass. "That's if I can get him to take a four-day weekend."

Damen smiles. "I think I can be persuaded. I've heard so much about American Thanksgiving, and I don't think I've ever had pumpkin pie in my life."

Whoa. That's not what I expected to hear, and maybe he's just playing along. But it would be fun to cook for Damen. And what better way to thank someone for all they've done for you than with a thankful meal.

The pleasantries continue as the drinks flow and the appetizers are brought out. Damen explains that he had a few traditional

Polish appetizers made for the evening, including hush puppies, pierogi, and potato pancakes.

"So how did Damen end up asking you out? It must be quite a story," Caroline says.

"It's crazier than you think," I tell her. "My ride left me at the party, so I asked Damen if he could give me a ride and he said yes. We got to talking and one thing led to another."

Damen's body vibrates with laughter as he curves his hand around my hip to settle at the small of my back. "I can confirm that's exactly how it happened."

"When is your baby due, Caroline?" I ask.

"This is baby number two, and he's due in about six months. I was way overdue with our daughter, Leanna. I'm hoping this guy comes when he's supposed to."

"A boy and a girl, you must be so excited."

"We are. We just found out the sex right before our trip here."

"So, what brings you two all the way here? Damen hasn't told me a thing about your business dealings."

Brant snorts and looks at me. "I've been pursuing him for a few months. I told Damen that I didn't care what it took, but I wanted Cardwell Bourbon to be the official house bourbon for the Aldon. Then he finally agreed to meet with me, but it ended up being a video conference since he was about to board a flight to the States."

Caroline laughs. "Yeah. So here we are, literally in his backyard, and he's flying to ours for a last-minute trip. But it all worked out."

I look between the two men. "And how did it work out exactly?"

"Cardwell is the official house bourbon, and we're going to make a hell of a lot of money," Brant says. "And in the process, we're going to donate part of the proceeds to charity. Doing good to promote international business while giving back."

"Amen to that." Caroline raises her sparkling water into the air, and the rest of us do the same.

Amen indeed. Damen smiles at me and my insides turn to mush. It's probably premature to feel this happy. But the fact that Damen wants me here with him and entertaining is kind of a big deal. Right?

For now, I'll just enjoy the moment.

CHAPTER
thirty

Damen

Long after my guests had departed and unable to sleep, I wander into my study and pour myself half a glass of vodka.

Impressive doesn't begin to cover the way Lauren handled herself during tonight's dinner. She might be young, but she holds a conversation seamlessly. It was easy to see that Brant and Caroline were charmed by her.

I clip the end of a cigar, settle back into a leather armchair facing the fireplace, and stare into the flames.

Earlier I'd received an update on Gregory and his list. After hours of persuasion, he'd managed to get Detective Fleming to call off the investigation, assuring her that Lauren was safe. He told the detective that Lauren had been through too much trauma and didn't want the public to know she'd been trafficked.

Gregory also provided the detective with information, albeit inaccurate, about Lauren's kidnappers. I'm not going to let the authorities handle taking down my father.

I'll manage that myself.

My phone pings with a message from Riks letting me know that Lauren's passport, driver's license, and a copy of her birth certificate are being sent overnight. The birth certificate is an overachievement for Gregory. That has earned him bonus points.

I send a message to Riks: *Bring Gregory any meal he wants and close a window.*

My eyes stare at the shadowy flames as I puff on my cigar. I'm distracted when I see Lauren standing in the doorway. Her supple frame taking up a fraction of the space. She's wearing a sleep shirt that hits at the top of her thighs. When she comes closer, I read the words: *Born to Sleep* in block lettering.

"What are you doing?" Her voice is low and husky.

Enjoying the view comes to mind.

Not waiting for my answer, she picks up my glass and sniffs the contents. "Not sleeping. I'm shocked. Are you a vampire or something?"

"Not a vampire."

"Good to know you won't bite."

Tease.

That makes me chuckle. "I never said that."

Lauren takes a sip of my drink and then returns it to the coaster.

"Are you getting a taste for expensive vodka?"

"I don't know. Maybe."

I pour some liquid into a glass and hand it to her.

"Thank you." She smiles and takes a seat next to me, tucking her long legs beneath her, giving me a flash of black fabric.

Fuck me. I should send her back to the guest room immediately.

"How old are you, Damen?"

The question takes me by surprise. "I'm thirty-two."

Lauren takes a small sip. "Wow. All this"—her hand sweeps around the room—"and you're only thirty-two. So young. It's impressive."

"I told you that I'm young." My lips break into a smile around my cigar. "And I didn't do all of this on my own. I had a little help from my mother."

"How's that?"

"When my mother passed, she left me and Wystan a huge trust. Wystan invested in his club, and I invested in the Aldon."

She chuckles into her glass. "There's a rumor that you won the Aldon in a poker game."

I blow a ring of smoke into the air. "Who told you that?"

Lauren lifts a shoulder. "Kilan Dimants."

Disgust bubbles in my veins. But also like the fact that while she was with him, she was thinking about me. Something hot and ugly flares to life beneath my skin. As if I have any claim on this woman. But jealously gets the better of my control.

"I don't like hearing his name on your lips. Did he touch you?"

My muscles tighten, revolting against the idea that Kilan had laid hands on her.

She stares at me for a beat. "No. He never touched me. He was way too busy fucking waitresses in the halls of his house."

"You mean his father's house," I correct.

A smile pulls at the corners of her full lips. "Right."

Lauren rises from the chair and walks toward the fireplace. Flames lap up her long legs and a rush of heat snaps up and down my spine. As well as other places.

She's smooth and untouched, but I know there's a fire that burns inside her beautiful body. I want to see how hot that fire burns.

I shouldn't tempt the flames. I've had my hands on her. My mouth on hers. It unnerved me and consumed me all at once.

I'm Icarus flying too close to the sun.

Lauren moves from the fireplace and runs her finger along the top of my desk and then turns her attention to the books housed in the large bookcase. She still rolls up on her tiptoes despite her height, giving me a prime view of her ass covered in black cotton.

The devil on my shoulder taunts me.

Just another touch.

A small taste to suppress the hunger.

My brain and my cock are in an epic battle for control.

"Have you read all these books?"

I shake my head. "They're mostly for display."

She cocks a brow and pulls a book from the shelf. "Nonfiction. I see *mostly* war stories. Do you take notes before you charge into battle?" Amusement filters in her voice.

"What do you know of my battles?"

She turns to face me and her thigh bumps against my desk. The computer screen comes to life and my heart thumps out of sync.

Fuck. I forgot to turn off the monitors.

Her head swings to the screens and a gasp falls from her lips. "Is that Greg?" Lauren asks, bending to get a closer look. The ends of her blond hair sweep along the desk.

I don't move from my chair. Instead, I lazily puff on my cigar.

"Yes. He and I had an interesting chat, and now he's doing some work for me."

"Why is he half-naked?"

"Do you really want to know?"

She eyes me over her glass. "Did you hurt him?"

"What makes you think that I would hurt him?"

"Are you going to continue to answer my questions with questions?"

"What would you like to know?"

She saunters toward me, setting her glass on the coaster next to mine. "Did you tell Greg that I'm alive?"

"Yes."

"What else did you tell him?" Her pink-painted toes dig into the thick rug.

"I told him you were no longer his or your sister's concern."

She swallows, and a smile plays on her lips. "Am I your concern now?"

That slow smile says nothing but trouble. Temptation rises up and I'm not sure that I have the strength to squash it.

She knows I'm unraveling. I can pretend that I haven't wanted her from the moment I saw her at the table with my father.

I can pretend that I haven't dreamed about pushing deep inside her and making her mine.

Lauren knows better. Even in her relative innocence, she knows my truth.

"You asked me for protection and with protection comes concern. Your safety is my concern."

"Is there anything else that concerns you, Damen?" She steps closer to me and a hint of vanilla and jasmine washes over me.

My father is still a threat. The fact that I haven't heard anything so much as a whisper about Lauren from his camp heightens my suspicions.

I've never met anyone who hasn't suffered his wrath from taking something from him. I'm not exactly convinced that he's done with Lauren, even though he'd have me believe that she was just a means to an end.

More than her photographic memory, Lauren possesses something else that my father can easily profit from—her virginity.

"A few things, yes. What about you?"

"I don't know. I guess feeling normal again."

I flick the end of my cigar into the crystal ashtray. "What does normal feel like to you?"

She chuckles and walks toward the window. "Dinner and conversation felt normal. Although I could kill you for not telling me that it was Caroline Cardwell coming to dinner. She's one of my favorite designers."

"I apologize for leaving out that bit of information." I stand and grab our glasses from the side table.

"You're forgiven."

I hand her the glass. "Good. And as for normal, you'll feel it one day. When you're far away from here. When you're out with your friends again and having the time of your life."

She stares at me with those gorgeous blue eyes wet with unshed tears. Even her sadness is beautiful.

"Being out with a friend, someone I thought was my friend having the time of my life, got me drugged and kidnapped. As much as I want out, I don't think I'll ever see the world the same way I did. I always thought I was safe. But now, I fear I'll be looking over my shoulder. Maybe I should just stay here."

I let out a ragged breath. "This world isn't for you, Lauren."

"Why? Because you think I'm some young, naïve American?" she snaps. "I know what goes on here."

"What goes on here and your perception might be two entirely different things," I say softly, wiping away the tear that spilled down her cheek.

She takes a small sip of her vodka. "I know the world isn't all sunshine and rainbows. I knew that before I was kidnapped. My dad beat me every chance he got, and my mother did nothing about it. I know terrible things happen. My sister sold me to a mobster, for fuck's sake."

Her father hit her.

Anger rages inside me. I want to board my plane and fly back to Chicago to track down Lauren's father and beat the shit out of him.

"He would go to the bar and drink," Lauren tells me. "He would come home at all hours of the night. Yank me from my bed and tell me to make him some food. He did the same thing to Kat."

With each word she utters, the urge to beat up her father turns murderous.

"When I was fourteen, he brought home a strange man." Her voice shakes a little. "Dad said that the man's snowmobile broke down and he'd been stranded in the cold for a while. He warmed up by the fire and then the man came into my room. He said he was looking for the bathroom, but when I told him it was across the hallway, he still didn't move."

"What's his name?"

"I don't remember, honestly."

I take a breath, keeping the rage at bay, even though it wants to rise up and crush the glass in my hand. "Did he touch you?"

"No. His hand skimmed up my leg, but Kat came in with a baseball bat in her hand and told him to get out of my room."

"It was a good thing Kat was there to look out for you," I tell her.

She laughs. "A lot of good that did me. I should be able to protect myself. Teach me how to shoot a gun."

My head rears back. "You want to learn how to shoot a gun?"

"Why not? If you won't teach me, I'll just walk right up to one of your armed guards and ask them."

"You will not go near my men," I growl.

The thought pierces my chest, spreading something greedy and possessive throughout.

"Easy with the alpha male act," Lauren teases and glances back out the window. "But I can't say that I don't like it."

Her words slide through my veins like hot water. Scalding me with an odd sense of pride.

Lauren is Lauren. And I want to know absolutely everything about her. Fucking Lauren isn't my motivation. I don't care that she's a virgin. I just want her, and I realize that wanting her, having her, and making her mine are three very dangerous things.

Temptation slithers inside me and I feel like a snake in the Garden of Eden. I give myself a few moments to indulge in the fantasy.

My hand spears over the curtain of blond that shields her face. "What else do you like?"

As soon as the words left my mouth, I knew the devil had won.

CHAPTER
thirty-one

Lauren

I'M NOT PREPARED FOR THE LUST THAT SURGES BENEATH MY SKIN AS he stares at me.

The two of us have been dancing around on the razor's edge of our truth. The truth of our strong desire pulling us toward one another. And that pull wreaks constant havoc on my body and my mind.

I feel it every time he looks at me. Touches me. Talks to me.

"You're beautiful, Lauren," he says. His finger trickles down the side of my arm, and he plucks the glass from my hand.

It's nice to feel beautiful. Wanted. Desired. Damen makes me feel all those things.

All the while my body screams, *"Take me! Rip the albatross that is my virginity from my neck."*

"You're so sexy," I tell him.

A ghost of a smile hits his lips and I feel foolish because Damen is eight years older than me. He's probably been with dozens of women. Experienced women. Women who know about sex and all things pleasure.

How can I even know what to do with a man like Damen Kallas? I can't possibly give him what he needs. I've only given a few hand jobs. Did I even do it right? Was I any good?

Damen would have to teach me. Tell me what he likes.

Embarrassment crashes into me and I feel ridiculous at the thought of asking Damen to show me what he likes. I've been a tease, playing with a heat that is just too hot.

His hand settles on my waist and goose bumps pulse from under his hand and across my body.

I smooth my hand up his arm. It seems like the natural thing to do, though I know it's not.

His hand strokes lower, inching the fabric of my nightshirt up and over my hips. Air rushes along my skin, making me shiver.

"Tell me something, Lauren. How wet are you right now?" The lazy grin that stretches over his face sends shivers rippling down my spine.

I don't have an answer. What am I supposed to say? I know that my panties are soaked just from him touching me. He hasn't even kissed me, and I feel the wetness spreading.

I've lost control of my body.

Will he make fun of me like my high school boyfriend did? In college, a guy I dated told me to change my underwear when he kicked me out of his bed.

Ugh.

His lips hover over mine. "Tell me that you're not wet for me."

The ache grows stronger, sending a rush of dampness against the fabric. My body betraying me and crumbling with the intolerable need.

"I'm not . . . I'm not wet for you."

"You're a little liar, Lauren. I knew it the moment I met you." His hand skates over my stomach and up my ribcage. Every inch he travels sends sparks along my skin; unlike anything I've ever felt in my life.

His tongue licks over his bottom lip. "You want this. You want me. You want us, but you shouldn't."

I tremble. Lusting for him at the same time loving the forbidden rush.

"I should punish you for lying to me," he whispers in my ear. "I should spank—" Suddenly, he freezes and then slowly pulls away.

I know what he's thinking. My eyes find his in the moonlight.

"Don't stop," I tell him, grasping his wrists. "Please don't stop touching me."

"Are you sure?"

"I'm not sure about a lot of things, but I'm definitely sure that I want you to keep touching me."

His knee nudges against mine, forcing my legs apart. With seamless control, he presses his hard body against mine. His hips crash into mine.

My mind goes blank with the absolute-numbing pleasure.

"Tell me again how you're not wet for me." His hooded eyes imprison me. "Lie to me again."

"I may have lied to you about my name and my reason for being here," I breathe. "How I came to this place, but I don't want to lie, especially not to you."

"Fuck, Lauren," he rasps. Whispering his lips over my cheek, bringing them closer and closer, the tip of his tongue tastes the corner of my mouth.

Yes.

Damen's mouth hovers over mine for a split second, and he stares at me with those dark blue eyes, practically drowning me with his all-consuming attention.

My heart chases the anticipation. Finally, after what feels like an eternity, his mouth crashes onto mine and he kisses me. His fingers thread through my hair, pulling me closer—dominating my mouth with his, owning my tongue with his savage rhythm.

I don't want his lips to leave mine—ever. I never want to let him go. We kiss like starved fiends, the passion igniting between us, setting every part of my body ablaze.

Our tongues clash together, forgetting everything but the electric energy between us.

My back hits the cold glass, and he pushes my nightshirt up to my waist. I want him all over me. I suck in a breath as I feel his cock hardening against me, and I know he wants me too.

All shyness evaporates when I rock against the hard length of him, hinting at what I want. What I've been needing from him.

"Tell me a secret. A dirty, dark secret, Lauren," he whispers against my lips.

"I can't."

"You can."

Every pulse of his hips draws a quickening in my core. As he slides a finger between my thighs, my entire body shakes against the glass.

"I . . . think I had a sex dream about you in your bed."

His eyes fill with a fire and his fingers feather over my damp panties.

"*Fuck*. I like hearing that. Did you beg me to fuck you? I want to. I want you begging me to fuck you."

His fingers scatter my thoughts, probing against the thin cotton of my underwear. His touch is electrifying. I want more. I want it all. I want everything.

Shamefully, I arch into his touch, seeking more. I groan, my thighs ache, the heat between them insufferable.

He touches me like he knows just what I need. Where I need him. Like maybe he's imagined this too.

I gasp, breaking our kiss. I need to breathe before my knees give out.

"You can either take your panties off, or I'll cut them off you." His dark gaze slides over me.

Saying nothing, I slide the fabric over my hips and down my legs. I step out of them, and Damen picks them up and shoves them into one of his pockets.

My eyes go wide. "Um. Will I get those back?"

"Maybe," he hisses, followed by a litany of words I don't understand. "*Kopalnia.*"

Damen kisses me. A whimper escapes my lips when he pushes a single finger into me. My hands claw at his shoulders when he adds a second finger—stretching, filling me. It's so good.

"Oh god, Damen," I cry, feeling my muscles tighten and coil. He flicks his wrist, and his thumb circles my clit.

Stars flash behind my eyes when he increases the tempo. Pleasure cascades through my body and my legs shake as the tingles radiate up and down.

My eyes screw shut as my orgasm crests deep inside. "I'm not going to last."

"Good," he breathes. "Soon, I'm going to strip you naked, spread you wide, and fuck you. Make you come all over my cock."

My head falls back, smashing against the window. My heart explodes into a mess of passion and frenzy.

Oh my god.

"*Kopalnia. Kopalnia,*" he inches out in between curses.

I turn rigid before detonating into tiny fragments. Every thought, every inch of my body, is stolen by his mind-blowing touch.

I've never felt anything like this.

Of course you haven't.

Damen releases the hold he has on me, my body still shaking. Seconds later, I feel him pick me up and carry me, and then he's laying me onto something soft.

When my eyes crack open, I realize he's situated us both on

the leather couch in his study. A warm blanket covers us, and his hands stroke lazily through my hair.

"What does *kopalnia* mean?" I ask, feeling sleep take hold.

He presses a kiss on my shoulder. "Mine."

Sunlight streams through the gauzy curtains, beating my skin with severe, annoying rays.

I do not like sunshine.

I do. But in small doses.

I've often wondered if I'm meant to live in London or Seattle. Gloomy days are more beautiful to me than sunny ones.

But I won't say no to a beach vacation.

I stretch my arms over my head and smile at the sight of the beautiful room spread before me. Beyond exhausted, I slowly push the thick blankets off my body, still sore from the night before.

You mean a few hours ago.

When I glance at the nightstand, I spy a note from Damen with instructions to take two ibuprofen and drink the entire glass of water.

While brushing my teeth, I mentally replay the events of last night in my head. I've never felt so much all at once. Never felt so connected to another person, and I didn't want to let it go.

Noting the time, I decide to wait to shower. I pull on a pair of joggers, a slouchy cashmere sweater, and a pair of UGG slippers.

"Good morning, Dorel," I hum as I walk into the kitchen.

"It's afternoon. But there is fresh fruit, bagels, and coffee," she says and mutters something about America under her breath.

"Where's Damen?" I ask, pouring a cup of coffee.

"He's not here," she snaps.

Hmm. Okay. Well, obviously, someone pissed in her Fruit Loops.

After I pop a bagel into the toaster and garnish it with an obscene amount of cream cheese, I decide to take my food into the dining room.

"Nie. *No.* Dining room is not for breakfast or lunch."

My brow scrunches. "Sorry. Where should I eat?"

"Right here."

"Thanks." I take a seat at the island.

I take in my surroundings, which somehow look completely different today. I finish my bagel, and one of the staff offers to take my plate.

"Thank you."

The young woman smiles and then says something I don't understand.

"English, please, Polina," Dorel swoops in and chides.

"Dorel. Do you know when Damen will be back?"

"No. I'm not his timekeeper."

I hear the familiar sounds of nails tapping on the hardwood. *Luka.*

He runs up to me and I lean down to scratch his ears. "Would it be okay if I took Luka for a walk?"

Dorel's gray eyes narrow at me. "Fine. That would be fine. His leash is there on the wall."

"Okay, buddy," I tell him. "Let me get my coat and you and I can go for a walk."

Before I stand, Dorel shoves my coat into my hands. "You must dress warmly. Gloves left pocket. Hat right pocket."

"Thank you." I trade my slippers for a pair of Sperry boots.

Walking outside, I inhale deeply and sigh. I tilt my head back and peer into the gloomy, snow-filled heavens. The sunshine has run away.

Luka hops through the snow and then takes off toward the dense forest of trees. I'm trying to keep up, but he's surprisingly strong. My arms jerk and we take off running.

"Slow down, Luka."

He tugs on the leash and dashes forward. "Maybe I should've learned your language before taking you outside."

Searching my brain, I try to remember what commands they said last night. *"Peatus, Luka. Peatus."*

The dog comes to a halt, and I manage to break my fall in a snowbank.

Luka sniffs around the tree line while I push up and dust myself off. He lifts his leg and paints the pristine white snow a shade of dark yellow.

"Good job, buddy."

An electric charge suddenly fills the air. Worry creeps into my body.

Luka barks. He feels it too.

Fuck. Is someone out here?

I tug Luka's leash. "Hello, is someone there?"

My heart skips a beat as a tinge of fear fills me.

Go.

Run.

I look back toward the house to see if I can see any of Damen's men. No one is visible from where I'm standing.

Stop overthinking it. *Run.* The dog will follow.

No. I won't leave Luka.

"Come on, Luka," I gently tug the leash. "Let's go home."

The dog continues to bark into the snowy wind. I trudge through the snow and place my hand on his back. "Let's go, buddy. Gotta get back to where it's warm."

Luka doesn't move. He stiffens under my touch.

A branch snaps and snow falls from the sky, landing inches from the two of us.

I freeze and look through the tree line. My back crawls with the fear that I'm being tracked.

No one is there.

No one is there.

I push again, coaxing Luka to ease closer and closer to me and the path we came from.

Come on. Come on, Luka. Please.

My breath comes in icy puffs. The chill of winter steals the air from my lungs. With my heart in my throat, I keep tugging silently, praying one of Damen's men sees us.

Finally Luka moves toward me, and I persuade him to come closer. "Good boy, Luka. Let's run. What do you say?"

Luka darts past me and I charge ahead. With snow lapping at my calves, I kick up and look back one final time.

My heart beats a furious rhythm in my chest.

You are safe.

With a shaky breath, I climb up the stairs onto the gray stone patio. I shake the snow from my clothes and dust the snow from Luka's fur. "We're okay. Nothing there. Just my mind playing tricks on me."

"Ms. Sanders, is everything okay?" one of the men in black asks before crushing out his cigarette.

Nodding, I try to catch my breath. "I think Luka saw something in the woods. Spooked him."

"I'll have two of the men go check it out."

"Thanks."

Luka runs toward a big pile of snow near the hot tub. He digs his nose into the snow and tosses it up into the air. "Oh, you like that. Okay, let's play this game."

I grab a fistful of snow and toss it to Luka. The dog jumps with glee and tries to catch the snow in his mouth.

Shaking the weird feeling, my mind relaxes, and I toss a snowball at my new furry friend.

CHAPTER
thirty-two

Damen

THE PACKAGE ARRIVES JUST AFTER FOUR.

I will be able to return something to Lauren—her identity.

Soon she'd be able to do anything with her life that she wanted. Go back to Chicago. Get a job. Return to her world.

But first, I want her to know that she'll have a place here if she wants to stay. I'm offering her parts of myself that I've never given anyone.

Parts of myself that I shouldn't. For her own safety.

But the thought of another man touching Lauren makes my chest flare with anger.

What happened last night can't happen again, I remind myself. My heart pounds, prickly heat coats my arms, and I'm sure my blood pressure rises.

I drag my gaze back to the screen. Gregory is nearly done with his list.

Rich people doing rich people things. Money always wins. I

knew he could get it done. Everyone has a price. Even those who think they're in it for the greater good.

People can make their rules and their laws. But the rich will always find a way around them or a way to break those rules. Which is why people like my father need to be stopped.

My eyes cast down toward the yard to see Lauren outside, just off the patio, playing with Luka—again. This is the third time they've been outside today. At least Luka has been keeping her company while I've been tending to business.

She tosses a snowball up and he tries to catch it in his mouth. She throws her head back in a fit of laughter and Luka jumps on her, sending her flying backward into the snow. He licks her face, and she reaches back to scoop up some snow and then blows it in his face.

Your dog even likes her.

The slam of the front door and the heavy thud of boots rip my head away from the computer screen.

Jonas appears in the doorway. "Sir, a moment."

I nod and walk toward my desk. "What is it?"

"Earlier, Ms. Sanders took Luka out toward the tree line that borders the east end of the property. She told us she thought there was something in the forest. We found something."

I take a sip of my tea. "What was it? Let me guess, a pack of gray wolves?"

"A dead girl . . . *woman.*"

Well, that's new and unexpected.

"You're telling me there's a dead body on *my* property?"

"Unfortunately, yes."

"Does she have any identification on her?"

"No. What do you want to do?"

I spear a hand through my hair. "Get a few of the men to help—"

I don't get a chance to finish my sentence when Lauren

165

interrupts. "Is it true? There's a dead woman on your property. That's what Luka sensed earlier."

"It's true."

"No fucking way," Lauren murmurs. Her hands tremble as she brings them to the sides of her face.

"Okay. Take a deep breath."

"I . . . want to see her." Her voice shakes.

"No fucking way. Not happening."

"Please. What if it's . . . *she's* someone who was with me in Belize?"

That thought hadn't occurred to me.

"What if this is some kind of warning from your dad?" she whispers.

I bite back a laugh. Only because I feel like she's seen one too many mobster movies. But if she's right, this could be the beginning of war.

"I see you, Damen." She jabs a finger at my chest. "I'm being serious." Her blue eyes widen. "This could be your dad's doing."

I pull Lauren close. "I'm sorry. I don't mean to disregard you or this woman's life."

"Jonas, take a team out and recover the woman's body. Take her to the stables."

"Right away, sir." Jonas leaves the room and Lauren exhales a deep breath.

"This is insanity. That poor woman."

I squeeze her tighter before loosening my grip. "Insanity. Or just a freak accident."

Lauren swallows, and I release her. "What are you going to do?"

"I'll take care of it."

Her brows furrow. "What does that mean?"

"It means that I'll take care of it. Trust me."

She glances at my computer screen. "Gregory has empty food cartons surrounding him and he's got a shirt on today."

I incline my head. "Yes. He's almost done with his list of tasks." I pick up the envelope that holds her belongings. "This is for you."

"Me?"

"Yes. Go on, open it."

She pushes back the flap and reaches inside. Her face beams when she pulls out her passport and the other items. "You got my stuff back."

"Those are replacements. And that's a copy of your birth certificate."

She frowns. "I don't have any stamps for my passport. Ugh. I only had two, but they were mine. Proof that I'd been somewhere."

"I think you need to look at the very last sheet in the booklet."

"There's a stamp," she exclaims. "I've been to Vutreila. Officially."

"*Officially*. And let me just say, welcome to our country."

She laughs and then throws her arms around my neck. "Thank you, Damen. This means the world to me. It makes me feel . . . I don't know. Just happy, I guess."

"Happy is good."

Jonas darkens my doorway. "Sir, we've moved the young woman into the stables."

I grip Lauren's hand. "Are you sure you want to do this?"

She nods. "Yeah. If I can identify her, I want to help."

CHAPTER
Thirty-three

Lauren

I'VE NEVER SEEN A DEAD BODY BEFORE.

The closer we get to the stables and the dense forest, the more anxious I become.

But I'm with Damen and I feel safe in his grasp. I know if anyone is out there—a killer, Damen won't let me go, and the men with guns will protect us both.

The sweet scent of hay and pine wraps around me when we step inside the elaborate barn. We walk down the center of the barn and one of Damen's men directs him to the stall at the end.

"Are you ready?" Damen stiffens, obviously sensing my fear. "You don't have to do this, you know."

I nod. "I can do this. I promise."

My eyes land on a large navy blue blanket with a gold letter *K* embroidered on it and under that gorgeous blanket is a body.

Swallowing thickly, I cast my glance toward the man in the stall. We step up and he pulls the blanket back.

"Oh no," I gasp, and my free hand flies to my mouth.

"You know her?" Damen asks.

"Yes," I nod as tears spring in my eyes. "She was with a Russian guy at the Aldon. She's the one who told me about the high-rise apartment."

"Okay. Now we have somewhere to start. Run her face and fingerprints through our software," Damen orders. "No one calls the police until we have a name."

He exits the stall, forcing me to follow him down the aisle.

I can't stop shaking. "Zabek says the girls in the high-rise are *your* girls. If they tie her to the high-rise, won't that mean you're responsible for her? What if this is Valter's plan to frame you for murder?"

"Has anyone ever told you that you have a wild imagination?"

"Actually, no."

My instincts are going haywire, and I don't know how to convince Damen I'm not some young, naïve girl. I thought that he thought more of me.

"You know, just because I'm not a mobster or son of a mobster doesn't mean I don't have thoughts about the dark side," I toss the words over my shoulder as we make our way back to his ice fortress.

Damen snags my hand. "What's wrong?"

"You're dismissing my feelings, and that hurts," I hiss. "I'm not trying to be a brat, I swear. And let me remind you before you go and sound off with some bullshit about me being young and inexperienced—I spent a good amount of time locked in a room with criminals, and then I had to spend time around your father. So while you think I have a *wild imagination*, I assure you that's not the case. I'm worried that something will happen to you."

"I'm sorry, Lauren. I don't mean to make you feel less than. And nothing's going to happen to me. This place is more than secure."

"But you can't say that for sure. If something happens to you,

I won't be able to forgive myself." I glance back toward the stables. "I can't help but think I asked too much of you."

Until this moment, I haven't admitted that to anyone. And hearing the words out loud, it stings. A tidal wave of emotions swamp me.

"Lauren," he sighs and tucks his fingers under my chin, forcing me to look up at him.

"Yeah?" I steady my breathing and dig deep for some calm.

"I know you think you're alone in a strange place, and I understand that you're afraid. I'm not going to lie to you—this world, *my* world is dangerous. And the truth is that you shouldn't be here. But you're here and you're asking me to teach you how to shoot a gun and you're dealing with some dark shit. I can't imagine what that's like for you. I'll keep us both safe. I swear."

"God. I'm a mess. I don't know what I'm doing anymore. I feel nuts."

"I promised you a relaxing weekend. Definitely not any of this." His husky voice cuts through the air, and he gestures back to the stables.

"This wasn't on my bingo card either. But, hell, being here with you wasn't either." My teeth chatter and I curl into Damen's side, seeking warmth. "I know I shouldn't be here. Maybe I should leave."

"If that's what you want."

"Your world would be easier if I left and never came back."

"I don't know if that's entirely true. My world will always be what it is."

His world will always be dangerous. Damen's father is the head of the Kallas crime family. And Damen isn't exactly innocent with his business.

So why am I still here?

"Do you want to leave Vutreila?"

Do I?

His words bounce around my brain, but everything scrambles. My chest tightens and I try shaking it off. My head tilts back and I breathe in the icy air.

His chuckle brings me out of my haze. When I glance at Damen, I watch his fingers flying over the screen of his phone.

"Are you booking me a flight?"

He chuckles. "Not unless you tell me to. Come with me." He grasps my hand, and we trek up the stairs and into the house.

We walk up the stairs to his bedroom. His fingers dig into the tight muscles in my neck and shoulders.

"What are we doing in your bedroom?" My voice shakes a little.

"Not what your dirty little mind is thinking." He winks and raises a brow. "Unless—"

I pound my fist on his chest. "You're hilarious."

Damen tugs me across the room into the bathroom. It looks just like the one in my room except holy freaking bathtub. It's huge. I mean ginormous. And I laugh a little at the thought of a man like Damen soaking in a big tub.

The entire room is glass except for one wall. It reminds me a little of the room I stayed in at the manor.

"Holy freakin' soaking tub. And this view."

"You can use it anytime that you're here. I even have bath salts," he says, shaking a glass jar filled with blue crystals.

"Do you soak in this thing? I can't picture a man like you having a bathroom like this or bath salts."

"I have bath bombs and bubble bath too. I've heard women love all these things."

A pang of jealously hits deep in my chest. Has Damen done this for other women? Why would he have this stuff on hand?

Okay, jealousy, keep quiet and just enjoy the moment.

"Why don't we see what's behind door number two?" He gestures to a set of double doors on the other side of the bathroom. "This way."

The doors open to reveal an elevator. We step inside, and he keys in a code. His phone chimes, and he keys in another set of numbers.

"Where are you taking me? To your bat cave?"

He chuckles. "There you go again with that imagination of yours."

When the doors open, we step into a room that looks almost identical to the spa at the Aldon. It's gorgeous, with another soaking tub overlooking the property, two massage tables, and a waterfall behind a glass wall. And a woman in gray scrubs stands in front of us. "This is Meri. She's here to give you a massage. Enjoy and relax."

"Right this way, Miss Sanders," she says in an eloquent English accent. "Your stress will be gone in no time."

The familiar smell of jasmine and botanicals envelops my senses. Meri directs me to the changing room.

"When you are ready, lie down on your back and pull the sheet around you."

Once I strip out of my clothes, I climb onto the table and situate myself under the silky black sheet.

"I haven't had a massage in a long time," I tell her.

"I will take good care of you," she says.

Meri starts to work on my shoulders and neck, and my muscles uncoil instantly. Staring around the room, I let my mind wander, and of course it goes right to the man who brought me here to this hidden oasis.

I close my eyes and forget about what happened today. I try to stop thinking about all the sordid things that have set my nerves on edge.

Damen lives in a dangerous world. Do I really want to be here?

My mind transcends and I think about fluffy clouds, a warm salty breeze, and the gentle lapping of water.

CHAPTER
thirty-four

Damen

"WHO WAS SHE?" I ASK MAREK.

"Elske de Lange. Twenty-two. Citizen of the Netherlands. She left The Hauge Airport in early October for Tulum. She was first reported missing in Tulum on October fifth. Her friends said she didn't return to their hotel after a night out. I've sent her file to you."

I push up from my chair. "Cause of death?"

"The coroner thinks it was most likely an overdose. There were no signs of forced trauma."

"Have you found the high-rise apartment yet?"

"We're working our contacts. We have her on video at the Aldon with Ivan Popov. Jonas is combing through the security feeds. So far, we don't have anything that shows how she got here."

Blowing out a deep breath, I spear a hand through my hair. "Thanks for the update. Let me know when you find something about the high-rise."

"You got it, boss."

A dead girl on my property. So young and with her entire life ahead of her.

I pour a healthy amount of vodka into a tumbler. I spend the next hour staring out into the horizon and thinking.

If this woman, Elske, was one of the escorts for my father, why kill her? Dead girls don't make money.

My father loves money. Power. Control.

Could Elske turning up dead on my property be a warning? But for what?

Why kill a woman that means nothing to me?

It's intimidation. Or it could be nothing.

Elske could have been Lauren.

Even though I haven't known Lauren that long, I feel a deep sense of responsibility for her. It would be easy to say that it's just lust.

She's gorgeous, but there's more to her than looks.

Obviously, there is an innocence about her, but she has good instincts.

Getting kidnapped will heighten your senses.

I'm sure that even her brother-in-law sees the world a bit differently now.

My fingers skate over my keyboard, and I check the monitor in the spa. Lauren is resting comfortably in one of the heated stone lounge chairs.

We're not so different. I'd been innocent once, but that changed when I saw my father murder his mistress. He shot her in the head down by the docks, execution style, when he found out that she'd been sleeping with a door attendant at a club downtown.

But my first lesson was one that haunts me to this day.

"Are you going to let this dog get away with biting you?"

"It was an accident, father. I spooked him."

"You're bleeding. When your enemies bite you, will you not bite

back? You show them that you are the bigger dog. The top dog. Makes all the other dogs fall in line."

"He is not my enemy, father."

"Is he not?"

"He is not. I see no enemies here."

"Very well."

When I refused, Valter dismissed me. I had my back turned for a moment. When the shot rang out, I knew what had happened.

I didn't look back. I didn't let Wystan look either. I remember clamping my hand over Wystan's mouth, muffling his cries. As much as we cared about the dog, we couldn't let our father know it affected us.

"Don't show him that you care, Wystan. It's okay to cry, but you can't let Father see you."

After that day, every chance Valter got, the two of us were there by his side in all the ugliness. Showing no emotion when he took, tortured, and killed.

What my father doesn't know, or maybe he does, is that I've kept a list of all his crimes, and I know where almost all the bodies are buried.

The dog, Vlad, is the first name on my list. Today Elske de Lange's murder has been added to that list. Even if it wasn't him who gave her the lethal dose of heroin or whatever drug made her heart stop. I'll make sure he pays for it.

It's not that I've spent a lifetime exacting revenge on my father. I've shown Valter mercy. And until now, he hasn't given me a reason not to.

With the betrayal of my mother, Lauren's kidnapping, and countless others—this is the beginning of the end for Valter Kallas.

My phone vibrates on top of my desk.

Riks: Gregory has completed his list. Her bank card will be there first thing Monday. I've uploaded everything you asked for to the drive.

Once I confirm the list, I send Riks a message to release Woodward.

Remind him that if he talks to anyone, he will live to regret it.

CHAPTER
thirty-five

Lauren

DAMEN STANDS BESIDE ME, ROLLING A CIGAR BETWEEN HIS fingers. "Good. Just like I showed you. You've got this."

I stare straight at my target and take a deep breath. I'm finding it hard to focus. All I think about is how good his hands felt on my body.

Aside from these little touches, he hasn't tried to kiss me or anything. I didn't see much of Damen for the rest of the weekend except for meals and at night for an hour or two after dinner.

I want him to kiss me. When I saw Damen after my time in the spa, I wanted him to rush me into his bedroom and kiss the hell out of me. But something has stopped him, and I don't know how to change it.

"Curl your finger around the trigger," he instructs. "Yes. Now make sure your grip is tight."

Taking my time, I position the gun at my target several feet away.

This is my second lesson. When Damen isn't busy with work,

I've spent time learning from him. I want to help him break up the trafficking ring. I want to protect myself.

And if it comes down to it, I want to know that I can protect him.

"Now, aim and shoot the gun, just like I've taught you."

I move the gun, lining up my shot. I'm a few inches off to the right. I position it right where I want it, then I take aim and fire.

I count silently to myself. One. Two. Three. Four. Five.

"Good job. Dobra robota."

"Thank you. Dobra robota. Polish," I tell him.

"Very good. Now reload and try again."

In addition to shooting, Damen is teaching me the languages of Vutreila—Estonian, Polish, Russian, and Latvian.

As instructed, I check the magazine, load it, and chamber a round. I catch a glimpse of Damen with a cigar between his lips.

So damn sexy.

"Stop staring at me, and fire at your target." He smirks and takes a long puff.

Blushing, I take aim again, fire, and hit all my marks.

"Well done." Damen claps, and I engage the safety before placing my weapon back in its case.

When Damen and I get back up to the main house, Wystan is waiting for us.

"So, how's the shooting going?" Wystan asks.

"She's a natural, and that's a little scary." Damen chuckles and places his leather gloves on top of the desk.

"Well, I think it's hot," Wystan says, pulling a manilla envelope from his jacket. "And speaking of hot. I'm wondering if you recognize this woman, Lauren."

Wystan sets a photo on the table, and I nearly jump out of my skin. "Yeah. That's Bianca. She was . . . we were in the same room together for a while in Belize."

"She's been in the club a few times," Wystan tells us. "Last night, she was with Kilan."

Damen rolls his eyes.

"Bianca was the first one sold," I explain. "The only reason she's here is because of your father." Disbelief swims in my chest. "She might be one of the women at the high-rise. If I can talk to her, she'll tell us where the penthouse is. *Maybe.*"

"What do you mean maybe?" Damen's dark brows knit together.

"From what Bianca told me when we were together, she doesn't have a very good home life. Bianca was hoping to get sold to someone wealthy." My stomach twists as I recall our conversations. "Someone who could take her away from her troubles and her mom's sleazy husband."

"And now she's with Kilan," Wystan grumbles. "One of the biggest slime balls we know."

Damen swings his gaze to mine. "So you think she won't want to leave if she's happy at the high-rise."

I nod. "Yeah. I'm afraid that could be true."

"Well, we won't know until we talk to her," Wystan points out.

"Do either of you have a plan?" My gaze pings between the two of them.

Wystan runs a hand through his longish hair. "Should we ask Kilan about her?"

"Not unless we have to," Damen says. "Why don't we have dinner at le Rideau Bordeaux tonight. If Bianca shows up, it will give Lauren the perfect opportunity to talk to her."

"Great. I'll make sure the private dining room is yours."

Damen shakes his head. "No. Give me any table in the executive dining room."

"Done," Wystan says. "And what about . . . the other room?"

"Other room?"

"He's talking about Rideau la nuit tombée."

"English, please."

"Rideau After Dark. It's a sex club."

My head snaps to Wystan. "You have a sex club?"

Wystan scratches his beard; an amused smile plays on his lips. "There's something to be said for people who want to branch out of their normal bedroom routine and try something different. I understand that clubs can be filled with wannabees who think they want the dominant or submissive life. That's not what happens in my club. And I'm not in the business of flesh peddling. I'm an opportunist."

Damen steps toward me. "I'm sure you understand that people have particular fantasies they need to partake in."

My throat tightens. "Right. Threesomes, gang bangs, bondage, whips, and chains. I've seen porn."

"You'll be surprised at your expectations versus the reality," Damen adds.

"Expectations of kinky sex? I can assure you that I have no desire to participate."

"And you don't have to participate. Most people like to watch anyway." Wystan waves his hands in front of his body. "It's not what you're thinking. My place is exclusive. NDAs. Extensive background checks. I've got policies in place—members have to apply for a room seventy-two hours in advance. Drug tests are mandatory. And no one is allowed to be drunk when they enter the club. If anyone is out of line, their membership is revoked indefinitely."

My voice turns to ice. "So what I'm hearing is that Kilan is a member of your club, and he could potentially take an unwilling participant to your secret sex dungeon. What if someone had taken me to Rideau After Dark? I wouldn't have had an ID. There's always fake, I guess."

"We've never seen anyone in distress."

"That's because you probably weren't looking."

"I hear what you're saying. It's not a perfect system, but maybe with your help, it can be better."

"You want me to help at your sex club?" My hands push into my hair.

Wystan lifts his shoulder. "Aren't you looking for a job anyway?"

"No fucking way," Damen snaps. "Lauren isn't working at Rideau."

All the confidence I felt while shooting the gun drains away. I asked for Damen's protection, and after everything that's happened, I know it's a risk. But the puzzle pieces are starting to come together. Valter's not going to tell us where the high-rise is or why Elske is dead. Bianca is my best chance for the missing pieces.

The sooner we get those pieces, the sooner I can move on with my life.

And Damen can move on with his.

"I'll do it."

"With her photographic memory. It's ideal," Wystan says.

"You don't need her photographic memory. You've got a security system," Damen counters.

"She can be a host. Think about it this way; a lot of information passes through my club. Lauren's an extra set of eyes and ears."

"I understand what you're telling me." Damen's hands land on his hips. "Do you feel comfortable doing this, Lauren?"

"Yeah. I mean, not entirely. But it's only because I've never been to a sex club."

His gaze flicks to Wystan. "You make sure that someone's got eyes on her the entire time." His blue eyes turn dark.

"Relax. Lauren will be fine," Wystan says and pushes off the chair. "I'll see you both tonight."

Twisting to look behind me, I watch Wystan stride out of the room. I count to ten and then turn back to face Damen.

"Have you participated at the club?"

"No. I like to watch."

Blush runs up the back of my neck. I'm not surprised. If I needed confirmation that I have zero business being romantically involved with a man like Damen Kallas, this is it.

But what I wouldn't give to feel his lips on mine one more time.

CHAPTER
thirty-six

Damen

ON ANY GIVEN NIGHT, MY TABLE AT RIDEAU AFTER DARK IS MY best information gathering spot.

Wystan failed to mention earlier that tonight was booked for a private party. Depending on the guest list, some of the regulars might not be here.

My gaze slides to the frosted door, where I see Lauren conversing with Violet Henning, one of the hosts.

I'm still not completely on board with Lauren working here. But if normalcy is what she needs, then she can have it. I'll put Riks on her security detail.

I've been here for about an hour when I spot Petra Gataki. She catches my stare and gives me a silent nod.

In the public eye, Petra is your run-of-the-mill wealthy heiress. Philanthropist and businesswoman. Not so public, she's got a hotel and spa here in Stuvica. It's much like the Aldon, except Malabar doesn't have a casino and offers exclusive rooms by the hour, in addition to rub-and-tugs.

"You're staying late tonight," she mentions, tapping her long black nails against the table.

"Yeah, well, I'm bored as fuck."

She combs her fingers through her short jet-black hair. "Heard you're looking for some information."

"And who did you hear that from?"

Her dark red lips tip upward. "Word gets around."

I nod toward my butler for a drink, but he's already on his way with a bottle of Champagne for Petra.

"Dom Perigon Vintage. You remembered."

"What information do you have?" I ask, glancing toward the parting frosted glass doors.

"I dated the guest of honor years ago." Her hand flutters through the air as she rolls her eyes.

"Is that so?"

She nods before taking a sip of Champagne. "Yeah. There was a time when it would've been me with him in there, getting my pussy slapped with a finger in my ass."

"Jesus Christ, Petra."

"Right. Changing the subject," she says. "One of my regular clients went from a weekly rub-and-tug that he could barely afford to booking one of my luxury suites. Not only that, but he'd sometimes book the suite for a week."

I reach for the bottle of Beluga and splash three fingers into my tumbler as she continues.

"One night he was drunk or high, maybe both, in the lobby of Malabar rambling about a dick-sucking whore, E being gone forever and never coming back. Since he made such a scene that night, I had patrons canceling left and right. I had to do some checking after he left."

"Of course." I swallow a gulp, savoring the burn. "When did all this happen?"

"Just a few nights ago."

My eyes squeeze shut as my grip tightens on the glass. "What did you find out?"

Petra leans in closer. "Whoever this E woman was, she almost killed your father. I don't have a lot of details. But what I can tell you is that your father frequents the Vettriano. There's an exclusive brothel on the top floor."

The Vettriano.

"Frequents the Vettriano?"

"Well, yes, Valter owns the building. You didn't know?"

A sardonic laugh heaves from my lungs. "No."

"Rumor has it a woman named Em runs the entire operation. But that's where things get dicey."

"How so?" I ask the question knowing the expected answer.

"Another rumor—that you supply the woman for the Vettriano."

"I can assure you that I don't."

She smiles. "You're a lot of things, Damen Kallas, but a pimp you are not. No offense."

"None taken. Can you give me the name of your regular client?"

"He goes by Abel Niehaus. I wish I had more for you."

"Thanks. This is helpful."

Petra scoops up the bottle of Dom and rises from her chair. "Thank you for the Champagne."

She struts away and I take another sip of my drink. Even with this new information, nothing seems to tie together.

Obviously, the dead girl E is Elske. It still doesn't explain why she was found on my property. The interesting tidbit is that she tried to kill my father. But why?

At the infinite number of reasons that race into my mind, I chuckle into my glass.

And if someone like Petra knows that I'm not running the brothel, why does Zabek think that I am?

Wystan will definitely find all this interesting.

I haven't seen my brother all night. He usually stops by, but he must be tied up or busy having fun.

Come to think of it, I haven't seen Lauren in a while. I walk down the corridor and up the stairs to the balcony overlooking the main floor. There's a woman on her knees in the crowd with six men surrounding her, all jacking their cocks.

I make my way to the other side of the room, where I see a man hurling a barstool into the air. Other than the no fighting policy and the bartenders and servers losing tips, I'm not above breaking a few skulls since I know the owner.

A little bloodshed sends a nice message.

Until I catch a flash of blond hair ducking behind a curtain.

Oh, hell no.

A chair swings toward my head. I bob and weave through the crowd, and the chair cracks onto the floor. I land a punch to his jaw, and he stumbles back into Wystan's broad chest.

"I told you about fighting in my club," Wystan grinds out.

"He was licking my wife's pussy," the man grumbles.

"Yeah, and you were fucking *his wife* against the wall. If you can't handle it, then don't bring your wife here."

"Watch out!" The words and the voice grab my attention, and I glance over my shoulder. A skinny fucker with a knife comes at me. He swings and misses.

I step toward him, but I'm halted when Nikolas, the biggest bouncer, steps in front of me and grabs the guy by his upper arms. Nikolas tosses him aside.

"You can finish him off if you like, boss." Nikolas chuckles before kicking him in the ribs.

As satisfying as that might have been, I drag my gaze to Lauren. "That's okay, Nik. You take the trash out."

The situation seems to have cooled, but when I reach Lauren, someone jumps me from behind.

"You asshole, you could have killed my husband," the voice shouts.

All it takes is a single move to peel her off me. Nikolas grabs her before she can come at me again.

CHAPTER
Thirty-seven

Lauren

"A RE YOU OKAY?" DAMEN'S VOICE IS HOARSE, AND HIS CHEST heaves from exertion.

My eyes must be the size of dinner plates. I've never seen a fight up close and personal. I don't even know how to process seeing two naked men try to beat the shit out of one another.

When I don't answer, Damen grips my arm and shakes it. "Lauren, are you okay?"

The adrenaline that had been pumping through my veins disappears. Damen's hold relaxes me and the concern in his voice brings me back to center.

"I'm okay."

"No. You're shaking."

"I swear I'm okay. Who wouldn't be shaking? That was intense and super weird."

"Let's get out of here," Damen says.

"Okay. But this won't keep me from working here."

He chuckles. "I had a feeling you'd say that."

Wystan steps up and grips Damen's shoulder. "Thanks for helping out back there. We haven't had a fight break out in months."

"Why were they fighting naked anyway? Fighting, in general, is dangerous, but naked is a whole other set of problems." I shake off the weirdness and adjust the silver necklace I'm wearing.

Damen's thumb runs along his lower jaw. "Sometimes people come here with something in mind, but when they get into the reality of it, they can't handle it."

"Or they come down from the high and realize their good idea or fantasy isn't what they really wanted," Wystan adds.

Damen flicks his gaze toward his brother. "You got *this* handled?"

"Of course. Nikolas has them in the back room now. I'm going to call Zabek."

Damen looks down at me. "I'll call you later. I have more important things to worry about right now."

Wystan might have smiled or laughed or said something, but I can't seem to break away from Damen's stare.

He finally looks away and leads me down a dimly lit hallway.

"Where are your things?"

"Wystan locked my purse in his safe."

He slides his key into the elevator and then keys in a seven-digit passcode that I catalog to memory.

"Don't bother," he hums. "The passcodes change every six hours."

"I figured as much."

After what feels like an eternity, we walk in silence down the corridor toward Wystan's office. After he unlocks the door, I step inside, getting a whiff of his cologne.

"Bring the car around," Damen barks into his phone. "We're leaving."

My eyes meet his in the mirror as I shrug on my coat. "I'm serious about coming back here to work."

"And you will, but I think you promised me a Thanksgiving meal tomorrow," he reminds.

"Wow, is tomorrow Thursday already? Geez."

We step into the private entrance and wait for Kacper.

"Do you have everything you need to make the meal?"

I shrug. "Probably. I haven't checked. I gave my list to Dorel because she insisted, and I was afraid to argue with her."

Damen laughs. "That's why she's the head of the house."

"Because it's her way or no way?"

Ignoring my question, he opens the heavy metal door, and the frigid air hits my face. The light from the canopy above glints off the shiny chrome of Damen's Bentley SUV. The man has a fleet of vehicles.

Damen waits until I'm settled before joining me in the backseat. While Kacper drives us to Damen's house, not the penthouse, I scroll through my appointment calendar. I actually have a schedule. Things to do.

Work.

Shopping.

Cooking.

The only thing missing is a friend to have lunch with me.

Slow down. It's a marathon, not a sprint. This is just the start of getting your life back to normal. When Damen had given me my credit cards and debit card earlier in the week, I felt relieved and beyond grateful.

I thought for sure, given Kat and Greg's money problems, they would have cleaned out my bank account and used my credit cards to pay off their bills.

"No luck spotting Bianca?"

"None."

"Aside from the fight," Damen drawls in his elegant accent, "did you enjoy your evening?"

"You know that I did."

"And nothing odd happened?"

I laugh. "Odd. Hmm. You mean aside from the naked brawl. Or all the people having sex with strangers, lovers, or whomever."

"You'll get used to it, especially since you're going to be working there."

Which reminds me, now that I have a job and my money back, I should think about getting my own place. I want to stay and see what the city of Stuvica has to offer me.

It's a whole new world.

New job.

New city.

New people.

It's a lot to take in all at once.

I distantly remember the Bentley SUV coming to a stop.

"Lauren, are you coming inside?" Damen's smoky voice breaks me out of my momentary haze.

"Uh, yeah, for sure."

He chuckles and we walk up the steps where one of his bodyguards greets us.

"Mr. Kallas," the man's deep voice says. They exchange a few words in Polish and the guard nods.

"Have a good night," Damen says.

When the front door opens, I take a step forward, and Damen's hand settles on the small of my back, steering me across the porch. The sensation of his touch in such a vulnerable place ripples through me.

We reach the foyer, and his hand falls away.

I glance at Damen as we hang up our coats, trying to read

him, but even though he is looking at me, his gorgeous face gives nothing away.

"Would you like a glass of wine?" He nods toward the living room.

"Sure. That sounds nice."

After flipping on the fireplace, he shrugs out of his suit jacket and hangs it on the chrome coatrack.

Fuck my life. Damen stands at the bar pouring a glass of wine and I can't help but notice how much I love the way he looks in a vest and dress shirt.

Strong shoulders. Check.

Beautiful, flexed biceps. Check.

Let the record state for the zillionth time that Damen Kallas is gorgeous with a lethally hot body. I've seen him look this way several times, but tonight it's as if I'm admiring him all over again for the first time.

I have no idea what I'm doing with him, and I don't know if I can stop the wild mess of emotions vibrating inside of me.

He hands me the glass of wine. "Thank you."

"You're welcome." He motions to the couch.

Surprise hits me when Damen takes a seat beside me. He has such a profound visceral effect on me. God, he smells good too.

It's just lust. I remind myself. Yeah, my hormones are out of whack because I'm going to start my period soon.

Sure. That's it.

How can I be so turned on by a man who likes to watch strangers fuck? A man who doesn't even flinch at the sight of a deadly weapon.

I want him. Bad. But I have no business being with him.

"Look at me, Lauren."

My eyes close against the surge of arousal I feel at the sound of authority in his tone.

"What?"

He stares, his icy gaze searingly intense. "What's on your mind?"

My heart pounds fiercely against my ribs before diving into my gut. Taking a long sip of wine, I think about all the things I want to tell him.

"I was just thinking about our kiss and other things," I whisper. "And how I want you to kiss me again."

"You want me to kiss you?"

I nod. "I do."

"I can't do that, Lauren."

Hurt fills my chest.

"Why?"

"Because."

"Just because? That's all?"

"I shouldn't have crossed that line with you."

Rejection hits me hard, and I wonder why I even bother to lay my feelings bare to him. Anger compounds as my cheeks flame with heat.

"You're lying. You said that you wanted to fuck me. You said a lot more too, Damen."

"I did, and it was a moment of weakness. I'd been drinking. I'm sorry for that."

"Oh, please. You knew what you were doing. We both did. There wasn't that much alcohol involved." I push up from the couch, tempted to toss the wine in his face.

"Do you think that if we fuck, I'm going to fall in love with you or something?"

His humor flees as he stands, his eyes darken.

"Forget it." I set the wineglass on the table. "I think we need to reevaluate the terms of our arrangement."

He contemplates me with narrow eyes. "And what do you want?"

I want you to kiss me. *Damn it.*

Shutting out my feelings, I dig deep. Confidence roars through me and I grab hold and leap.

"I want to rent an apartment in the city. I think it's time I leave. I've obviously read this situation entirely wrong. I'm throwing myself at you because you've rescued me or something like that," I sigh and walk toward the hallway.

Suddenly my legs feel like jelly. My hand rests on the carved wooden door as I try to calm my nerves.

I feel him come up behind me. "Turn around."

"Why? So I can look at you while you stand here and lie to me about how you don't have feelings for me? So you can humiliate me more than I already am?"

The strength of his presence is only compounded by his closeness. It has me contemplating my own self-preservation.

"We do have undeniable chemistry," he whispers. "But *fuck,* Lauren. When I'm with you, I'm happy. When you make me smile and laugh, it brings the sunshine out in me. When I see you and our eyes meet, it's like something I've never felt before. I'm not a *sunshiny* man. If I let you in," he breathes, and his lips brush behind my ear, "what makes you think I won't fall in love with you?"

My stomach churns at his words. Mainly because this whole time, he's seen me in an entirely different light than I ever imagined.

"Damen, please don't say things like that." I hear the agony in my voice.

One of his hands presses flat against my stomach, and he urges me back against him. His cock hard and thick against my lower back.

"If this is goodbye," I whisper, "kiss me one last time."

Silence stretches for what feels like an eternity. Tension radiates in waves.

"Lauren?"

"*Kopalnia.*" The word fell out of my mouth without conscious thought.

"Turn around."

Embarrassment and regret stir inside me as I turn in his grasp and sag against the door.

He groans, tilting his head before crushing his lips to mine.

CHAPTER
thirty-eight

Damen

S HE'S RIGHT. YOU ARE A LIAR.
Kopalnia.
I'm not ready for her to leave yet.
Kopalnia.
I don't want her to go.
Maybe ever. Kopalnia.

Lauren tears her mouth from mine. "I shouldn't want you, Damen. I know that I've got no business being with a man like you. You're everything out of my element."

"You're out of mine and I love it. I want you, Lauren, and that's the fucking problem."

"I love it when you say my name," she admits. "Your accent comes out, and it's so damn sexy."

Her hands slide up my chest and I tense beneath her touch. I want to kiss her again, to feel her lips pressed against mine.

"If we take this further, you should know something," she whispers, and her cheeks tinge pink.

I shake my head. "Unless you're going to ask me when the last time I had sex was, I don't need to know anything."

She arches a brow and smiles. "When was the last time you had sex?"

"A few weeks before I saw you sitting with my father at Wystan's club."

"Um. I do have something I feel needs to be said." She drops her gaze to the floor.

"Okay. Tell me." I reach to cup her cheek, forcing her to look at me. Her skin is porcelain smooth.

"I've never had sex before, and I think you should know that before . . . we take things further."

Without blinking in surprise, I keep my eyes on hers. Years of being around Valter, I've trained myself from showing any emotion. And I am not without my cracks, but I can't lie to her. I can't pretend that I don't know. "Well, in the spirit of honesty, I know."

She rears back, and a strangled laugh leaves her throat. "How could you know?"

My hands slide into her hair and down her neck. "My father. He was crude the night of the Serpent Ball. He tried to bait me, and I told him to go to hell."

Lauren reaches up, wrapping both hands around my neck and dragging my face to hers. Our lips connect, and her hot little tongue slips inside my mouth.

I slide my hand lower, cupping her ass and lifting her off her feet. Her legs twine around my waist and she flexes against my cock.

"You're a greedy little thing. Aren't you?"

Her gaze heats, and I know her inexperience doesn't matter. "Only for you."

I sweep my tongue over the seam of her mouth. "I can't wait to fuck you."

"You're probably going to be really disappointed. Bored even."

"I wasn't bored when I had my fingers buried deep inside your pussy. I wasn't disappointed when you came all over them."

"Oh god, Damen," she rasps, then forces my mouth open with her tongue.

Fuck.

"You are so beautiful it hurts. I have tried to fight it, this urge deep inside me to fuck you, claim you, make you mine," he whispers. "You're all I can think about."

Her hand slides down my cheek, and then she presses her soft lips to mine. "I've been fighting my attraction to you, but I don't want to fight anymore. Why waste time denying ourselves what we want?"

We kiss for a long time until we're breathless and wanting more.

And more is exactly what I want right now.

CHAPTER
thirty-nine

Lauren

I DON'T REMEMBER HOW WE GOT HERE, BUT MY BACK HITS THE mattress, and Damen's on top of me, and I'm naked, drowning in need.

With a boldness I've never had, I reach between us and palm his cock, giving it a gentle squeeze.

"I want a hell of a lot more than your hand on my cock," he groans into my ear.

"I want that too."

"But first—" He shifts his hand to cup my pussy. Heat blooms between my legs and only becomes hotter when one finger strokes up and down my slick heat.

"So fucking wet. You want to come on my hand again? Fuck my fingers until you're begging for my cock?"

His dirty words push me to the edge because I want that and more. My hips buck and surge forward when he pushes his finger inside me.

"Fuck, I forget how tight you are. You'll strangle my cock when I finally bury myself in your sweet pussy."

Oh my god.

Words aren't possible. Damen sends me over the end when his thumb circles my clit, adding the pressure where I need it most.

"We'll work on your stamina," he feathers kisses down my cheek. "Or maybe we won't, and I'll know that every time I see you, I can make you come so fast your head spins. It'll be so satisfying knowing that I can just lift your skirt," he groans against my skin. "Slide my fingers inside you. Play with your clit. Tease you."

Damen plunges two fingers back inside me, thrusting in and out. "Just like this, Lauren." His fingers work a magical friction, making my body hum and tighten with intense lust.

Moaning, my inner muscles clench as my orgasm takes hold again. My fingers dig into his shoulders, and I bury my face in his neck and scream.

When I come down from the euphoric bliss, Damen withdraws his hand, bringing it to his mouth, sucking his fingers clean.

Holy shit.

"I love how you taste," he murmurs against my lips.

The action and words should flame my cheeks with embarrassment. I've never had a man taste me. My heart rages against my ribs, thumping so hard I wonder if he can see my pulse thrumming in my neck.

His mouth moves down my chest and my fingers weave through his dark hair.

"And now I'm going to devour your pussy," he says and inches his way down my body. Kissing across my abs and down my thighs.

"Spread your legs, *skaists*," he commands. "I want your knees up and your feet flat against the mattress."

I follow orders, and his tongue lashes me from top to bottom. "Oh."

Within moments, I'm grinding against him of my own

accord as his moans send vibrations rocketing through every nerve ending.

"*Laba meitene*. Good girl."

"How many languages do you speak?" I pant.

"I'm going to eat you until you scream and that's what you're thinking about?"

I lever up onto my elbows and stare down at him. "What I meant to say is . . . I'm going to love watching you eat me."

Damen's eyes flare with heat. "I've been thinking about this since the moment I laid eyes on you."

"You have?" Shock evident in my voice.

"Fuck yes. Would you like me to tell you all the things I want to do to you?"

"Yes. But I'd rather you show me."

Who am I right now?

Damen's eyes flash as dark as the night sky before he dives in, licking and sucking my clit. I become an incoherent babbling mess when his mouth lands on my pussy. Long laps of his tongue drive me wild.

My back arches up off the mattress and Damen grips my ankles trying to anchor me in place. I'm lost in the sensations.

Like a possessed beast, he licks and sucks until I'm moaning and writhing against his face. I can't believe I came again. This isn't at all how my friends explained their sexual experiences to me.

"You feel so good," I tell him.

Damen pushes himself up and off the bed. Heat flows through me as if someone turned up the temperature in the fireplace.

He shoves off his pants, and I expect to see boxers at least. Instead, there is Damen. A whole lot of Damen.

Huge dick Damen.

My eyes bug out when he strokes himself. Just when I think he can't get any bigger, I watch his length grow. I like naked

Damen. If he wants to walk around naked all the time, I will not mind one bit.

He crawls up my body and then leans down, pressing his mouth to mine in a brutally hard kiss. Damen slides his cock up and down my slit, coating himself in my wetness.

"Next time, you're going to ride my face," he says.

"Ride your face?"

His chuckle fills the room as he climbs back onto the bed. "Yeah. I'm going to lie on my back." He slinks toward me. "And you're going to fuck my face with that sweet pussy of yours."

My thighs press together instinctively.

"You're so damn sexy."

My eyes drift up and down his body. "So are you."

"This is how sexy you are, Lauren. I'm so fucking hard."

I wrap my hand around his solid shaft. He's hot and his skin feels like velvet and steel all at once. I lick my dry lips and swallow.

"I've never . . . I mean, I've never sucked dick before."

He layers his hand over mine and we move together. "It doesn't matter."

"You're going to have to tell me what you like."

"This is a good start," he whispers against my lips. "I'll teach you how to suck me deep and swallow me down. Is that what you want?"

"Yes. I want to make you come. I want to wreck you." My lips pull into a tiny smile, feeling more confident.

"Then, by all means, my cock is yours."

My hands shake as I guide him right where I want him, and my palm flattens against his chest. "On your back, handsome."

It seems better than yelling, *Gimme that dick.*

Damen relaxes back onto the pillows and then reaches for the nightstand. Music pipes around the room and the fireplace roars to life.

My head fills with the hypnotic melody, which swirls with

the smell of sex. I settle between his muscular thighs as he did with me. His hand reaches to cup my breast. He pinches my nipple and the pleasure zaps straight to my core.

"I want you here." Damen pats the mattress on his right side. "I want to play with your pussy while you suck my cock."

Oh my.

Hovering over him, I do as he tells me. When I'm settled on my knees, I grip his pulsing cock with two hands. And then I go for it. I lower my head to circle the tip of his dick with my tongue. I remember seeing a woman on her knees tonight. Flashes of the way she looked poised and unashamed enter my mind.

I glance up at him and he gives me a roguish smile. Heat blooms between my legs again. His fingers whisper over my ass, and then he's slipping a finger inside me again.

"Still so fucking wet."

I circle the head again, flicking my tongue at the pre-cum that beads on the tip. My friends have all kinds of stories about what cum tastes like. I thought it would be gross, but Damen . . . I don't know how to describe it.

My mouth closes over the head of his monster of a dick. Keeping the same pressure with my hands, I bob my head, working my tongue along the soft skin.

I think I'm doing this right?

A long moan escapes Damen's lips. "Fuck, that feels good. Keep doing that with your hands and mouth."

His finger pumps in and out of me, and then he's sliding up toward my ass. In a heartbeat, he's right there circling my most sensitive spot.

And holy fuck. It feels *good*.

Damen groans as I suck the head into my mouth, teasing. I waste no time taking him deeper.

I rock against his touch as he continues his leisurely strokes from my pussy to my ass.

Damen buries his other hand in my hair, guiding me with my movements.

"Take me deeper."

His hips shoot up and I nearly choke. My eyes sting with tears. He swipes his thumb across my cheek. I nearly lose my rhythm, but Damen guides me when I falter.

Something primal strangles his voice as he pumps in and out of my mouth. "Fuck, I'm gonna come," he rasps, with a warning, and then he pulls out.

"No. I want you to come in my mouth."

With a wolfish grin, he nods. "Whatever you want, skaists."

I wrap my hands around his cock, stroking softly before closing my mouth back over the head of his dick. Then I suck and stroke until he loses himself under my touch.

He doesn't hold back, and I swallow every drop that coats my throat.

"Fuck me. For someone who has never sucked dick. That was very good." He pulls me close and kisses me. "Are you okay?"

"Yeah. I'm more than fine. But I want you to fuck me."

I've never said anything so bold in my entire life. But with a man like Damen Kallas, it feels so natural.

"I'm glad you said that. I don't care if the world burns around us, because I'm dying for you, skaists."

"English, please."

"Skaists. Beautiful."

"It's Latvian. And for the record, I speak six languages." He flips me onto my back. I feel two fingers slide through my wetness and his thumb strums my clit.

My head falls deeper into the pillows when he pushes a finger inside me. The feeling is supremely decadent, reviving all the nerves that had been overwhelmed from my earlier orgasm. He pumps his finger over and over, and I feel like I'll combust.

"You're so tight," he whispers against my lips. "Gotta get you ready for my cock."

A shiver rolls through me as my hands glide over the hard planes of his abs. His mouth covers mine and he kisses me hard.

"Don't come, beautiful. Breathe. Look at me." Damen slides his dick through my folds. "I want to fuck you with nothing between us, and someday I will when you're ready."

"I've got an IUD if you're worried about—"

He cocks a dark brow. "Are you sure?"

I nod. "I'm very sure."

Slick with my arousal, his dick slides lower, nudging the head of his cock between my ass cheeks, brushing part of me that only he has ever touched. My body flinches at the contact, but not from fear, just sensation overload.

"And one day, I'll take your ass. Your sweet little asshole." His eyes darken. "I'm the only one who's played with your ass, aren't I?"

"*Yes*. You're the only one, Damen."

"It's sexy as fuck to know that I'm the only man who's ever fingered your ass."

A riot of sensations and emotions ricochet through me. He slides down my body once more, dropping his mouth to my pussy. He teases my clit with his tongue and then spears two fingers inside me.

"You're almost ready for my cock." He rises above me again. "I can't wait to be inside you. When my cock slides inside you, you'll drown in a pleasure you never knew existed."

Yes. Please.

Everything in my body feels like it's moving at the pace of a tsunami. Even my blood pumps hot and wild.

Inch by solid inch, Damen pushes himself inside me. I'm more than ready, but it still burns and hurts like a bitch.

Damen moans and all the pain is worth it. My nipples bead

with a tight ache as he fills me. Twinges of sensation wobble between pleasure and pain zigging through my body.

It's too much. It's too good.

I need to concentrate and make this feeling last.

My hands claw at the sheets beneath me as I fight the searing pain of him splitting me in two. Remembering what he said earlier, I breathe, trying to relax my muscles.

"So. Fucking. Tight."

So you keep saying.

His fingers dig into my hips, and he moves with long, slow strokes. Damen bends to suck my nipple, biting on the sensitive skin. So many sensations course through my body.

"Fuck," he groans. "Don't tense, Lauren."

"Sorry."

"Don't be sorry. Just move with me," he says.

His thick cock stretches me, and my body finally relaxes, allowing him to go deeper and faster with every stroke. My mouth drops open, and I suck in a breath as vibrations ripple through me.

"Please. Don't stop, Damen," I beg.

"Not a chance in hell, beautiful."

Damen mutters a string of words in what I think volleys between Polish and Latvian. It doesn't matter. Nothing matters except this moment.

"More," I hiss the request.

"You give me more, Lauren. Use my cock," he says as he pushes deeper.

My fingers slide between us, and I play with my clit. Rubbing in fast, tiny circles.

"Fuck me, Lauren. You're so fucking sexy. If you could see what you look like . . . blond hair fanned over my sheets, biting your lip, and strumming your clit. It's enough to make me blow my load."

Something inside me snaps, and I buck upward. My gaze

drops to watch his cock slide in and out of me. I'm coming un-glued and he knows it.

"Oh, Damen, yes," I cry out through broken moans.

He pushes forward, burying his cock inside me, balls deep, and I scream, diving over the edge into devastating bliss. Blood roars in my ears when Damen's thumb brushes over my clit, driving me to another orgasm.

When Damen howls out his own release, his cock pumps inside me and my body goes limp. Everything drains from my limbs.

Holy fucking shit.

Virginity time of death: 11:52 p.m. local time.

CHAPTER
forty

Damen

I SPENT THE MAJORITY OF THE NIGHT IN MY STUDY WORKING. I DID manage to get a few hours of sleep. Before sunrise, I climb off my leather sofa and head downstairs.

Dorel is prepping the staff for the day's events, including breakfast.

"Good morning, Dorel."

"Good morning, Damen. Did you sleep . . . *well* or at all?" She gives me a cocky smirk.

"More than well," I assure her.

Dorel hands me a cup of tea. "Would you like to go over the menu for today?"

"You'll need to take that up with Lauren. She gets full approval, and don't make it difficult for her."

"Yes, sir."

I walk into the living room and flashes of Lauren's body bowing against the door as our lips fuse together wash over me.

Everything I've ever wanted and never knew I wanted existed right here with Lauren. And now I have absolutely no idea what to do next. I've never done the domestic aspect of a relationship. I've had girlfriends, but in order to keep them safe, I kept them far away from Valter.

As far as my romantic life went, I didn't have a plan except for staying unattached.

No wife.

No kids.

Until now, the plan has been solid. Now, I'm on a shaky foundation, all because of Lauren. Marriage? Maybe.

Kids? I can't say that the thought of Lauren carrying my future child didn't cross my mind last night.

Call it fucking crazy.

I stand near the fireplace sipping my tea when suddenly the mug is plucked from my grasp. A smile tugs at my lips when I see Lauren. Her smile is so broad that it sets off the dimples in her cheeks, making her look years younger than she is. I've never seen anything so gorgeous in all my life.

"On *Thanksgiving,* we drink mimosas," Lauren chirps, setting the cup on the mantel. "Not tea." She's freshly showered and wearing slouchy black pants with a long-sleeve T-shirt.

I band my arms around her. "Good morning."

"Good morning." She rises on her toes to kiss me.

"Are you sore?"

Her cheeks flame pink, and I can't help the smirk that paints my face knowing that she still feels me with every step. "A little. Nothing a few cocktails can't cure though."

"I'm sorry, beautiful. I should've taken it easier on you."

"You better never take it easy on me. Is it wrong that I want to drag you back to bed?"

"Let's put a pin in that idea. Dorel's awaiting your holiday marching orders." I nod toward the kitchen.

"Okay. Thank you for letting me do this."

"You're welcome."

She pulls out of my grasp and spins toward the kitchen. "When do we start decorating for Christmas?"

I shake my head. "Whenever you want."

Did I just say that? *Who am I?*

"You want any help, Lauren?"

"No, we've got it," she calls out from the kitchen.

Lauren and Dorel are cruising around the kitchen. I've been in there twice, grazing the appetizers. Lauren smacked my hand when I tried to steal my third double fudge cookie.

Since we're ahead of the States, I've got last Sunday's NFL game on the TV in the living room.

The house is filled with laughter, music, and way more noise than I've heard in a long time. And the smell of apples, cinnamon, and butter fills the air.

Lauren invited Wystan and told me to invite Ingrid, my secretary, to dinner. She also suggested that I let the guards come in and eat in shifts.

"There's plenty of food."

"I can definitely get used to this," Wystan says from the chair beside me.

"Me too," I admit. Luka trots into the room and curls up by my chair.

"So, what's the deal with the two of you?" Wystan asks before taking a drink of his bourbon.

"The same deal that's been in place for weeks. She asked me for protection and I'm honoring that."

With a knowing smile, he says, "Whatever you say. I've seen the way you two look at each other. Are you catching feelings? That's what the young kids are saying these days."

"What have I told you about watching too much reality TV?"

Ignoring my question, he just chuckles.

From the kitchen, I hear Dorel cursing in Polish.

"English, *please*, Dorel," Lauren singsongs. "If you're going to swear in front of me, you might as well give me the fucking translation."

Dorel howls with laughter. "You are a . . . hoot, Lauren. And I don't mean hoot like an owl. People say hoot like a funny person."

"Yeah. Yeah. I've heard the expression. You should visit the Midwest sometime, Dorel. You'll fit right in. There's a huge Polish community in Chicago."

This exchange goes on through the end of the second quarter and into the half-time report.

Mia, one of my housekeepers, enters the living room. "The food should be ready in about thirty minutes," she says. "Miss Lauren wanted me to let you know."

"Thank you, Mia."

Wystan stretches his arms over his head. "I'm going to check in on the club. Make sure the place isn't burning down without me."

"Yeah, I should check in too."

Neither of us gets very far when Marek appears and hands me his iPad.

While Valter Kallas is alive, Damen Kallas, the billionaire's oldest son, is seemingly untouchable. But recent speculation suggests the owner of the Aldon hotel is being questioned about the murder of a young Dutch woman. According to sources, the woman, Elske de Lange, was found dead on the hotelier's property. While the police have made no arrests at this time, they say that the billionaire playboy isn't being ruled out as a suspect.

A detailed history of the Kallas family, including Wystan, our uncles and their families, follows.

I've never been the subject of negative headlines. Wystan and I have only ever graced the society pages.

Not even in the years when my father was accused of the same crimes. With Valter, the charges just disappear. Not even Lorence has had prison time.

"Well, this is new," Wystan quips.

"Are the police at the Aldon?" I level my gaze to Marek.

He shakes his head. "No. Our sources on the inside say there's nothing about you even on their radar."

My mind reels. "This piece is all gossip. The language is speculative at best. Even if the part about Elske is true."

Wystan levels his gaze to mine. "Valter planted this story. He's trying to discredit you. This is another seed of doubt. First the high-rise and now this. What's next?"

I lift a shoulder. "I need to get Zabek on the phone. Tell him that if he needs anything, I'm cooperating fully. Everything else gets handed to my lawyer."

"I'll get word to your lawyer," Marek says, and leaves the room.

Wystan and I walk into my study and close the door.

"Are you worried?" Wystan asks, refilling his tumbler with bourbon.

"I'd be lying if I said no."

"Valter has always been Valter, but he's still our father. Let his own son go down for murder? A murder you didn't commit. No fucking way."

I let out a deep breath. "It's time to let Valter know that I'm serious about taking over the family business."

"What about the Aldon?"

"What about it? It practically runs itself." My knuckles press to the top of my desk. "He's a step ahead of me. Maybe ten. For years he's been running a trafficking ring and a high-stakes poker game under my nose. There are only two things Valter understands in this world. Money and family."

Nodding, Wystan's brows shoot upward. "What are you thinking?"

"Inviting him here today for *Thanksgiving*." The words taste like acid on my tongue.

"Have you lost your fucking mind?"

"Probably. Unless you have some suggestions?"

"This is Lauren's day," he reminds. "Fuck. Putting her under the same roof. In the same room . . . at the same table as the man who kidnapped her. That could trigger her trauma. You should talk to her."

"Valter will see through her façade. Just like I did," I point out. "If I tell Lauren that Valter is coming to dinner, she'll have time to prepare. I need her raw and vulnerable. And I need to pretend that I don't give a shit about her or her feelings."

His eyes close and he hangs his head. "That's ruthless, Damen. *Jesus*." He spears a hand through his hair. "Maybe you're more like Valter than you know." He laughs darkly.

"Remember Vlad? The dog Valter shot."

Wystan flicks his gaze toward the window and sighs. "Yeah. I remember."

"I need to show Valter that I don't care about Lauren. If he believes it . . . even a fucking ounce, it'll send a message. This could be the leverage I need."

"At least that's your hope," he scoffs.

"You can't change things from the outside, Wystan."

"There's always the *other* option."

Killing Valter.

"I don't think it's come to that yet."

"What are you most afraid of, brother? Are you afraid that Valter will kill Lauren? Kidnap her? Sell her again?"

"All of the above."

He levels me with a poignant stare. "Then you can send her

away. Someplace she wants to go where she can happily live the rest of her life."

I squeeze my fist tight, shaking with the urge to shut him up. He speaks rationally and makes sense. Complete sense. Because I have had the same exact fucking thought.

"Or . . ." Wystan sighs, dropping his voice above a whisper. "*Or* you can marry her. You keep her and fall in love with her—if you haven't already. Then she would have the Kallas name, and she would be untouchable. Connected."

I shake my head. "I don't know, Wystan. Don't you think that would only give Valter more incentive? Have you thought about marriage? Kids?"

"Family is important to Valter," he points out.

"Not in any real capacity though. Everything with the two of us has always been a lesson. If we have kids, he won't be that sweet grandfather reading to them, teaching them to ride horses, or even putting together a puzzle. Everything would be a lesson, and you and I would be the assholes who exposed our kids to their nightmares."

"Therapy is expensive." Wystan raises his tumbler in my direction. "I hope you know what you're doing."

That's the issue. I don't know what I'm doing. With any of this. I haven't been able to stop thinking about Lauren and what transpired between us. There's something there. It's something I haven't felt before, and I know that I want more. For the first time in my life, I've thought about having a future.

The flames of the fireplace hiss and crackle as if delivering a message straight from hell. I just hope Lauren can forgive me and understand what I'm about to do.

CHAPTER
forty-one

Lauren

SOMETHING IS OFF.

The earlier light and happy mood is now ominous, and I can't shake the feeling of darkness that's crept in.

Damen has barely looked at me since he sat down at the table. Wystan can't stop looking at his phone.

Okay. Calm down. This isn't their holiday, it's yours, and they need to work.

"Sir," Dorel says from the doorway. "Your guest has arrived."

Guest? My gaze swings around the table. I thought he had only invited Ingrid. Damen's staff, including the guards, ate in shifts in the kitchen.

My holiday joy vanishes.

Valter Kallas darkens the doorway, and all the air leaves my lungs. He's dressed in a gray suit. The only splash of color is the red pocket square in his left breast pocket.

Damen doesn't look at me. Instead, he stands and greets his father.

The staff hurries through the dining room, setting a place for Valter next to me.

Next to me.

What the fuck is Damen doing?

"You permit your pet to eat at the table?" Valter scowls.

I look around the table, but I don't see Luka on the floor next to Damen or Wystan.

"Today, Lauren is a guest, just as you are," Damen says flatly.

I'm the pet.

With a smugness that makes me want to slap him, Valter reaches over and squeezes above my knee. His touch sends shivers of disgust through me. Damen sits at the head of the table, with cold vacant eyes, allowing Valter to touch me.

I want to run. I want to scream.

Why is Valter here? Why is Damen sitting there letting his father touch me?

Valter grumbles something in a language I don't understand. I expect Damen to say, *"English, please."*

Instead, he replies in the same language. At least, I think it's the same dialect.

Have I been played? Damen sleeps with me and then invites his father into his home to sit next to me. To touch me. To mock me.

To share a meal with me.

A meal that I prepared for Damen.

What is fucking happening?

The three of them make conversation and carry on as if Ingrid and I are not in the room. Confusion winds through me, and I swear my blood stills in my veins, turning to ice.

Valter's phone buzzes, and my heart leaps in my chest. "I didn't know that dinners were such an informal affair these days."

Fuck you.

The staff enters the room to refill our water glasses and wine goblets. I look down, noting that I've only eaten a few bites of my potatoes and turkey.

My gaze swings across the table to Ingrid. She smiles before taking a bite of the vegetable medley Dorel prepared.

Valter's eyes glint. "How long do you plan to say in Vutreila?"

Until you die.

But I realize that Valter would have never known about me unless Kat and Greg hadn't lost their asses in a private game. Maybe Valter is not totally to blame.

"What did you do? Turn her mute?" Valter chuckles, and the ice clinks against his glass.

Shut up. Shut up.

I could end you. I could pick up my knife and jam it in your throat. But I won't.

"Lauren, my father asked you a question," Damen says. "Don't be rude. Answer him."

I resist the urge to smirk and slam Valter's face against the table. Under the table, my fingers fly over the screen of my phone. Ingrid waits a beat before giving me the signal.

Two can play this game.

"I don't know. I've been thinking about leaving soon. Maybe at the end of the month. I've always wanted to spend Christmas in England."

Check and mate, Damen.

CHAPTER
forty-two

Damen

MY FATHER CARRIES ON ABOUT SOMETHING, BUT I CAN BARELY focus on the conversation. Suddenly the anger in my veins evaporates, leaving me nauseated.

"Let's talk business," Valter says and pushes up from the table.

I thought he'd come here to eat, make small talk, and leave. Hell, I half expected him to have a phone call interrupt the meal and then tell us he had to leave for an emergency.

No such luck.

Instead, Valter took his sweet time eating the main course and drawing out dessert. He spent the majority of the meal staring at Lauren, which I hated.

When Valter left, I planned to spend the afternoon making it up to Lauren. I can still taste her pussy on my tongue. Her orgasm in my mouth.

Fuck.

And I want to do it all again.

Instead of finding Lauren, more time ticks by. Time that I

should be spending with her. Talking. Not talking. Worshiping her body.

Now I have to entertain my father in a business meeting. I lead the two of them to my study, where we have conducted many meetings over the years.

It will all be over soon. Just play the damn part.

Wystan pours the vodka and hands a glass to each of us. Valter offers a toast, and then we drink. The alcohol does a nice job of coating my brain and relaxing me.

"So, Damen." Valter sits in the leather chair opposite my desk. "I'd like to buy Lauren from you."

What the fuck?

"I'll give you a million dollars."

The grip on my glass tightens as my gaze lands on the silver letter opener on my desk. My hand itches to grab the shiny metal and stab his eyes out.

"Lauren isn't my possession. She's here of her own free will. But you can talk to her and offer her the money. I don't think she's interested in being your whore."

My insides snarl, and I fight the urge to jump over this desk and end his life here and now.

"You seem annoyed by her free will. Let me take the girl off your hands. I will give her a life fit for a princess. That's what I originally promised her."

My fingers drum against the top of my desk. "As I said, you'll have to discuss that with Lauren. But I think she's set on going to England."

"Maybe she'll fall in love with a duke or an earl and become a real princess," Wystan quips.

Valter nods. "Perhaps. But I think I can give her a better life. All my wealth would be hers."

"Are you dying?" This comes from Wystan.

He laughs. "No. Though I'm sure you'd be happy if that were the case."

Valter doesn't move. He's still talking about Lauren, and I swallow down a groan of madness and frustration.

How can she affect me so much? Why does my entire body feel battered and bruised at the thought of her leaving?

I take a moment to check my phone and smirk. *Good girl.*

"There is something that I've been wanting to discuss with you."

"What's that, son?"

"I want in on the Vettriano. And don't lie to me and tell me nothing is going on there. A dead woman turned up on my property and I know that she was one of your girls."

"No deal," Valter says.

"Why?"

"Why?" he repeats. "Because right now, I have one business partner and a small overhead. Bringing you in on the deal is less money for me."

"If you don't bring me in on the deal, the entire world will know that you killed Elske de Lange. Now that might not be enough incentive for a man like you." I rise from my seat and switch on the television.

Valter stiffens in his chair. "What is happening?"

"Oh, *this*," I mock. "This is the location for tonight's private game. The games you've been running for years. I'm not opposed to private gambling, as long as they're within the parameters of the law. Meaning you don't fucking take people as payment for a debt." I slam my fist onto the desk.

"Six, zero, land, rubber gloves, powder keg," Lauren taunts from the doorway.

Valter's eyes narrow and his gaze pings between me, Wystan, and Lauren. "What the fuck is this?"

"You're out, Valter," Lauren states. "While you were busy

stuffing your face with food, you forgot that I have a photographic memory. I memorized the passcode on your phone. Then I slipped your information to Ingrid, who gave it to Marek, who did his techy magic shit, and *boom*, baby." She leans in, bracing her hands on the armrest. "We. Got. You. By the balls, asshole."

He opens his mouth to argue, but I finish, "What she's saying is we've got your phone records. Text messages. Passcodes. Bank accounts. Your emails. Lots of interesting fucking shit."

Wystan hands me a cigar. "Fascinating shit that the local police, the FBI, Scotland Yard, and Interpol would love to hear about. And right now," Wystan says, looking at his watch, "all the women you've got locked in your Vettriano high-rise are being set free."

"But my phone never left the table," he protests. "*I* never left the table."

"You sure about that, Valter?" Lauren baits him. "All we needed was your passcode. You're smart with the two-factor authentication. But Damen is smarter."

"This is illegal. This is unfathomable," he stammers, red-faced. "My own sons have betrayed me."

Illegal? I laugh. Might as well add salt to the wound.

"And one more thing, Em and Abel, they're on their way to jail," I inform. "I bet your name comes up a lot."

"You've got two choices, Valter," Lauren says. "One, you go to prison for murder, racketeering, kidnapping, trafficking, etcetera, etcetera, and you lose everything. Including your position as head of the Kallas family. You're going to lose your properties. If you have any, your friends will leave you."

Wystan waves his cellphone in front of Valter's face. "There is another option. I can make a phone call right now. You still lose everything, but you'll be miserable and become a distant memory."

I slide a piece of paper in front of Valter. "Sign this contract. It puts me and Wystan in charge of the family business. You're going to retire to a nice quiet life somewhere away from Vutreila. Maybe Siberia."

Valter pushes up to his feet. "You think this is over?" he growls and steps closer.

I pull my 9 MM from the holster. "It's definitely over," I assure.

Valter picks up the contract, examines it, and then plucks the pen from the desk. "This is . . . outrageous."

Lauren pours herself a vodka. "What's it going to be, Valter? Option one or option two?"

Valter swallows hard as sweat forms on his brow. There's a pained look in his eye, but there's zero chance that's it's remorse.

"You might want to make that decision quickly because the police are about to be on their way here to arrest you," Wystan says.

Valter will pick option two.

He knows he's lost.

"Fine. Option two. But I'm not going to Siberia." He signs the paper and tosses the pen back onto the desk.

Wystan chuckles and taps his phone screen. "We'll see about that, old man."

Three of my guards enter and escort Valter out of the room. "Are you okay?"

"I can't believe we did that," Lauren squeaks. "My heart hammered in my chest the entire time during dinner. *Fuck.* I can't believe it worked."

"I'm sorry you had to go through that with my father."

"It was worth it once I figured out what was happening."

"All I want to do is keep you safe," I tell her.

"Where are they taking him?"

"I've got a holding cell in the basement. Valter and I have some business to discuss."

"Are the women at the penthouse really free?"

I nod. "Yes. They're all being examined by doctors, and we've got therapists for them too. Your friend, Bianca, was there."

A sad smile crosses her face. "When can I see her?"

"In a few days. I promise."

It's just one of many promises I intend to make and keep for Lauren.

My father's reign has come to an end, and soon I'll extinguish every fragment of his cruelty.

CHAPTER
forty-three

Lauren

ADRENALINE SPIKES IN MY BODY. I FEEL LIKE I CAN RUN A MARATHON. I shut the door and pace back and forth across the tiny living room area in my bedroom.

It's over. Almost over. We still have the trafficking ring to dismantle. I'm sure that's what Damen and Wystan are doing right now, getting Valter to confess everything.

After a long shower, I climb into bed, but I can't sleep. A whirlpool of emotions zaps through me.

It's late when Damen comes upstairs. I stare at him and neither of us speaks. Whatever he is feeling bubbles close to the surface.

The moonlight passes over his face when he steps in front of the window. I study his neck and his five o'clock shadow. Dirty thoughts surface, thinking about his face between my legs with that scruff rubbing against my most sensitive spots.

"I missed you," I tell him. "Are you okay?"

"I'm here," he whispers and climbs onto the bed. "I'm fine now that I'm with you."

His hands weave into my hair as his lips slant over mine. Every bit of emotion that has been flying between us bursts into heat.

Damen's hands drop from my hair to reach under the backs of my thighs. He shifts and settles between my legs.

"Do you think we'll be able to break up the trafficking ring?"

"I hope so. But right now, I don't want to think about that." The intensity in his eyes turns molten.

"What do you want to think about?"

"All I can think about is fucking you." He kisses me and then shifts up and off the bed.

Heat pulses between my legs as he unbuckles his belt and then kicks off his pants. After he pushes off his boxers, he climbs back onto the mattress.

"Everything about you makes me want to fuck," I moan against his lips, tugging the shirt away from his shoulders, and his hand slides between my legs.

"No panties? You're a little vixen, and you're so damn wet."

The heat of the blush burns over my cheeks, and I moan in response, spurring him on.

"Lauren." My name spills out with a rough edge to his voice. Damen kisses down my neck and then back up over my cheek. His lips hover over mine, and then, in a heartbeat, his mouth is on mine.

The pulses between my legs reach a fever pitch when he drags the tip of his cock through my folds and his hot mouth closes over my nipple. His eyes flash and darken with heat. I lift my hips and rub myself against him. A silent plea.

"Damen, I want you." He presses two thick fingers inside me, and my body weeps with temporary relief.

His lips capture mine. I lose myself in the kiss, digging my nails into his broad shoulders. Damen's tongue sweeps inside my mouth, teasing before his teeth nip at my lips.

"I can't stop thinking about you," he whispers. "I need you."

My heart clenches, and I throb with ache. "I need you too." My hands wrap around his cock, and I stroke him slowly.

"You're so damn hot. You drive me crazy," he moans against my skin.

"Show me how much," I tease, continuing my sensual torment.

"I'm going to own every inch of you tonight," he growls and pushes inside me. One slow deep thrust and Damen is buried to the hilt.

"Oh, you feel so good." I wrap my legs around his waist, and my heels dig into his ass.

The heavy ache of my orgasm builds with every thrust. My nails claw and dig into his muscles.

"Damen!"

His name rips from my throat in a hoarse cry, but he doesn't slow. He pushes harder, making contact with my clit, pushing me closer to the edge.

"Please, *please*." I don't care that I'm begging.

"You want more?"

I nod.

"Tell me. I need to hear you say how fucking bad you want it."

"I need it. I want it, please."

"And I want you to scream. I want this tight little pussy of yours to squeeze the fuck out of my cock when you come."

Decadent pain and overwhelming pleasure slams through me when his fingers find my clit.

His lips find my neck, and his teeth scrape along my pulse. My eyes squeeze shut as my orgasm slams into me, and Damen comes with a roar as he fucks into me harder.

For a long stretch of time, neither of us moves. Before Damen pulls out of me, he lowers his mouth to my ear. "You're mine in all the ways you don't even belong to yourself."

CHAPTER
forty-four

Damen

"I HAVE SOMETHING FOR YOU."

"For me?" Lauren stretches her long legs, flinging one on top of mine. My hand massages slow circles into her hip.

I reach for the drawer in my nightstand. We managed to make it out of her bed and into mine.

I hand her the box, and she stares at it with her mouth agape. "What is it?"

"Well, I'm going to tell you. Just open it." My fingers skim over the curve of her hip, drifting up her ribcage. Cupping her breast, my thumb traces her nipple, coaxing it to attention.

She hums in response, tearing at the ribbon on the box. "A necklace . . . is this a bullet?"

Smiling, I kiss the top of her head. "It's a dagger. Dorel's niece is a jewelry designer. This is from her latest collection."

"I love it." Her fingers skim over the ivory cardstock in the box. "Nevertheless she persisted."

"Dorel said it reminded her of you," I tell her. "And I couldn't agree more."

"So is this from you or Dorel?" Her face twists up.

"It's from me."

"Thank you for this. It's just gorgeous." Lauren unclasps the hook and I help her put it on. "I didn't know Dorel had a niece." She shifts her position on the bed to look at me.

My lips trace the smooth expanse of her shoulder. "Dorel has a big family. I can put you in contact when you go to England."

"I'm not going to England. At least not anytime soon," She shoves a hand through her blond strands, sweeping them around her shoulder.

"No?"

"We've got work to do. I still want to work at the club."

Lauren twists out of my hold, rolling up to lean against the headboard, which is still intact.

"And I want to talk to Bianca. Let her know that I'm here for her in any way she needs."

I glance over my shoulder. "She's lucky to have a friend like you."

She rolls the silver dagger between her thumb and index finger. "Well, I only knew her for a brief time. But I did feel a kindred spirit between the two of us. I don't suppose you'd be willing to have another house guest?"

My hand slides over the curve of my jaw. "If Bianca wants to stay here, there's plenty of room. You can move into my room."

Lauren slides down and rolls onto her side, her blue eyes bearing into mine. "I've never lived with a guy before."

My hands tangle in her hair, and I pull her face to mine. "Good. I like knowing that I'm the only one."

She leans in, kissing me softly. "Such a caveman. Were you always like this?"

"Nope. I've only been a possessed, territorial caveman with you."

She laughs and her hand covers her face. "I feel so silly asking this because you're you, and I'm me, but—"

I pull her hand away. "Ask me anything. I'll talk to you about anything."

"Tell me about your life," her finger touches my jaw. "What's your favorite color? Your favorite movie. Did you go to college?"

"You're adorable. My favorite color is black. My favorite movie is *Knife in the Water*. And I went to Cambridge. Although my first choice was Harvard."

"Wow. I'm super shocked that black is your favorite color. What's *Knife in the Water* about?"

"It's a thriller. A couple picks up a hitchhiker on the way to their yacht, and well, there's a violent confrontation."

A slow smile spreads across her lips. "You're kind of predictable. Although I would have thought a mobster movie would be more your favorite."

"Okay," I say, pulling her against my chest. "What's your favorite movie?"

"*Sweet Home Alabama*. Have you ever seen it?"

"Yep. Confession. I have a huge crush on Reese Witherspoon."

She props herself up to look at me. "I think you have a thing for blonds."

"I think I do. But there's only one blond for me—and it's you."

"Good." She turns on her side and flips off the light.

The smile that crosses my face has to be one of pure smugness. Wrapping myself around her, I tuck my cock between the sweet cheeks of her ass. Lauren shifts against me, and I nuzzle my face into her hair.

Jasmine and lavender washes over me.

Whatever this is between us feels like a real honest

relationship. Despite the drama. Despite the darkness that still hangs over us. The shadows of the Kallas crime family are never far behind.

My father is out of the picture, so he can't hurt Lauren or anyone again.

I'll see to that.

Soon I'll send him across the border to Ostad or Livachet. But not until I find out where the traffickers in Belize are located.

CHAPTER
forty-five

Lauren

I WAKE WITH A MOAN AS DAMEN'S HARD COCK PRESSES INTO MY ASS. His fingers strum my clit and my legs part instinctively, inviting him to settle between them just like he's done for what feels like the hundredth time.

With a smooth motion, he's buried inside me.

But it's not enough.

"Need more. Deeper," I pant.

He pulls us both up so that I'm on my knees with my ass in the air. Damen pounds into me, never letting up with the pressure on my clit.

"Oh god, Damen . . . *yes*, keep doing that."

Desire winds through me. When he presses his lips between my shoulder blades, my entire body shakes. My nails claw at the sheets as he drives into me with piston-like strokes.

"Damen." His name comes out in a desperate plea, wanting him to soothe the ache . . . the needy deep ache inside me. The ache is all his doing.

He slows his speed, making me drunk with lust. Each thrust sets my nerves on fire with anticipation.

The heavy throb of my orgasm builds with every pulse-pounding thrust. Damen pushes deep and I scream into the pillow. Damen fucks into me harder and comes with an animalistic roar. It's fucking hot.

He pulls out and flips me onto my back.

"Christ, woman," he breathes out. "You're amazing."

My hands skate up his chest and over his shoulders. "No, you're the amazing one."

The way he's got me feeling right now, I feel so alive. I want him more than I want my next breath.

Morning sex is the best. As I lie there trying to catch my breath in my post-orgasmic haze, Damen thoughtfully cleans me up with a warm washcloth.

"What day is it? What time is it?"

"Saturday, and it's almost nine," Damen says, pressing a kiss to my lips.

I spring upward and roll out of bed. "Shit! I'm going to be late."

"Relax. You've got plenty of time."

"You relax." I turn around to look at him. "I'm finally going to see Bianca."

"I'm taking you, remember?" Damen's laugh echoes off the walls and I melt. I love hearing that sound. "What? Why are you looking at me like that?"

I slink toward him. "I get it. Black is your favorite color. And you say you're not a sunshiny guy, but you've got this amazing laugh. It's what some might call infectious."

He cocks a brow. "Infectious also caused the plague."

"Fine. Stay dark and dangerous."

He comes up behind me and hauls me over his shoulder.

I smack his ass before he settles me onto my feet in the giant shower.

The warm spray washes over us and he cups my face. "As long as I've got you, my world will always have sunshine."

An hour later, I walk into the Diamond Suite at the Aldon.

Bianca leaps to her feet when she sees me. "Oh my god, Lauren. I just can't believe it. You're here."

I wrap my arms around her, and she holds me tight. "It is so wonderful to see you, Bianca."

"Come sit," she gestures to the table. "I ordered a ton of food already. I hope you don't mind."

I laugh and set my clutch on the table. "I don't mind at all."

She unfolds her napkin and places it on her lap. The server comes over and pours us both a glass of bubbly. Bianca looks amazing. Her dark hair is swept into a high ponytail and she's wearing a bright green top that matches her eyes with a slim-fitting pair of gray pants.

Bianca looks like she's ready to conquer the business world, not brunch. Happiness swirls inside me. She seems the same. And god, I hope and pray that she's not been subjected to demonizing shit.

"Okay," she says, raising her glass to mine. "This calls for a toast. To surviving and thriving."

I tap my glass to hers. "I agree. So, how are you doing? Do you mind talking about it?"

She shakes her head. "I don't mind. Honestly, the high-rise with Madam Em wasn't that terrible. Brutal honesty, I spent most of my time babysitting men. Her clients. A lot of them just wanted to talk."

"Are you fucking serious?"

She nods. "Trust me. I couldn't believe it either. I did have a regular client, Kilan."

My face twists in annoyance. "Yeah. I know Kilan. I had to, uh . . . let's just say, pretend to date him for a while when I first got here."

"Did you sleep with him?"

I nearly choke on my Champagne. "No."

She holds up her pinkie finger. "Good for you. He's not very impressive in the girth arena. He's got a long cock, though."

I chuckle a laugh. She's exactly the same as I remember in Belize. Full of confidence. Humor. Strength.

How?

"How are you doing, really?"

"You know. I'm okay. At least I think I'm okay. I wanted to be taken away from my old life, but I kinda miss my mom," she admits. "On the other hand, they gave me a laptop, and I searched the internet for my name. There wasn't much, just that I existed and then I disappeared. I stumbled upon an interview with my mom . . ." Her voice lowers. "She was dazed and glassy-eyed. Ken sat beside her, tears running down his cheeks. And that's when I knew that fucker was the one who had me kidnapped." She waves her hands in front of her. "I can't prove it, obvi. But I think he was bleeding my mom dry, and he needed the money."

A gasp falls from my lips. "My sister and brother-in-law were the ones responsible for my kidnapping."

Her green eyes widen in surprise. "How do you know?"

"My captor. Valter Kallas." I clear my throat. "He's the one who bought all of us—including you. He admitted it to me. Later, with the help of his son, Damen, that's when it was all confirmed."

She taps her finger to her lip. "Yep. Valter. He came to the high-rise apartment a lot. Elske was his girl. He fucked her every time he was there. I still can't believe she's gone. I hate Valter for many reasons. But when he found out Abel was screwing her too, he made Abel choose—his life or hers."

My eyes close and I want to vomit. "It's so cruel."

"She was a good kid," Bianca admits. "Elske didn't deserve it."

My hand covers Bianca's. "None of us did."

Over brunch, Bianca fills me in on everything that went on in the high-rise. Nothing she says surprises me or alarms me.

"So, *Damen* . . . is it true," Bianca says, tearing off a corner of her croissant, "that you're involved with the guy who runs this place? The son of the big bad man."

I clear my throat and take a sip of Champagne. "It's true. I confessed everything to Damen one night, and after some light convincing on my part, he agreed to help me. Valter is a connected man, I guess, or I don't really know the lingo where the mafia is concerned—but he is . . . *was* head of the family."

She cuts into her stuffed chocolate French toast. "Well, cheers to you and Damen. Does he have a brother by chance?"

My eyes meet hers. "Actually, he does. Wystan. And, girl, I think that you caught his eye. He snapped a photo of you at le Rideau Bordeaux one night with Kilan."

Bianca's eyes go wide, and she points her fork at me. "No way. Are you talking about the tall guy with the tats and the long hair?"

I lift a shoulder. "I think so. Do you want to meet him?"

"Hell yes, girl."

Bianca's excitement is contagious, but my mind is on something entirely different.

Valter.

"Are you sure that you're okay?"

She nods. "Things could have been a lot worse, but thankfully none of us were subjected to rape or torture. It might take me a while to adjust to normal life again, but this is a good start."

I smile, knowing that Damen has made all this possible.

It's nearly four in the afternoon. Bianca and I are happily buzzed and walking the casino floor without a care in the world.

"Do you want to go shopping?" I ask.

Bianca chuckles and stops to put some money in a slot machine. "Oh crap. I don't have a cent to my name. Look at us. Fucking walking out in public. Come get us, motherfuckers."

"Shh." I pinch her. "This is what got us kidnapped in the first place."

She eyes me over the rim of her wineglass. "Being hot and loud? I know. *I know.*"

"It's a crime against humanity."

Which, in its most basic definition, is absolute reality.

"I've got an idea," I whisper and motion to Riks. "This is my bodyguard, Riks."

"Hello, Riks," Bianca says.

"We want to go to le Rideau Bordeaux, but the after dark part," I tell him.

Bianca gasps and giggles. "Riks, we would like to go to the sexy club and watch people do it."

He rolls his eyes. "I think you're drunk."

Bianca stiffens her spine. "Maybe you're drunk."

We're going to have to take a break and drink some water before we go, because the two of us are definitely wasted.

CHAPTER
forty-six

Damen

MAREK STEPS INTO MY OFFICE AS I HIT SEND ON MY LAST email. "They're leaving the Aldon for le Rideau Bordeaux."

I nod and type a text to Wystan letting him know that Lauren and Bianca are on their way to his place.

Wystan: I'll give them your table.

"She's not going to make this easy on me, is she?"

He laughs. "No, sir. I think Lauren is a bit of a wildcard. Respectfully."

I wave him off. "I know what you mean."

Marek shrugs. "You know women. They've got to do things their own way. Sometimes they need to just drink or dance it out."

I cock a brow. "Is that so?"

"It's what my fiancée tells me."

"And that works for you?"

"Well, I think so." He scratches the back of his head. "She hasn't called off the wedding yet."

I walk to my bar and pour two tumblers of vodka. "Well, congratulations, Marek. Here's to you and your fiancée."

We swallow down our drinks, and then Marek tells me about his fiancée and their wedding plans. Not that he knows much, but happiness is apparent in his voice.

"Thanks for the drink," he says.

"My pleasure. What's going on?"

"I have news regarding your father. I'm afraid it's troubling. Years ago, he purchased a private island. Men with enough money come to the island to live out their deepest fantasies. The men bid on the women and girls—"

My eyes close, and I hold up my hand. "I get the point. My father buys and sells young women, forcing them into a living nightmare."

The nerve of the bastard. My mother is screaming from beyond the grave.

"Is this the same island with the shell corporation?"

He levels me with a heavy stare. "No. This island is in the Indian Ocean. It was a territory of Sardones. When the monarchy dissolved, your father bought the island."

"That has to be over thirty years ago."

"It seems that way."

"Okay." I weave a hand through my hair and blow out a deep breath. "Get the lawyers on it. I need to find out what my options are. And I'm going to go have a nice long chat with Valter."

Marek leaves my office, and I grab my suit jacket off the coatrack.

Just as I'm about to leave, Ingrid knocks on my door. "Sir, have you seen the news?"

"No. What's going on?"

Her face pales. "They found your Uncle Lorence's body this afternoon."

Everything in me stills except for my heart pulsing in my ears. "What? He's dead?"

"They're saying suicide," she whispers. "Maybe murder. Nothing has been ruled out. But that's not all."

I curl my fingers into my palms. "Go on, tell me."

"He wasn't alone. He was with his mistress and an unidentified woman. Both are dead too. Shot in the head. Execution style."

Lorence. Murdered.

Why?

Who?

The questions pour into me like a high-speed train derailing and falling off a cliff.

This is war. No one is safe.

"I've got to go," I tell her. "Go home. I'll send Olev with you. Lock your doors and don't let anyone in."

"Okay. Be careful," she says as her voice shakes.

My fingers fly over my phone screen, and I text Olev to come up and escort Ingrid home.

Me: Stay with her until you hear from me.

Olev: Yes, boss.

When I exit the Aldon through my private elevator, Kacper is waiting for me. I yank the back door of the Bentley open.

"My house. Now."

Kacper meets my gaze in the rearview and nods. "Yes, sir."

While Kacper weaves through the traffic, I send Wystan another text message.

Me: Lorence is dead.

Wystan: What? How?

Me: It's all over the news.

Wystan: Shit. Valter?

Me: Probably. I'm going to see him right now.

Wystan: If Valter ordered the hit. That means we've got big trouble.

Me: You got your eyes on Lauren and Bianca?

Wystan: They're not here yet.

Me: Let me know when they arrive.

My next message is to Riks.

Me: What's your location?

CHAPTER
forty-seven

Lauren

"Excuse me," a woman with red hair steps in front of Riks. "Can you take our picture?"

Riks shakes his head. "Sorry, ma'am, I don't work here. Ask someone wearing a black vest."

When we get to the hallway that leads to Damen's private elevator. Riks shoves his keycard into the panel and then enters his code.

Everything is eerily quiet. The hairs on the back of my neck stand up.

Bianca smiles at me and I shake off the weird feeling.

The doors open and Riks steps in first to hold the doors open for us. We step inside and just as the doors close, the woman with red hair appears and tosses something inside.

It's a white canister. I freeze and Bianca's green eyes snap to mine.

The whole elevator fills up with smoke and fear grips my heart.

"Oh my god."

"No."

Bianca's scream shreds through the air. Another blast rings out. My eyes blur and then I hear a thud. That's when everything goes black.

My head throbs with ache.

Blinking through the haze, I see Bianca sitting beside me. Her eyes are puffy, and her mascara trails paths down her cheeks.

I glance at my surroundings. We're in the back of an SUV.

"What the hell?" I whisper.

Bianca shakes her head. "It's happened again. The woman with the red hair and some guy. They're talking to the pilot right now."

"Pilot?"

She nods toward the jet on the runway. That's Valter's plane. I remember it from the night after the auction.

"Where's Riks?"

She lifts a shoulder. "I don't know. Probably dead."

Jesus. No.

"I can't believe it," I huff under my breath. "Damen will find us."

"I fucking hope so," she breathes.

"Have you overheard anything?"

She nods. "The guy keeps calling the red-haired lady Inga. Which makes her super mad."

Motherfucker. I should have known.

"Shut up back there," the driver grinds out.

"Fuck you," Bianca snaps.

Surprisingly, a quiet laugh escapes me.

"Inga pretended to be my friend, *Cynthia*," I tell her. "She works for Valter."

"That arrogant bastard has kidnapped us again?" She shakes her head.

Our hands are bound in front of us, and I try to wriggle free. My eyes dart to my silver ring. It's an open finger ring. Diamonds decorate the crescent moon and star.

It's another one of Dorel's niece's creations. I twist it off my finger and squeeze it in my palm.

"Time to go, whores," the man says when the back door opens.

"Where are you taking us?" Bianca demands.

When our driver opens his door, I drop my ring on the floor of the SUV. My door flies open, and he yanks me from my seat.

"You'll find out when you get there," the driver scowls.

If I know Damen, the cameras caught the license plate and at least he'll have some clue that I was here.

Kidnapping 101—leave a trail.

CHAPTER
forty-eight

Damen

DREAD CURLS IN MY VEINS AS I DIAL RIKS AGAIN. "WHY AREN'T you picking up your fucking phone?"

We pull up to my house and I push the door of the Bentley open. When I see two of my men lying face down on the porch and blood splattered everywhere, panic pounds in my chest.

I motion for Kacper to draw his weapon and stay low. He nods and ducks behind me.

"Fuck." I sprint up the stairs and draw my gun from its holster. Two more bodies and then I see the front door is cracked open.

When I look over my shoulder, Kacper reaches down and inspects the first body. He shakes his head.

Damn it.

With Kacper covering me, I rush toward the other body. It's Tannil. He's dead.

Fuck. Fuck.

The other two men are dead as well.

It takes everything inside me to harness my anger because

my brain is running a billion miles a minute. Ice-cold rage floods my veins at the realization of what has happened.

This is a hit. My father killed Lorence and now he's coming for me.

We keep low and move toward the side door that leads through the mudroom. The door is on the ground. Ripped off at the hinges.

Motherfucker.

"Sir, Marek and Jonas are activating contingency plan, B57. What else do you need?"

"Good." I nod, knowing that we're clearly outnumbered. "Call Wystan. Tell him to bring backup and have them do a quick perimeter sweep. And have Jonas keep dialing Riks. I need to know where Lauren and Bianca are."

Gun drawn, I ease inside the house. I scan the foyer and then the kitchen. Everything is trashed. Glass fragments and utensils scatter the floor. The rack over the island that holds all the pots and pans dangles empty. Traces of blood line the walls and the floors.

Blood roars in my ears when I see Dorel lying on the floor in the dining room. She's facedown and streaks of dark red pool around her body.

Please be alive. Please be alive.

She's alive, but her breathing is shallow. I sink to the floor beside her and that's when I see Luka wedged behind the hutch near the curtains.

"Hey, boy," I whisper and motion for him to stay.

Inside, venom and hate erupt like a raging volcano. Not *my* dog.

Footfalls echo and I roll underneath the table. My gaze darts to Luka. "Stay. Palieciet, Luka."

"It's just me," Kacper whispers. "Wystan is on his way."

"Good."

"What should we do?"

Before I can answer, Dorel coughs and gasps. "Kill the bastards. That's what you do."

I can't help the smile that breaks on my lips. "Dorel. Are you okay?"

"I don't know," she groans and rolls onto her side. "I was in the kitchen peeling potatoes when the whole house shook. I jumped out of my skin and when I rushed into the hallway, they stormed inside."

Fuckers.

"I'm pretty sure they got your father out of the holding cell." Dorel levers up onto her elbow.

"Is anyone else here?"

"As far as I can tell, just Tannil and his crew. I don't know if anyone was out in the stables."

I nod and help Dorel to her feet. Her legs wobble beneath her and she falls back. I tighten my hold on her and Kacper helps me move Dorel to the sofa.

I look at Luka, but he slinks behind the curtains. *Hmm.* His canine senses are on high alert. Something isn't right.

"Stay with her and Luka."

Whispers echo down the hallway, and I move to shield Dorel. Kacper crouches on the other side of me.

I stand up and whirl around when the voices get closer.

"Fuck. I could have shot you, brother," Wystan grinds out.

"Well, you didn't, and for the record, I could have shot you."

Wystan laughs. "Are you guys okay?"

I don't get a chance to answer him when Luka whines. I rush to him. "You okay, buddy?"

His tail wags and he crawls toward me on his belly. That's when I notice the blood on his fur. I check him for any injuries. When he doesn't yelp, I take that as a sign it's not his blood.

"How is she?" I ask Kacper. "Slice to the arm and looks like she's got some bumps and cuts. Just need something to bandage up the wound."

I hook my thumb over my shoulder. "Bathroom, there's a first aid kit."

"There's one under the sink in the kitchen too." Dorel laughs. "I tripped over the rug and landed there. But I played dead, and so did Luka."

"Probably saved your life," I tell her honestly. "I'm so sorry, Dorel."

She waves me off and laughs. "Aww, kiddo. I've known you since you were ten years old. I know the world we're living in. I'm here by my own choice. And that blood isn't mine. It belongs to the man I stabbed. I've always hated that rug."

I shake my head and chuckle. "Let's get that cut cleaned up and how about an icepack?"

"Fine. Fine. But we have a lot of work to do." Her hand sweeps around the chaos. "I will make calls."

While Dorel rallies the troops and calls in the staff that had the day off to put the house back together. Wystan and I step into my study.

He levels me with a grim look. "Valter is definitely gone."

"I assumed as much," I admit, tapping against my keyboard to bring up the security feed. "I should have known. Here's Valter sitting in the cell and then you can see here he jumps and that must have been when the house shook. Then everything goes off-line."

"Fuck." Wystan runs his hands through his hair. "How many people did we lose?"

"We lost Tannil and three of his crew."

My brother swipes the vodka decanter from the bar cart. "We drink to Tannil and the others."

We swallow down the vodka and get back to business. I dial Marek and his voice pipes through the speakerphone.

"Boss, I'm sorry, but someone kidnapped Lauren and Bianca leaving the Aldon. Riks is in the hospital. He's pretty beat up."

"Fuck. Goddamn it."

An anvil lands on my chest. Anger and more anger funnel through my entire body.

"Do you have any more information?"

"We have a black Escalade SUV driving erratically in the underground parking level. When I ran the plate, it says it was rented by Cynthia Lincoln. Cynthia's address is in Chicago."

"Cynthia Lincoln is an alias." My fist slams onto the desk. "A million dollars says that her real name is Inga and she's one of Valter's employees."

"I'm hacking into the street cams, and I've got my contact with the police out looking for the SUV. I will let you know when we have something."

Tension builds in my shoulders and rolls down my back. "Fuck. Fuck. She's out there . . . fuck knows where. Valter could have them both down at the docks right now slitting their throats." Murderous rage consumes my vision.

"We'll find them, Damen." Wystan grips my shoulder. "Come on. I'm driving."

The two of us sprint out the door, my adrenaline running overtime.

This is war. It ends with death.

Possibly my own.

CHAPTER
forty-nine

Lauren

M Y HEART SKITTERS IN MY CHEST WITH EVERY JOLT OF turbulence.

Who knows how many time zones are between Damen and me?

He'll find you. He's coming. Damen will save you and Bianca.

I chant the mantra over and over.

The plane swoops and the travel bug inside me fizzes and pops with amazement as I look out the window at the earth below.

Bursts of azure blue and mermaid green peek through the clouds. White sand stretches far and wide.

The entire flight has been peaceful. Aside from mundane conversation, Bianca and I have sat quietly except for our meals and trips to the bathroom.

Inga didn't board the flight. Neither did the guy who was with her at the airport.

As far as I can tell, there are only four passengers, including the pilot and a flight attendant.

"Ladies," the cheery flight attendant says. "We'll be arriving shortly. The pilot has asked that you make any final trips to the toilet now."

"Thank you," I tell her.

What else can I say? I wanted to ask her for her cell phone. I wanted to ask her why she flies kidnapped women around the world. I wanted to ask her to knock out the pilot and let us run free when we land.

But I knew none of that would happen.

Bianca levels me with a heavy stare. "What do you think this place is?"

"If I had to guess, I'd say Valter has shipped us to his sex island."

Her brows shoot upward. "Sex island?"

"Yeah, it's a playground for the rich and famous to live out their fantasies. I can only assume that men will pay top dollar to have sex with us. But don't worry, I know Damen. Once he finds this place, he will come for us."

The plane dips and Bianca grips the armrests. "What if that's not where we are? What if this isn't our final destination? What if Valter ships us back to Belize? What if we die here or worse?"

Emotion clogs my throat and I want to tell Bianca that we'll be okay. But everything isn't okay.

Leaning forward, I whisper, "Bianca, remember when you told me to get rid of my fear?"

She nods.

"Embrace your fear. You and I will fight like hell to survive whatever they have planned for us."

Her eyes close and a tear slides down her cheek. "I thought I was so strong. I thought this life would be better than the one I had. I prayed every night for someone to take me away from my mom once I knew that shitbag, Ken, wasn't going anywhere. Be careful what you wish for." Her words come out in a bubbled laugh.

I grasp her hand. "We didn't ask for this. You didn't ask for any of this when you dreamed of a happier life."

The speaker crackles and a second later, the pilot speaks, "Good afternoon, it's just after noon here in sunny Cadena Soleada. It's a warm eighty-eight degrees with a light breeze from the Northeast. I hope you enjoyed your flight."

Jesus Christ.

My insides roil as the jet drops and lands on the runway. After what feels like forever, the plane comes to a halt inside a large airport hangar.

The door opens and before we can unbuckle our seatbelts, two men dressed in black board the plane.

"Let's go, ladies," one of the men says.

"Welcome to paradise," the other one chuckles.

Neither of us protests because we know putting up a fight at this point is useless. We've both been captives. It's better to stay quiet. Observe. And stay strong. We have no choice.

CHAPTER
fifty

Damen

W E DRIVE THE STREETS OF STUVICA AND END UP HEADING to each one of his properties. Including the house where he first had Lauren.

I bang on the door and a woman with blond hair and blue eyes answers the door.

"Ahh, yes. I've been wondering when I'd see the two of you." Her voice drips with a strong Polish accent. "If you're looking for your father, he's not here."

My brows pinch together. "And you are?"

"I'm Anja. Valter hired me a few months ago to take care of this place."

Wystan nudges past her and walks inside. "And what exactly is this place?"

"This is the manor," she answers, matter of fact.

"I'm going to need a little more than your first name, Anja," Wystan quips. "For starters, you can tell us where Valter is."

Anja laughs under her breath. "I don't know. I haven't seen

him for a while. All I get is a text message that tells me to come here and clean. So I do."

"What about Lauren?"

"What about her?" She levels me with a pointed stare. "She left and Valter told me to box up all the clothes."

"Where are the boxes now?"

"I don't know. They were collected a few days ago." She stares down at her watch and then grabs her purse from the credenza. "And if we're done here, I must go to my next job."

"Thank you for your help, Anja." I turn and walk back outside.

Wystan scoffs. "Yeah, thanks for nothing."

"Well, that was interesting," I say and exhale a deep breath.

Wystan nods and unlocks his SUV. "Where to now?"

"Let's go to the Aldon. We can talk to parking garage attendants. Look at the security footage. Something. Anything."

Wystan grips my shoulder. "Isn't that what Marek and his team are doing?"

"I can't sit back and do nothing, Wystan."

"Okay. Let's go." He nods toward his Range Rover.

The parking garage attendants are useless.

"Black SUVs come in and out of here all the time. It's virtually impossible to remember driver and passenger details."

Five black Escalades drove into the parking garage yesterday. Three the day before and six the day before that.

And to make matters worse, someone hacked the security system at the Aldon. There is a ten-minute and twenty-four-second span of time that Marek identified as being looped.

"This is a dead end," Wystan says.

Wystan and I trek along the walkway up to the executive

parking level. That's when I see a man with a camera. When his gaze meets mine, he bolts.

"Hey, stop," I yell out and jump over the railing.

Out of the corner of my eye, I see Wystan running up the ramp.

Rage spurs me forward. The smell of car exhaust and dampness hangs in the air. The guy trips and rolls onto the pavement.

Wystan pulls him up and slams him against the concrete pillar. "Who the fuck are you?"

He stammers a string of curse words in Polish. "I don't have to tell you shit. I'm a patron."

"Then why did you run?" Wystan demands.

I study his face as he struggles against Wystan's hold. I pull out my phone, snap his picture, and send it to Marek.

"You don't need to tell me who you are. I've got people for that."

I type a quick message to Marek and tell him to run this guy's face through our software. Security runs toward us.

"Put this guy in cuffs and take him to the holding cell."

"Right away, Mr. Kallas."

The private elevator is still under repair. Instead of taking the service elevator, we hike down to the main level and enter through the lobby.

Wystan follows me up to the mezzanine level to the other private elevator.

"You got a plan?"

I look at him. "Yeah. Get information."

Wystan chuckles. "So we beat the shit out of him until he talks?"

"If that's what it takes."

We enter the room and Wystan settles into the chair behind our shutterbug. After I shrug out of my Prada coat, I roll up the sleeves of my dress shirt.

"Where is Lauren Sanders?"

"I don't know who this Lauren person is."

"You know something. Innocent people don't run," I sneer.

I step back and nod to Wystan, who unlocks the drawer on the wall. My brother slides a silver box onto the table. Opening the box, I rummage through the contents and then pull out a white cloth spreading it across the table.

"What's in the box?" he asks.

I smile. "Blades. Knives. I've got a big collection."

His brows raise, and a flash of horror crosses his face. Something tells me that I'll get my information without cutting off fingers. I place my favorite blade on the cloth.

Wystan grips the man's shoulders. He jumps in his seat. "Shiny, right? Sharp too. I bet it cuts through skin and bone like butter."

The man's face pales, and it looks like he may piss his pants.

"Would you like to have a closer look?" I bring the knife up and the light kisses the silver metal.

"Okay . . . *okay*, fine." He shakes his head. "I'll tell you whatever you want to know. Just don't use any of those on me. I need my fingers. All of them."

Satisfied, I step back and appraise him with a smirk. "That's good to hear. Now let's start with Lauren Sanders. Where is she?"

"If I tell you. Will you leave me out of it?" His voice shakes.

Wystan doesn't flinch. He grips the guy's shoulders with more pressure. "You're not the one asking questions. Answer him and we'll think about it."

The guy winces in pain. "Fuck, man. Okay. Okay. I got it. Lauren and the other girl, Bianca, are on a plane to the island."

"What island?" I press.

"The island that Valter owns. It's in the Indian Ocean."

Wystan uses a bit more force before locking him in a chokehold. "Not good enough. We need a name."

"It's in my phone. I can get it."

Wystan uncoils the hold he has on him and then unlocks his cuffs.

"What's your name?" I ask again.

"It's Martin," he answers and then swipes open his phone. "Cadena Soleada Island. It was once a part of—"

"Sardones." I snatch the phone from his hands and glance at the location.

"Who do you work for, Martin? And don't leave anything out, because I'll know if you lie to me."

"A lady named Inga recruited me. She hired me a few years ago. I'm supposed to bump into girls at clubs or wherever and spike their drinks. It just knocks them out and they go to sleep. No one . . . uh, hurts them."

"What the fuck?" Wystan hisses under his breath.

Martin's head swivels around. "Look, it's not just me, man. She's got an entire operation."

I lower my head to look him in the eyes. "Except that's the thing, Martin. These women that you drug. They do get hurt. In unspeakable ways. This follows them for the rest of their lives if they're lucky enough to survive."

"I'm sorry. It's good money, and I've got a family to take care of, too."

Wystan grabs his chin, angling it toward him. "If anything happens to Lauren or Bianca, I will hunt you down and you will wish that you'd never been born." Wystan slams his head on the table. "You're a world-class piece of shit."

Blood drips from his face as his head lolls from side to side. "Fuck, man. I think you broke my nose."

"Get this fucking asshole out of my sight," I bark at the guards.

As I was thinking of all the ways I wanted to tear Martin limb from limb for hurting Lauren and the countless number of other women, my phone rings. I answer and put it on speaker for Wystan to hear.

"We found the SUV," Marek informs. "It was abandoned out by the airstrip. Our team searched the entire vehicle. They found a silver moon and star ring in the back on the floor. I'm sending you the picture now."

I glance at the photo and confirm what my brain already knows.

"It's Lauren's. Smart girl leaving a trail. This guy we brought in, Martin. He confirmed that the girls were being taken to an island in the Indian Ocean. Cadena Soleada Island."

"Marek," Wystan chimes in. "We need a plane. We're going to Cadena Soleada."

"On it."

I end the call and turn to my brother. "Do you think Inga is acting alone, or is Valter calling the orders?"

Wystan shakes his head. "I don't know. There's no way we'll know until we get to Cadena Soleada."

"Unless we wind up dead before we can ask."

Wystan scoffs. "We're not the ones coming back here in body bags, brother."

Silence passes between us as an eerie chill settles in my gut. "Let's finish this war."

CHAPTER
fifty-one

Lauren

BEADS OF SWEAT FORM AT MY TEMPLES AND DOWN MY BACK.

The boob sweat is real.

We boarded a yacht shortly after landing. No sign of Valter or Inga.

Fear and anxiety coil in my stomach and I feel like I'll throw up.

The yacht slows and then comes to a stop.

We're here.

I take in the scenery. Dazzling shades of blue and green ripple around us and the palm trees dance in the breeze. But for as gorgeous as this island is, something wicked vibrates in the air.

"Miss Sanders, Miss Thompson, the tender is ready. Alejandro will take you to the island." This comes from one of the crew members.

I take a deep breath before getting on the tender behind Bianca. For a moment, I think about jumping into the water and swimming, but it won't do me any good.

And given the fact that I'm dressed in pants and a collared shirt, I would not make it very far.

I sit next to Bianca, and she squeezes my hand.

Several minutes later, we close in on the island, and a dock comes into view. Hammocks hang between palm trees. A large white building with a thatched roof sits on the beach.

As Alejandro slows near the dock, a man in black shorts and a white shirt approaches and ties off the boat.

"Welcome to paradise."

His black eyes and Spanish accent let me know that he'd probably worked his way up the ranks. He looks like a kidnapper.

"I'm Rohan, the director here at Cadena Soleada. Just follow me and I'll escort you to your bungalows."

Cadena Soleada? I've never heard of this place. It's beautiful.

We trek along the pier toward the white building. We step inside and I'm hit with a blast of cool air.

A server carrying a tray of Champagne smiles and offers us both a glass.

I shake my head. "Not drinking anything that I didn't see poured or made." I glance over my shoulder at Rohan. "Last time I was kidnapped, they laced my Champagne with drugs."

He laughs. "I assure you we would not do that to you, Miss Sanders."

"I think bottled water is fine for now, Rohan."

Bianca nods in agreement.

"As you wish, Miss Sanders."

In a flash, Rohan instructs the bartender to bring us two bottles of sparkling water.

"I'd love to give you a brief rundown of the island," he says.

"Is it possible to skip the welcome tour and negotiate our freedom? Or better yet, I think I'd like to make a phone call."

His lips twitch into a small smile. "I bet you would. We do

not allow our guests to keep cell phones. They are locked in the safe until your departure."

"Guests? We didn't book this damn trip," Bianca snaps. "Trust me when I tell you this is no vacation for the two of us."

"We don't have cell phones. In case you were misinformed, we"—I gesture between the two of us—"were kidnapped. Brought here against our will. I'm sure you're familiar with the concept. That's how you got this job, right?"

Rohan's lips twist into a sneer. "Miss Nowak hired me because I'm discreet and graduated top of my class in management and hospitality. I assure you that you will be treated extremely well as long as you stay here. I will take you to your bungalows."

Miss Nowak? Not Valter? What the actual fuck?

"Excuse me if I don't believe you, Rohan."

Ignoring my harsh words, Rohan leads us down a winding path underneath a canopy of colorful floral plumes and palm fronds.

Soon, we're walking toward a string of over-water cabanas. The walkway splits into a "Y" and Rohan stops.

"You are in this bungalow," he says, handing Bianca a key-card. "And you are in this one on the left."

Rolling my eyes, I take the keycard from him.

"What are we supposed to do now?" Bianca asks.

"Anything you want. Explore the grounds. Play in the ocean. Have a cocktail. I recommend the Blue Ice Martini. Miss Nowak requires you to be in the formal dining room at seven-thirty for cocktails. Dinner will be served at eight. Your luggage has been unpacked, and you should find your accommodations to be perfect. I supervised everything myself."

Luggage? I shake my head. That means someone has already purchased clothes in our exact sizes. Just like when you were brought to Vutreila.

Rohan walks away, leaving us alone with the sunshine and

water. The sea stretches far and wide. There is nothing, not even a boat in sight. The view is spectacular.

I'm captive on an island.

Where are you, Damen? Have you figured it out yet?

"Should we check out the bungalows?"

Shrugging, my eyes latch to Bianca's. "What else are we gonna do?"

We open the door to Bianca's assigned bungalow.

It's airy and spacious. There's a bathtub that overlooks the infinity pool and the ocean. The floor-to-ceiling glass windows allow for lots of light.

Artwork of blue, orange, and white shapes decorated the ivory walls.

King bed.

Plasma TV.

Indoor and outdoor shower.

We stride outside past the gauzy neutral curtains onto the private sundeck and drop onto the double lounger.

"If we weren't kidnapped and brought here under malice, I might fall in love with this place."

Bianca shields her eyes from the sun and glances at me. "Me too."

"I have a weird question. When they rescued you from the Vettriano, did you call your mom? Or your friend to let them know that you were alive?"

She lets out a deep sigh. "I thought about calling my mom, but I decided to search the internet to see if she was even looking for me."

I nod, snaring my bottom lip between my teeth. "Yeah, I did the same thing. What'd you find out?"

"Nothing much. Just a Facebook group started by my friend, Daisy. Not Janie. Which I thought was odd. But what was even more strange is that I went to look up Janie's social media and it had all been deleted. Of course I can't call her because I don't know her number."

My eyes close and my head drops back onto the blue cushion. "I hate to say it, Bianca, but I think your *friend* Janie probably had something to do with your kidnapping."

"I hate to say it, but you're probably right. What are you going to do when we get out of here?"

I look up through the piercing rays of sunshine. "I'm going to make sure Inga, Valter, and whoever is involved with this sick and twisted nightmare go to prison. I'm no murderer, but if anyone tries to fuck me, I'll kill them."

I just hope and pray Damen finds us before it comes to that.

Staring into the closet, my suspicions are confirmed. Every article of clothing and shoe is in my size. My exact size.

Anger rises in my throat. My temper so close to snapping.

Save it for Miss Nowak.

I pluck a floral print maxi dress from the closet and hang it on the dressing table mirror.

I hate that I can't chuck them into the ocean and let a shark gobble them up.

But it would be my luck that a sea turtle would get stuck and twined into the fabric. I'm the kind of person who cuts labels off all my plastic bottles. I even cut paper sacks and boxes so there's zero chance an innocent animal will get trapped.

When I hear a knock on my door, my eyes sweep to the clock on the nightstand. I've got about fifteen minutes to finish getting ready.

It's probably Bianca.

The door swings open, and Inga appears in the doorway. I freeze as I lock eyes with the bitch. My nemesis.

One of many.

"Are *you* Miss Nowak?" I sneer through gritted teeth. "I'm sure that you are. You can leave now. I'll see you at dinner."

She stares at me with her spine regal, wearing an invisible crown of power. Smug satisfaction plays on her lips as if I'm elated to see her.

I turn away from Inga and she grips my elbow, jerking me backward. "Come on, Lauren. Don't be a little bitch. Let's have a nice little chat."

I yank my arm from the hold she has on me. "Nice. I don't have anything *nice* to say to you."

She smirks, her gaze flashing between me and the ocean. "When Valter told me about you, I almost felt bad that I'd be duping you into a false friendship, knowing you'd eventually wind up here on this island. That this would be where you'd live out your prime sexual years. I'll keep you here until you're twenty-nine at the very most. You'll be damaged goods. You'll hate sex once you're time here is done. And your pussy will look like tuna tartare after the men have fucked you like a toy."

My body is for Damen only. Only him.

"Fuck. *You.* You fucking bitch."

Her eyes latch to mine. "Oh, sweetie. It's you who's fucked. Literally."

"The audacity. How can you do this to other women? You run this goddamn island. You take away our bodies and our power. *How* can you do this?" I'm seething and my heart thumps into my throat, beating like a drum.

"I do this all for the money and the view. You see, my mother was a whore. She was a whore for all kinds of men and women. Then she met this man, my father." She pauses to smell the vase of orchids on the dressing table. "He was wealthy and handsome. And as you might have guessed, my mother was his dirty little secret. Therefore, I, too, was a secret. And while my brothers grew up in the lap of luxury, attending fancy boarding schools and universities, I went to public school. No college. Eventually, my father discarded my mother and me entirely. The man left us poverty-stricken. My mother died when I was nineteen. Chronic hepatitis. I told myself that I would never let a man dictate my life. Alone and starving, I got a job at a club. A club where the wealthy dine and drink. Eventually, I met Valter. I told him that I wanted to learn everything about his business. He was very surprised that all I wanted was to learn from him instead of sleep with him." Rolling her eyes, her fingers flutter in the air like the wings of a butterfly kissing the breeze. "After all my years of working in the club. I knew secrets. People tell you lots of secrets when they think you're a nobody."

"And those secrets." I tip my chin. "Valter used them to strengthen and expand his empire."

"Precisely, and I became a very rich woman. I'll never be cold or hungry again."

"Great. So you're rich beyond your wildest dreams. Why don't you stop this trafficking business?"

"Because it's good business. Lucrative. All the women here are well cared for. No one is hungry or cold."

I swoop toward Inga. Disgust roils through my gut. "Right. Just used and abused and mentally damaged."

"You're being overly dramatic, Lauren." She clicks her tongue.

"I'm dramatic because I don't want to be raped," I scoff. "Why me? I don't want to be here."

She studies me with her dark gaze. "Because you mean something to my brother. I hate him. I hate Wystan. I even hate Valter."

The news hits me, and a wave of nausea creeps up my throat. "Damen's your brother. And Valter is your father. I should have guessed."

"Half brother. Sperm donor. But yes." Inga studies her manicure and then plucks a piece of lint off her billowy green dress.

Bianca knocks on the open door and then steps inside. "What's going on?"

My fingers splay across my forehead. "Inga was just telling me a story from her childhood and how she's Valter's daughter."

Bianca's eyes bulge, and she shakes her head. "Yeah, that seems about right. Where is daddy dearest?"

Inga rolls her eyes. "Come to dinner and find out."

CHAPTER
fifty-two

Damen

THE JET ROLLS TO A STOP AND WE'RE LED FROM THE PLANE through a breezeway. My contact, Alex Robertsen, greets us on the other side of the gardens.

Alex owns Robertsen Security. I met him a few years back when I wanted to upgrade my security software at the Aldon.

"Alex, I can't thank you enough for your help," I tell him and shake his hand.

"Anything we can do. I loathe kidnappers. We've set up a command post here," he says and leads us inside a large teal and pink building.

I remember Alex telling me when his wife, Ella, was kidnapped in the early stages of their relationship.

"Nothing on this earth could have prepared me for the news about Ella's kidnapping. It was frustrating and I was scared out of my mind. But we found her, and her kidnapper went to prison. Even though I wanted to rip him limb from limb."

I know that feeling.

Wystan, Marek, Jonas, and I enter the conference room. I stand in the doorway, watching the scene in front of me unfold.

The din of multiple conversations carried throughout the room. Dozens of people were bent over laptops or on the phone.

"We're trying to get an accurate count of how many people are on the island. As of an hour ago, we have eyes on about twenty-two people. Mostly staff and security." Alex leads us over to a large oval table. "You're welcome to work here, or I can arrange for a private office upstairs."

"This will be just fine," Wystan tells him, and I nod in agreement.

"We're going to find Lauren and Bianca," Alex reassures. "And when we find them, their kidnappers will pay a very high price."

Murder crosses my mind. Prison is a far second. But until we find Lauren and Bianca safe and sound, nothing else matters.

Given that neither Wystan nor I have any military skills, I brought in Alex and his team. Sure I could have dropped onto the island with Wystan, guns blazing, but I know that would have been stupid.

I can't risk getting Lauren killed after all she's been through. And I don't want to die. I would die for her, but I'd rather take a bullet and make plans for the next chapter of our lives.

Together.

"Here's what we know so far." This comes from Alex as he pulls up a map. "We've got surveillance over Cadena Soleada. We've got three drones flying discreetly around the island. So far, we haven't encountered any issues. There are sixteen ocean bungalows and twenty island villas. We've seen movement around the main building here." Alex points to a white building with a thatched roof sitting on the beach. "Mostly staff going in and out. There are guards stationed discreetly around the island, from what we can tell."

One of Alex's men tosses a file folder onto the table. "Here's the latest pictures and video. There's something happening to-night. Every guest is going to the main dining room."

Alex opens the file folder and spreads the pictures out across the table. "Recognize anyone?"

I scan over the photos. "No. I don't see her or Bianca."

Alex straightens his shoulders. "You're absolutely sure that they're on the island?"

"I'm not sure of anything, but you've got to get me to that island."

Wystan grips my shoulder. "You go to that island, and Valter sees you, he won't hesitate to lock you up or worse. Then you'll never see Lauren again."

Tension ripples through the room, casting a heavy shadow of darkness.

"You're right." I rake a hand through my hair.

"Let's comb through all the data," Alex suggests. "We'll try to get some video surveillance up to get more information."

"Fine. Anything is better than nothing."

It's been hours, and with nothing new to report on the island. I step outside with a cup of coffee.

The sky is bright blue, and the warm tropical breeze rustles the palm trees overhead.

"Hey, Damen," Wystan says from the breezeway. "They're about to go around the bungalows again."

"Okay."

None of us got much sleep last night. We launched drone surveillance just before dawn. No sign of Lauren yet. I want to punch my fist through a wall.

It's pretty quiet on the island. Everything seems to unfold

at a slow, agonizing pace. Mostly staff and security milling about the place.

Tick. Tock.

Tick. Tock.

The longer time drags on, the more hope seems to leave my body.

The room is silent, and my eyes never leave the monitors. The drone swoops low, sailing over miles of water. Glimmering water and sandy beaches stretch for miles. A seaplane lands in the distance, and a yacht floats miles off the coast of Cadena Soleada.

"Coming up on the bungalows now," Alex says.

Tick. Tock.

Tick. Tock.

Come on. Come on, Lauren. *Give me a sign.*

I see a flash of blond hair whipping in the breeze on the sundeck of a bungalow.

"See that figure? That's got to be Lauren. Can you get closer?"

Alex nods at the guy operating the drone. "Going in for a closer view."

My eyes stay glued to the screen. It's got to be her.

My heart beats against my ribcage, threatening to punch through. The drone steadies and I get a good look.

"It's her. That's Lauren."

"We have visual confirmation that Lauren is on the island," Alex announces to the room.

Claps of satisfaction filter around the room, and Wystan grips my shoulders. "We're going to get her back."

Relief washes through me, but I know we're not done yet. Not by a long shot.

"All right," Alex says. "My team and I will continue to formulate the extraction plan. You guys coming with?"

Wystan and I exchange glances, and my brother gives me a nod. "Hell yeah."

CHAPTER
fifty-three

Lauren

Restless is how I slept with thoughts of Damen on my mind, heavy with worry.

Where is he?

Last night's dinner was uneventful. Nothing happened.

Inga was nowhere to be found.

We ate together at a table overlooking the ocean. We were the only two guests in the entire restaurant.

I think she wanted to torture Bianca and me. Keep us wondering and waiting for her to appear.

Cup of coffee in hand, I walk onto the sundeck. My eyes sweep to the sundeck of Bianca's bungalow. I wonder if she's up.

I'm about to take another sip of my coffee when I hear a noise.

It's a low buzzing. My heart rate kicks up.

Shielding my eyes, I glance upward. I can't see anything. Maybe it's a bird or a creature native to the region.

"Hey." Bianca's voice floats into the air. "Whatcha looking at?"

I laugh. "I thought I heard a buzzing sound. But I don't see anything. Do you?"

"Nope." She rises up on her tiptoes, looks around, and then bounces back on her heels. "Oh, you made coffee."

"Come on over and grab a cup."

About a minute later, there's a knock on my door. My heart pounds in my chest at the thought of Inga darkening my doorway like she had done last night.

Thankfully it's the person I'm expecting, and she swipes a cup from the rack and then fills up her mug. We walk back onto the sundeck.

We chat briefly about mundane things. How we slept. What we dreamed about. The weather and the beauty of this place.

Another knock at the door interrupts our conversation. When I open it, Rohan appears with two staffers carrying trays of food and juices. At his instruction, they place the trays on the rattan table. My stomach growls when I catch sight of the fresh fruit and assortment of croissants, pastries, muffins, and cakes.

"Good morning, ladies," he chirps. "I see that you've made use of the coffee maker. Wonderful. Here is your breakfast. If there is anything special you want, I can have it brought to you. Eggs benedict, pancakes, waffles, anything you want, you just ask."

"We don't need anything else. Thanks." I eye him over the rim of my mug. Suspicion churns in my gut.

"The only thing we need is to leave this place," Bianca interjects. "So if you can arrange that, *that* would be great." She cocks her hip and pops a piece of mango into her mouth.

He shakes his head and dismisses the staff with a wave of his hand. "You know you aren't leaving. You will be quite happy here if you just give it a chance. Take a look around. You are in paradise."

"Paradise. Hmm." Bianca stands and saunters toward Rohan.

"If you help the two of us off this island, I'll show you my tits. Would you like that, Rohan?"

"I'm afraid your efforts are wasted on me, Mistress Bianca."

"Mistress," she repeats, a hint of acid on her tongue. "Well, since we're into formalities and you claim to be the best man for the job. Why don't you get us some information?"

"Yeah. We could use some information," I chime in. "And for every piece of useful information you give us, you'll be rewarded financially. Maybe enough money so you can buy this island or one like it one day."

"Bribery will get you nowhere." His voice hardens. "You two really should try to make a life for yourselves here. It'll be a lot less exhausting if you do."

Ignoring him, I return my gaze toward the ocean.

"If that will be all. I will leave you to your day," he says. "Enjoy."

I follow him into the bungalow and through the main room. Once he leaves, I lock the door again.

"What do you think Inga has planned for us today?" Bianca asks, breaking off a piece of the muffin in her hand.

"I don't know. I'm sure she's auctioning off our bodies to the highest bidders."

"Maybe we'll get lucky, and they won't want to have sex."

A howl of laughter escapes me. "Bianca. People don't come here and not fuck. This island expects sex."

"Let's hope we get rescued before that happens."

My eyes dance over the blue and green tides. In the distance, I see a large island. If I could somehow steal a boat, or maybe Bianca and I can stow away on a yacht, we can get off this island.

What does it matter?

Nothing.

Everything.

All this beauty is wasted on immorality and crime. It's a shame.

"You want to explore the island?" Bianca asks.

"Yeah. We need information, and I guess our time is the best asset."

She polishes off her muffin. "I wonder if we're the only two . . . *mistresses*. I guess that's what we are. Better than being called whores."

That is true enough.

My eyes squint along the glassy turquoise water as a pod of dolphins breaks the surface. Innocent and free.

Damen will find us. He will set us free.

Come on, Damen. Give me a sign.

Bianca and I spent the day looking for clues and cataloging everything to memory. Building locations, faces, and any other useful information.

We stop in the Coco Restaurant to cool off and get something to eat. Aside from our sleuthing, I hate that this feels like a vacation.

The two of us are led outside and then down a flight of stairs to a table for two overlooking the lagoon.

"We should order some drinks," Bianca suggests. "They're not going to drug us. They've already kidnapped us. We can't go anywhere. Even if we try to swim to that island we discovered across the way. Someone would see us."

I hold my hands up in surrender. "I hear you. And what do you want to bet that Valter owns that island too?"

We order two turquoise lagoon cocktails. Bianca orders the shrimp tempura and I opt for the veggie spring rolls.

As much as I hate it, I'll give Inga credit. She does have a nice piece of land here. We sip our drinks and bask in the sunshine and warm breeze.

"I can't decide if I want to go swimming, take a nap, or shower. I just can't believe there aren't any guests here on the island. There's a hell of a lot of staff for the two of us."

A cool chill settles in my spine. I know this feeling. It's the same feeling I had when I met Valter for the first time.

"Well, don't forget that staff also caters to me and Inga."

Valter.

I'd know that cold silvery voice anywhere.

"You really do just slither in like the snake that you are," I huff.

He tsk-tsks as he shakes his head. "That's no way to talk to the father of the man you're sleeping with, is it, Lauren?"

"What the fuck do you want, Valter?" Bianca asks.

He eyes me while adjusting the collar of his shirt. "Did you find what you were looking for?"

Why? What?

His question hangs in the air, and I know we are being watched. Confirmed.

Lifting my chin, I answer, "As a matter of fact, we discovered a lot."

His cool stare meets mine. "Is that so?"

No. But I won't back down from you.

If Valter and Inga want to play mind games, so can I.

"What brings you to the island?" Bianca asks Valter.

"I own this place. I can come and go as I please. I own every inch of this place, including the two of you." His voice darkens.

A flock of birds takes flight nearby and a bizarre feeling washes over me. Suddenly, everything goes eerily quiet.

Bianca's eyes snap to mine, and that's when I hear it. A loud popping sound. Valter's head explodes.

Red coats the white umbrellas and splatters all over the two of us. I can smell the blood and fear.

Our shrieks cut the air, and my entire body shakes. I try to stand up, but my body won't move. All I can do is stare at the blood and brain matter sprayed everywhere.

"Jesus Christ!" Bianca shouts.

I glance up at her. Blood covers the side of her face and shoulder. My stomach heaves and threatens to empty the lunch I just ate.

Two feet from me, Valter lies dead.

Valter is dead.

Valter.

Dead.

Damen.

"Wait. Wait," I say and grip Bianca's arm. "I think they're coming for us. I think we're being rescued."

"Okay! Let's go," Bianca yells. "Now."

My feet still don't move. I can barely hear Bianca.

"Lauren. We need to get inside," Bianca shouts again.

Nodding, I dig deep, finding my courage, and we run up the stairs and into the restaurant. My lungs burn as we run through the dining room and into the kitchen.

It's not until we reach the bar that my limbs feel sluggish and heavy. I take another step and my legs threaten to give out. I miss a step and fall onto two barstools. Dread seeps into my veins.

Something isn't right.

My steps are uneven as I follow Bianca down the pathway. She stumbles and then drops like a bag of wet cement onto the sugary white sand.

I've got to get to the bungalow.

I can't leave Bianca here.

Backing up, I cling to a palm tree and suck in a lungful of air. Fuck. They drugged us.

My lips start to tingle.

No. No.

I shove my finger down my throat. Nothing happens. It's no use. The drug is winding its way through my system.

"Maybe you shouldn't have used so much?"

I cock my head up toward the voice. Two shadowy figures stand a few feet away.

Damen?

My thoughts are fuzzy.

"Bianca," I say and shove at her shoulder. "Come on, you gotta get up."

I'm not sure if I'm breathing. Everything around me buzzes. My heart drums in my chest and ears, and I think I might pass out.

My throat burns as I blink against the darkness.

Why can't I see? What's happening?

"Damen! Help! Damen!"

CHAPTER
fifty-four

Damen

"THE TACTICAL TEAM IS READY TO STORM THE BEACHES LIKE Normandy on my command," Alex says.

Wystan laughs. "I don't think Vutreila was part of that invasion."

Alex swings his gaze to me. "After the team has secured the perimeter, identified any potential threats, and cleared them, we go in and get your girl. Got it?"

"Yep."

"Sir, we've got chatter that shots were fired on the island." The voice belongs to Sofia, one of Alex's team members.

"What?" He walks toward the monitor.

An icy cloak settles over me and I prepare for the worst news. My gut churns with venom.

"Bringing up the visual now," she says.

My head throbs and a sharp pain pierces my heart. Not Lauren. *Please.*

"Unidentified white male is the victim. We can't run facial recognition." Her face scrunches up.

"All right. I'm sending in the team," Alex shouts. "Someone get in there and recover that body. Change of plans, gentleman. I'm going to bring up the satellite images, and you two are going to watch from here."

My hands grip the edge of the table until my knuckles turn white. "Fuck. Fuck." I push past my brother. My shoulder collides with Alex's. "No. No way. We're coming with you."

"Damen, I will find Lauren. My men will find her and Bianca. You need to trust me."

"Is she still on the island? Are *they* still on the island?"

Silence passes between us, and it stretches on for what feels like forever.

Lauren.

Lauren.

"Sir, the dead man is Valter Kallas," the sharp voice says.

Valter is dead?

"Who pulled the trigger?" Wystan barks.

"Unknown. Do you want us to recover the body?"

Alex's gaze pings between the two of us. Wystan shakes his head. I nod in agreement.

"Negative, Parkes. Get back to your boat."

Pop. Pop.

"Shots fired. I repeat, shots fired."

"Parkes and Kerr, get off the island," Alex orders.

My head pounds and my limbs are heavy. My thoughts are clouded. Volleying between Lauren and Valter.

"Boss, we've got eyes on two shooters," one of the men says over the radio. "We can take them out."

Alex's knuckles crack against the tabletop. "Do it."

Pop. Pop.

"Targets eliminated."

Everything in the room halts when the phone on the conference table rings. Alex punches the speakerphone button and my fingers curl into my palms.

"Hello, Damen," the feminine voice chuckles darkly. "Wystan. I'm sure that you're bristling with energy like a bull ready to run the streets."

Wystan's hand passes over his thick beard. "Who the fuck are you?"

"I'm your sister. Inga Nowak. But I should've been a Kallas like the two of you."

"Why did you kill Valter?" I roar.

"Because I wanted to," she laughs. "He was an old man, getting too greedy and getting in my way. Why do you care? Didn't you want him dead too? Consider this a favor."

I shake my head. "I don't want anything from you."

"Well, I want something from you. Get the fuck away from my island. Turn around and leave. If you step one foot on my shores, I won't hesitate to kill Lauren. I'll slit their throats and dump their bodies in the ocean."

"Inga, I'm sure that we can come to a reasonable arrangement," I begin.

"No. We will not come to any agreement. You owe me. Wystan owes me. Now Valter has paid his debt to me. I own the island."

Before I get another word in, the line goes dead.

Inga has just made a grave fucking mistake. I'll kill her with my bare hands.

"Alex, you've got to get me on that island."

He runs a hand through this dark hair. "Tonight. We'll go tonight."

Alex kills the motor about a quarter of a mile offshore, and then he drops the oars into the water.

The bungalows dot the shoreline in the distance.

We each take turns rowing toward the bungalow where we saw Lauren earlier. We get as close as we can and wait for instructions.

"Team Alpha is in place," Alex whispers and stops rowing. "Team Omega is ready to go."

Finally we reach Lauren's bungalow. I step out of the boat onto the steps that lead up to the sundeck.

"We don't have much time," Alex says.

I nod and Wystan is right behind me. "We'll be right back."

Guns drawn, we enter the bungalow and fan out. Quickly we check the small space and then arrive at the bedroom.

Lauren.

She's lying on her back. The moonlight casts a soft glow over her soft features.

"Lauren, don't be scared." My hand covers her mouth, and I gently lift her into my arms.

"Damen. Is it you?" My name rolls off her tongue in a slur.

"Yes. I'm here."

"I knew you'd come for me."

"We have package A acquired," Wystan says into the radio.

Lauren's arm shoots out. "No. We have to get Bianca. She's in the next bungalow."

I smile. "We're already on top of that."

"Kallas, hit the deck!"

My ears register the sound of Alex's voice before the gunshots ring out.

CHAPTER
fifty-five

Lauren

I PUSH UP FROM WHERE I LANDED ON THE WARM WOOD.

As soon as I'm on my feet, the earth wobbles, and I nearly fall into the pool.

"Lauren, get down."

I duck and cover my ears. Blinking through the black of night, I try to focus on Damen's voice. I stay low and crawl on my belly.

"Sorry, brother. Your girlfriend is my property now." Inga's lazy drawl reeks of cruelty.

"She is no one's property. Lower your gun and let us go." Damen's voice deepens.

My head bobs as I try to stand. "Inga. For fuck's sake. It's over."

Her laugh slices through the air, and I sway, stumbling toward her. All I see is red. Anger funnels through my body and I charge at her.

"I'll kill you!" I scream, and then we're floating and falling at the same time.

"Get the gun," I hear someone bark out.

Adrenaline spikes inside me, filling me and spurring me on.

The water keeps us weightless while I punch, claw, and kick her. Our bodies float but lock together in a battle. I shoot to the surface for air.

She grabs me from behind, dragging me back under the water, and I jam my elbow into her ribs.

Bullets fly around us from all directions.

"I've got a man with a gun aimed right at your precious Damen's head," Inga chokes out.

"No you fucking don't," I scream out and land a punch to her jaw.

We go under again. Inga punches me in the leg.

I break the surface. "I'm going to kill you," I snarl and reach for her, grasping her throat with both of my hands.

Before I know it, two strong arms pull me from the water.

"No. No. Let me finish this," I cry out.

Damen jerks me back, gathering me close in his arms. "Shh. It's okay. I've got you. You're safe now."

At this point, I am shaking and crying uncontrollably. As much as Damen tries, the sobs rack my body, and I feel like my legs will give out from underneath me.

Dripping wet, my chest shakes and my heart pounds fiercely. Damen strokes my soaked hair in an effort to calm me, but I'm too agitated.

"I want her dead, Damen. Dead," I whisper against his chest.

"I know you do. But she's going to live out the rest of her miserable life in a prison cell."

Before I can respond, chatter from the radio distracts me from evil thoughts of murdering Inga myself.

"Building one clear. Building two clear."

"We've got three women here in the main bungalow on the island's west side. Send the medic."

"Go. Go. Go. Secure the main building."

It is hard to tell who is speaking to who in the flurry of activity. Darkness and light swirl as the chaos unfolds around us.

"Inga Nowak," a deep voice says. "I'm taking you into custody for kidnapping and a long list of other shit that I'm not going to get into now."

"Who are you, American soldier?" she snaps.

"Alex Robertsen and your worst nightmare," he bites out. "Get this piece of trash out of my sight."

Inga curses as she's dragged across the sundeck and through the bungalow.

"You got a hell of a swing, Lauren. If you ever want a job in security, I'll hire you any day."

Under the moonlight, I look up to find a pair of glowing hazel eyes staring at me.

"Thank you very much for helping to save us." I stumble over my words, feeling the rise of heat in my cheeks.

"You're welcome. Let's get a medic over here to check you out." Alex waves his hand in the air and then barks some orders into the radio.

"Miss, I'm Charlee Rhodes. Let's get you inside," she says.

I nod and she grips my arms for support. I must have hurt my leg when I jumped into the pool.

She angles my face into the light and checks my eyes and then my pulse. "Yeah, you were definitely slipped something."

Charlee walks into the kitchen and pulls a mug from the cabinet. I hear the spray of water and then her boots stomp toward me over the hardwood.

"Here, drink this," Charlee says and hands me a glass of water. "This will help get the drugs out of your system faster."

"Thanks. What's in it?" I sniff the contents before lifting the glass to my mouth.

"It's totally natural. I promise." She gives me a small smile.

I swallow down the contents that taste a little like baking

soda. "Can you check on my friend, Bianca? She's in the bungalow right next door."

"Sure thing. I'll be right back." She pats my shoulder and drops a bottle of water onto the nightstand.

I never understood the freeing feeling of crying in the shower until now. My stomach roils in pain, and I throw up.

As I scrub out the blood and brains matted in my hair, I vomit twice more before Damen enters the bathroom.

He strips out of his clothes and joins me in the shower. "Let me do this for you." His words are soft and comforting. "It breaks my heart to see you cry."

"I've got pieces of your father stuck in my hair. It's so disgusting. And I'm so sorry that you lost him."

"Lauren, he wasn't a good man. I knew that. Wystan knew that, and you've always known that too. We don't have to talk about him."

"Can we talk about Bianca?"

He grabs the shampoo bottle and pours some liquid into his palm. "Of course. She's okay. Charlee gave her the special serum too. Wystan is with her. I think they're going to be good friends."

That makes me laugh. "Just friends?"

He tilts his head to the side. "Probably more than friends." Damen's fingers gently scrape against my scalp. "Okay, rinse."

When my eyes meet his, he buries a hand in my hair and tilts my head back. His mouth trails down my throat, and it sends shock waves of pleasure down my spine.

"It's over," he whispers against my wet skin. "You are safe. I promise you that."

"You gotta double pinkie promise," I choke out.

His forehead rests against mine. "Double pinkie promise and cross my heart."

My fist pounds against his chest and then he tilts my mouth to his. Our lips meet for a long slow kiss. Then he cups my ass, lifting me into his arms and taking my nipple into his mouth.

"Oh god," I rock against him, rubbing against his abs.

His cock slips between my ass cheeks. "You feel so good. I want you."

"It's been too long," I whisper against his lips.

"Are you sure you want to do this now?"

"I'm sure. I want to drown all the bad memories. I need to feel you. All of you." I buck against him.

"I'll give you what you need," he tells me and slides his cock between us, and I feel like I'll combust.

He moves us away from the spray and then spins me away from him. I glance over my shoulder and Damen shoots me a wicked grin.

Using his foot to widen my stance, he rocks against me. As I tilt back, seeking more friction, he groans. The sound of his groans and the feel of our wet skin gliding together make me wetter.

He guides himself inside me and I moan loudly. "Oh, Damen. You feel so good. I need you."

"I've got you," he whispers as his fingers circle my clit. With the snap of his hips, he's buried inside me, and we move together.

"Damen. Damen." I cry out his name as the orgasm rushes through my body at lightning speed. "Too fast. I'm sorry."

"Don't ever be sorry." Damen's husky laugh fills the shower. "I promise we're going to work on your stamina."

It's always so easy with Damen. Then again, I don't have any experience *except* with him. I glance over my shoulder to look at him and his mouth crushes to mine. The heat of his chest against my back is glorious.

He's alive. Living and breathing, and he's here with me.

Damen pounds into me and before I know it, he's roaring his own release. "Fuck, beautiful."

The water beats over us and turns cool. We cling to one another, but when the spray turns to icy needles, he flips it off. We step out and wrap up in the big, fluffy towels.

He cups my face in his hands. "It's been so long. I'm going to have you every day."

"I like the sound of that. All of that. Now take me home."

CHAPTER
fifty-six

Damen

Two Days Later

A FTER A LONG FLIGHT BACK TO STUVICA, WYSTAN AND I TAKE Lauren and Bianca to my country house.

Dorel is magic. My house doesn't look like a war zone anymore.

I step into the bedroom, and the faint light from the windows washes over Lauren's face. She's safe. She's here.

Knowing that Inga had drugged her still had me fired up with anger and rage.

But it doesn't matter because Inga is in custody and Valter is dead.

Turns out Inga, not Valter, killed Lorence. She wanted everyone out of her way that could interfere with the operations in Cadena Soleada and Belize.

Inga claims to be our sister. I had a DNA test administered right away. We should know the results soon enough.

As for the island, I'm going to figure something out with

CHRISTY PASTORE

Lauren and Bianca's help. I've got a couple of ideas brewing, but I don't want to make a move without their input.

Lauren's legs stir beneath the covers. "Good morning. How long have you been standing there?"

I smile. "Good afternoon. Not long."

"Afternoon!" Lauren shoots straight up. "Why didn't you wake me up?"

"Because it's Saturday, and it's okay to sleep in on a Saturday."

I shake my head and Dorel rushes in with a cup of coffee, setting it on the table in the middle of the room. "Drink coffee, and I make you anything you want to eat, Lauren."

She scoops the mug into her hand. "Thank you, Dorel. I think I could really go for some pizza."

Her brows scrunch. "How can you drink coffee and then want pizza?"

Lauren lifts a shoulder. "I dunno. My stomach wants what it wants."

Dorel waves her hands into the air. "Fine. I will make you a pizza. Cheese and veggies. It will be wonderful."

The sound of Luka's nails on the hardwood has me moving out of the way. As soon as we walked in the front door, Luka rushed to Lauren. Not me.

But I don't mind one bit.

"Luka," she coos and scratches behind his ears. "How's my good boy?"

He wags his tail and nuzzles into her. "That's a good boy. We'll go for a walk later. You wanna go for a walk, buddy?"

Luka spins around and then trots to the fireplace and lays down.

I bend to kiss her lips. "How are you feeling?"

"Fine. Better than fine."

"You sure?"

288

She nods and rolls up on her toes to kiss me. "I'm positive, but just in case. I'd like to see a therapist. Do you have someone on the staff like that?"

I wrap my arms around her. "I might know someone that can help."

"Good. I've got a few other things that I need help with too."

My brows rise as I tug on the strap of her nightgown. "Do you need me to get you naked? I can definitely help with that."

She rolls her eyes. "Later. We can do all of that later. Right now, I want to talk about what's next for me. For us."

She has a point. We haven't discussed any details yet.

"What do you want to do?"

Lauren pads around the room in a flurry of excitement. "I need to go back to Chicago and clear out my apartment. Someone probably needs a place to live, and my place is pretty cool for a single gal. And then I need to confront my sister. I want to look her in the eye when she tells me why she played god with my life. I need a job. I don't know if working at Wystan's club is the best use of my time."

I study her, absorbing everything she's saying. "I'll help you in any way that I can. Have you given any thought to where you might want to live here?"

She smooths her palms up my chest and over my shoulders. "Well, you haven't exactly asked yet, but I know that you really want me to stay here."

"Do I?"

"Yep. But if not," she says and spins out of my arms, "Bianca and I can always find an apartment together in the city."

"No way. Not happening." I step toward her and bury my hands in her hair. "I lost you once, and that's never happening again. You're going to have to move in here so that I can keep my eyes on you."

"Good. Besides, I think Luka needs me."

I lower my mouth to hers. "We both do." I kiss her lips, tasting the promise of the future—hope and love.

Yeah, I love her. I'll tell her. Soon.

CHAPTER
fifty-seven

Lauren

I STARE DOWN AT THE DELICATE GOLD BANGLE ON MY LEFT WRIST. THE afternoon sun glints off the sun charm.

I take a deep breath and wait for my sister to arrive. I'm sitting in a coffee shop by the front windows.

Damen, Wystan, and Bianca all came on this trip with me. We spent yesterday packing up my apartment. After I tie up all my loose ends here, we're going to do the same thing for Bianca.

Kat is forty minutes late. Part of me thinks that she won't show up.

The chime of bells rings out, drawing my eyes to the door. It's not Kat who stands in the doorway, it's Greg.

Anger surges inside me, and I try desperately to lock it down. Keeping my emotions in check, I ignore the stabbing pain in my heart.

Betrayal hits me all over again.

I roll my eyes. "She's not coming, so she sent you?"

"No. She doesn't want to see you." Greg takes the seat across from me.

My heart drops to the pit of my stomach. "*She* doesn't want to see *me*. That's rich. Well, funny enough, I don't want to see you. I came to see Kat."

"She doesn't want to see you," he murmurs. "You need to go and never come back."

My brows knit together. "So you keep saying. I'll be gone once I talk to Kat. All I wanted was to look her in the eye and ask her why."

"He was going to take our daughters. We had to give him something."

I swallow, trying to stay calm like Damen and Wystan taught me. "You mean *someone*."

"I'm sorry I can't give you the closure you're looking for. The closure I know you deserve. What we did was unforgivable. And for what it's worth, I am sorry."

"You've got that right. I didn't come here to forgive you or her. I just wanted to look my kidnappers in the face one last time," I tell him.

Greg shifts in his seat. "Keep your voice down."

The nerve. I pull my final punch with the evidence that Damen gave me.

I stand and scoop up my Strathberry clutch. "Drop out of the mayoral race, Greg." I pull the flash drive from my purse. "If you don't, this gets sent to the Times and three local networks."

"What is that?" He shoots up out of the chair.

"This is the video of you and Kat negotiating my kidnapping."

"But I was told . . ." He clears his throat. "I was told that if I did everything Saint Arthelais wanted, that would never see the light of day."

"Plans change. Kat should have thought about that before deciding not to show up today."

"You can't do this to me."

My eyes narrow. "I can't do this to you? After what you did

to me, you don't get to win. You don't get to have all your dreams come true and be a giant fucking success. You're going to put some good back into the world, Greg."

"I've worked hard to get where I am, Lauren. You know that. You watched me and Kat work and work. You can't discount that. We made a mistake. A giant fucking mistake," he says, his voice soft and unconvincing. "I know you're not going to believe me, but Kat and I've been really messed up about what we did to you. We're both in therapy."

"Spare me the bullshit. Your atonement is that you will have to live with the fear every day. The anxious feeling of looking over your shoulder and constantly checking social media to see if I'll blow up your life."

"Please don't do this, Lauren. Think of Cora and Thea." The desperation in his voice is apparent.

"You think about *your* daughters, Greg. Set aside a trust for the two of them. If you or Kat so much as hurt another person, cheat on your taxes, steal a cab from a senior citizen, or kick a puppy, I'll know about it and blow up your world."

"God, you really are a petty bitch."

"But I'm a petty bitch with all the power." I walk toward the door feeling empowered. "Goodbye, Greg, and go fuck yourself."

Sliding my sunglasses up the bridge of my nose, I walk out of the coffee shop. With a smile on my face and my shoulders straight. I don't shed one damn tear.

Five Months Later

I'm on vacation. *Again.* Except this time, things are insanely different.

Damen and Wystan turned Cadena Soleada back over to the

293

Sardonian monarchy after King Nicholas donated a very large sum to our new endeavor, Champion Hope Global. I'm excited about all the possibilities. But there is still a lot of work to be done.

We rented out the entire island, and we are celebrating Damen's birthday. We brought everyone, including Luka, who loves the sand just as much as the snow.

I thought that the fact that Valter was murdered here would be a trigger for stress and have me backsliding in my therapy, but it hasn't. The first thing Damen did before negotiating the deal with the royal family and government was tear down the section of decks where Inga shot Valter.

Speaking of Inga, turns out she is Wystan and Damen's half sister. Well . . . was, she killed herself two weeks before her trial.

I've never asked Damen and I don't think he'd lie to me, but I'm pretty positive Inga's demise was from another cause. But none of that matters.

"Dorel says the cake needs to be cut soon. She thinks the frosting is melting in the heat." Bianca's voice comes from the doorway, where she's dressed in a stunning lemony yellow sundress.

"She just wants to see the look on Damen's face when we all sing happy birthday."

Bianca hands me a glass of Champagne. "You're probably right."

"Let's cut the cake," I tell her.

We walk out onto the patio of the grand villa and Luka runs past the two of us, barking and jumping.

"Happy birthday, Damen." I wrap my arms around his neck, careful not to spill my drink.

His lips map over my cheek, kissing the corner of my mouth.

"I love you," he murmurs.

I feel those words deep within my bones.

"I love you too."

My life was turned upside down and flipped inside out. Who

knew that I'd be my own boss? With a very handsome boyfriend. And a family that I can't imagine my life without.

I can't imagine my life without Dorel and her constant Mother-Henning. I love it.

I can't imagine my life without Wystan and his watchful and playful big brother attitude.

I definitely can't stand the thought of not having Bianca in my daily life. She's become my most trusted friend and confidant. Aside from Damen. But Damen doesn't need all the girly stuff. And I mean the girlish of girly stuff.

Of course there's Damen. My life has changed dramatically, and even though he'll never take any credit for helping shape me into who I am now, he's the reason.

He's the reason I'm stronger

He's the reason I'm more confident.

Although he will tell you that it is all me. All my own doing.

If we're going down that road, I believe we all have the strength inside of us. And some of us are lucky enough to have a support system, which helps.

I think that's why I'm so excited and grateful to be taking on this important foundation. I want to be that support system for people.

Damen winks and pulls me into him so that my back is pressed against his chest. "You are the most amazing girlfriend."

"Yes, I am, and I'm going to let you prove it to me later."

"Happy birthday to me indeed," he hisses. "I know what I want from you tonight."

"You can have my ass. I'm ready."

"Happy birthday to you," Dorel emerges from inside the house with the gorgeous cake, and everyone starts singing.

"Thank you so much," Damen shouts and blows out the candles.

While everyone is distracted by the cake, Damen grasps me

by the hand, leading me away from the party and back to our bungalow.

We stop along the way, kissing and grinding on one another.

"I'm not wearing any panties," I whisper between kisses.

He rears back, mischief playing on his dark features. He lifts my skirt and slides his hand around my ass cheek, pressing the pad of his index finger against my most sensitive spot.

"Oh my god," he breathes and spins me around to face the palm tree. "You little vixen."

"Bianca helped me pick one out. Do you like it?"

He drops to his knees in the sand and spreads my cheeks apart. Flush blooms on my skin as Damen palms my ass and teases me with the jeweled butt plug.

"I'm going to use this to fuck your tight little asshole."

"Yes, please!"

He pulls it out and then pushes it slowly back inside. My muscles tighten even though I'm trying desperately to relax and let him push past my body's natural resistance.

"My cock is as hard as a steel spike," he says and bites my ass.

The toy thrusts in and out. Damen licks me *there* and I think I might die. He circles my tight hole and then moves to my drenched pussy, slipping through my wetness. My nipples harden to the point of pain.

"Jesus. Damen. It feels so good."

He takes the silver toy and pushes it inside, and my body opens to him.

My pleas turn into screams, and my entire body convulses with pleasure. Shattered from the orgasm, I feel Damen's finger sweep over my pussy, coating himself with my orgasm.

"Fuck that toy. This is mine," he growls against my skin.

He slips his finger knuckle deep inside me and after a few glorious thrusts, my asshole tightens around his finger. Wave after wave of pleasure washes over my body.

"Fuck me. You feel incredible," he says. His words are deep and seductive. "Do you feel that? I'm the only man who will ever fuck this sweet little ass. And that was just my finger. Wait until I get my cock inside you."

"Oh yes, fuck me."

Damen has awakened my senses and stirred my soul to new heights of pleasure.

"I know you liked that," he says, kissing me. "I want to hear that dirty little mouth say it. Tell me that you want me fingering that tight little hole."

"Yes," I murmur against his lips. "I love it when you finger my asshole."

"Good."

We both laugh before kissing, and then his fingers twine with mine, tugging me along the sandy walkway.

"Thanks for the best birthday ever," he says. "A very sun-shiny birthday."

"You're welcome. There will be many more happy, sunshiny birthdays."

He sucks in a breath and then kisses me. "I can't wait to have them all with you."

epilogue

Lauren

New Year's Eve

"I THINK TONIGHT'S THE NIGHT WYSTAN'S GOING TO POP THE question," Bianca whispers in my ear.

He's not.

Not tonight anyway. I know because Wystan asked me to help him pick out a ring. He's planning to whisk her away to Crete in a few weeks, and that's when he's going to ask her to marry him.

I still can't believe that these two have fallen so deeply in love. It's wonderful.

"You could do a lot worse than Wystan."

She laughs. "Don't I know it."

All these months later, I'm not surprised that Bianca is thriving and doing this well emotionally and mentally. When I met her in that room the first time, confidence radiated off her like waves.

She's taken back her life in spades. I'm so proud of her.

As for me, working to restore the lives of victims of sex

slavery and obtaining justice for survivors is a huge part of my own recovery. I, too, am thriving.

My past still shows up in flashes, mostly when I'm alone or at night, waking me from my sleep. But the nightmares of being kidnapped and subjected to Inga's betrayal and cruelty are few and far between. With Damen by my side, I know I'm going to be more than okay.

An email notification pops up and I click it immediately. A smile breaks across my face.

"What's up?" Bianca asks.

"We just reunited our one-hundredth person with their loved ones."

Bianca claps and bounces in the chair across from my desk. "That's impressive. This calls for Champagne."

Our little project has really taken off. We've been able to save many women and girls from a life of sex slavery.

Every day at Champion Hope Global brings different experiences. Most days are filled with hope and we're lucky that nothing has gone awry. I'm grateful to be alive and that I'm doing something meaningful with my life.

Bianca returns with two glasses and a bottle of Veuve Clicquot.

"Don't let Wystan see you drinking that," I tease.

"He's just going to have to deal with the fact that I like the cheap stuff." She pours the bubbly and then hands me a glass. "I'm so glad I met you, Lauren."

"Me too. Here's to us and saving more people." I lift my glass to hers.

"Cheers."

"Getting the New Year's Eve celebration started already?" Damen's voice lashes over me, making me shiver with anticipation.

My cheeks heat. He's so freaking gorgeous. How had I gotten so damn lucky?

"We just closed our one-hundredth case," I tell him.

His gorgeous face lights up with a smile. "Well, how about I take you somewhere to celebrate?"

My hands skate up his back. "I'd really like that."

Bianca swipes the Champagne from my desk. "I'll lock up. You two have fun."

When the door closes, Damen presses his mouth to mine. "I missed you today."

"I just saw you at lunch."

"That was hours ago," he counters.

I wiggle free from his hold and walk toward the bar in my office to grab the bottle of bourbon I keep on hand for him. He mutters something under his breath and follows me, his long stride gains on me. Before I can blink, I find myself pinned to the wall by six feet and some odd inches of hard, hot man.

Damen nips my lower lip with his teeth, then soothes the sting away with the gentle caress of his tongue.

Sliding my arms beneath his jacket, I hug him, soaking up the warmth of his lean hard body. Damen brushes the loose strands of my hair away from my temples.

"How did I get so lucky to find you?"

My heart aches in my chest at his words. "I'm the lucky one."

His mouth seals over mine and then his tongue thrusts into my mouth. Hunger surges through me, a need for him I can't control or fight.

"Get your coat. I need to take you somewhere."

I sit in the back of the limo with my hands tucked into my coat pockets, watching the snow fall. It's so thick it looks like a curtain.

The car rolls to a stop and Damen steps out first. When he

opens my door, I glance up at the building in front of us, but I have no idea where we are.

"Are we in an alley?"

"This way. We're going in through the VIP door."

I laugh. "Of course we are."

We step inside and I shake off the brutal winter chill. Although I do love all things winter in Vutreila.

"Are you going to tell me where we are?"

"You'll see." Damen keys in a nine-digit code, and seconds later, the door opens.

We walk into a hallway and then we step into a much larger room. Damen flips the lights and I'm stunned at the sight spread before me.

"What is happening? Where are we?" I stammer.

"This is a jewelry store," he answers smugly.

"I can see that. The diamonds on display were my first clue."

A man wearing a gray suit approaches us from the middle of the store. "Right this way, Mr. Kallas. We've been expecting you."

"Thank you, Cillian. I really appreciate this."

We follow Cillian into a small, private room adjacent to the showroom. The faint smell of cedar wood chips hangs heavy in the air. Inside the interior is warm and cozy with oversized ivory chairs, a roaring fireplace, and a huge bar.

When I turn toward the door, a woman walks in carrying a tray and then sets it on the counter. Then another woman enters with a tray and another. My breath catches in my throat as the light bounces off the diamonds."

The fireplace crackles in the corner and before I know it, Damen is on his knee in front of me.

"Oh my god," I gasp. "You're Sweet Home Alabama-ing me." My heart thumps out of sync against my ribcage.

"I figure that all this started between us because of a diamond." He lowers his lips to my ear. "The night you stole the

Dashiell Diamond and then begged me to keep you safe. This is the way I want us to begin the next chapter."

"I want that too. More than you know."

"Marry me?" he asks. The question is short and straight to the point. Very Damen.

"Maybe."

Damen traces his finger down my nose, over my cheeks, and across my lips. "How can I turn that maybe into a yes?"

"Say the magic words."

His dark brows crinkle. "I love you. Marry me."

"I thought you never wanted to get married?"

I'm teasing him. Making him sweat a little bit. After all, this is Damen Kallas, and I like knowing that I'm the only woman who can bring this sweet and strong man to his knees. It's very empowering.

"That was before you, babe," he says, his accent growing thicker. "Please. Just say yes. Pick one."

I laugh. "That's what I wanted to hear. I'm going to make you so happy, Damen Kallas."

He cocks his head to the side. "So that's a yes?"

I nod. "Yes. I will absolutely marry you."

Someone I once loved and cared for deeply handed me a box full of darkness. It took me a while, but after all this time I understand that this darkness—it was a gift.

A gift that led me here.

Here to Damen.

A life full of hope.

A life of happiness.

A life where a little bit of sunshine parts the darkness and you see things you never knew that you wanted.

afterword

Thank you for reading! I hope you were thoroughly entertained and enjoyed reading Damen and Lauren's story as much as I loved writing it. When it comes to reading books, you have unlimited choices, and I can't thank you enough for taking time out of your busy life to read *Dirty Gentleman*.

If you LOVED reading *Dirty Gentleman*, I hope you can spare a few moments to leave a few words on the platform where you purchased this book. Send me an email when you do, I'd love to hear from you.

You're always welcome to join my reader group on Facebook, Christy's Classy Lit Chicks.

Are you ready for more reading fun? How about another swoony gentleman? Check out *Wicked Gentleman!* It's a steamy, slow burn, billionaire romance. **https://geni.us/cpa_wg**

In the mood for a royal romance? Meet Prince Nicholas in, *Royal Gentleman*. **https://geni.us/RoyalGentleman**

books by
CHRISTY PASTORE

The Scripted Duet
Unscripted
Perfectly Scripted

The Harbour Series
Bound to Me
Healed by You
Return to Us

Standalone Titles
Fifteen Weekends (Women's Fiction)
Wicked Gentleman
Royal Gentleman
The First Lights

The Cardwell Family Series
Beautiful March
Sweet Agony
Copper Lining

Novellas
Double Contact
Snowed In with the Quarterback
Snowed In with the Boss

Be sure to sign up for my newsletter at christypastore-author. com for the latest news on releases, sales, and other updates.

acknowledgements

This book is the product of months and years of ideas, planning and plotting, writing thousands of words only to delete thousands of words, and then starting over entirely. Pretty much like everything I write.

First and foremost my husband Kevin and our feline tribe, Cheeto, Dorito, and Brew—I love you all so much. Thanks for keeping me sane during this process.

Beyond grateful for Linda, Missy, Robyn, Michelle (the Lacey to my Cagney), and Yolanda, when I needed you, you were there. I'm grateful to each of you for giving me your time and advice, but most importantly for your friendship.

From the bottom of my heart—Rachel, Danielle, AJ, Fabi, Cary, Brit, Gemma, and Patti, I can't thank you enough for always being in my corner and for believing in me. You all mean the world to me.

Immense thanks to Kylie and Jo at Give Me Books for helping me put this book out into the world. Your professionalism, transparency, and grace exceeds expectations, above and beyond. You two are truly a class act. Thank you.

And to the readers, y'all are the bees knees. I truly appreciate each and every one of you. Thank you for taking a chance on my stories.

Xoxo, Christy

about the author

International Bestselling Author and self-proclaimed french fry addict, Christy Pastore writes sexy, contemporary romance books that contain no nonsense (mostly) heroines and swoony gentleman with a naughty side. Readers so overwhelmingly embraced one Wicked Gentleman, Jackson Hart specifically, turning many of her #AuthorGoals into a reality.

When Christy's not turning her risqué thoughts into something worth reading, you'll find her geeking out on all things pop culture, obsessively stalking Pinterest for home interior ideas, lunching with friends, or researching her next vacation destination.

She has strong opinions about folding laundry, fruity wines, the Oxford Comma, fashion, and mixed vegetables.

Christy lives in central Indiana with her husband and their three loveable cats, Cheeto, Dorito, and Brew. But as cute as they are, please send scratching posts asap because they're slowly destroying the furniture.